Geoff Tristram has been a professional artist and ~~~~~~~ or over twenty-five years, working for a diverse range of clients including Embassy World Snooker, The BBC, Tarmac, Carillion, Past Times, Winsor & Newton, Trivial Pursuit and the television show, 'They Think It's All Over!', to name but a few.

He has painted celebrities such as Jonathan Ross, Ian Botham, David Vine, Alan Shearer, Ian Hislop and Gary Lineker, not to mention virtually every famous snooker player that ever lifted a cue. You may have even noticed him at the World Championships on TV, interviewing them as he drew their caricatures!

Geoff has designed many book covers, album sleeves for bands such as UB40, The Maisonettes and City Boy, (remember them?) and postage stamps, notably 'Charles and Diana - The Royal Wedding', 'Lake Placid Winter Olympics' and 'Spain 1982 World Cup Football' editions. He also writes jokes for the marvellously rude and irreverent greetings cards published by Emotional Rescue Ltd.

Geoff's younger brother, David, is a well-known and extremely successful comedy playwright, so it was no real surprise when Geoff eventually turned his hand to comedy writing, hence this, his third full-length novel, featuring the chaotic and accident-prone artist, David Day.

In order to make up for lost time, Geoff has now written four more novels, which follow this dreamy, scatterbrained character as he grows up and eventually gets a real job. Geoff's family wonder if he will do likewise.

# VINCENT GOUGH'S VAN
## Geoff Tristram.

First published in 2007 by Geoff Tristram Ltd.

Printed and bound by C P I Antony Rowe.

ISBN 0-9551428-2-2

ISBN 978-0-9551428-2-6

*Cover illustration by Geoff Tristram.*

Contact the author on gt@geofftristram.co.uk

**With sincere thanks to the incredibly clever Aileen Fraser for editing my books and never asking for a penny, which is just as well.**

vi

Dedicated to the memories of
Mike Timmins and Russell Waldron.

## Dramatis Personae

David Day, an Art Student

Dylan Weldon, Friend to David Day

Suzanne and Kathleen, Girlfriends to David and Dylan

Ruby, Len and Paul Day, Parents and Brother to David Day

Kim Hobbins, a Police Officer

Laz, Musician and Friend to David Day

Olga and Helga, Café Proprietors

Jimmy Triplicate, a Bus Driver

Claude Beardsley, the New Head of Art College

Kingsley Hamphlett, the Previous Head of Art College

Gertrude Hamphlett, Wife of Kingsley

Jack Hamphlett, Son of Kingsley

Laurence Fuchs, an Obnoxious Fine Art Student

Leonora Fuchs, a Pre-Raphaelite Dream Rabbit

Mrs Fuchs, Mother to Laurence and Leonora

Wilfred Fuchs, a Doddery Old Bore

Kieron Hastings, Head of Fine Art

Katie Black, an Art Student

Duncan Lake, a Rock Singer

George Jameson, another Rock Singer

Ken Stephenson, a Drunken Bassist

Nick Chinn, a Drummer

Mrs Timmins, a Sweet Shop Proprietor

Donald and Reg, two Beat Bobbies

Mrs M, a Psychic Sewing Teacher

Mike Sambrokes, a Photographic Technician

Vincent Gough, a Florist

Rosie Krantz and Gilda Stern, two Lesbian Assassins

Jim Weston, a College Lecturer

The Weird Woman, a Weird Woman

Mo, A Road Manager

Desdemona Wilcox, Mo's Girlfriend

Dougie and Horace Graves, two Gas Fitters

Bernie and Doris Woods, Landlords of the Castle Pub

Glenn, a Barman

Billy the Convict, a Nightclub Doorman

Jodie Stone, a Large Breasted Student

Dom Bentley, a Lecherous Lecturer

Edwin Binks, a Spotty Faced Herbert

The Limp Lisper, a Fantastic Fop

Quentin, The Limp Lisper's Boyfriend

Martin and Kirsty, Picture Framers

Barry, Proprietor of The Spray Bay

Mrs Westfield, a Sad and Lonely Housewife

Tim Finlay, a Ceramics Student

An Unnamed Pest Control Officer

Plus;

A One-Eyed Snooker Club Proprietor, Several Strange Commuters, An Assortment of Odd-Ball Café Customers, Bit-Part Players, Molly the Cat, and Jennings the Hamster R.I.P.

No hamsters were killed in the making of this novel, which was filmed entirely on location in Wolverhampton, Kinver, Stourbridge, Stratford upon Avon and Dittisham, Devon.

David was convinced that Laurence had been tampering with his tip.

# CHAPTER 1

## The Long Hair of the Law

David Day studied the policewoman from behind as she stood looking longingly at the window of Tweedledum's Coffee Shop. A devilish grin spread across his face as he approached her. Treading carefully now, like a cat burglar, he was so close that he could smell her perfume. Had she been on guard, she would have noticed his ominous, looming shadow reflected in the window, but her mind was focused on other things. The frosted apple turnover seemed to be calling to the depths of her soul. She had skipped breakfast that day because the alarm clock had failed to go off, making her late for work, and now, at eleven-thirty a.m., she was ravenous.

He was inches away now, admiring that incredible hair. It was in a bun, of course, as she was in uniform, but still shiny and wonderful. It had fascinated him throughout his infant, junior and grammar school days, all three glorious feet of it. When unfurled, it covered half of her athletic six-foot frame. He had often imagined her naked, her modesty both above and below protected by this vast tidal wave of hair. She could have played the part of Lady Godiva, or featured in those sensual T.V. hair shampoo advertisements, but neither career options held any fascination for her. Ever since junior school, she had confided in David that she wished to join the force. He remained convinced that she had been brainwashed in those impressionable years by the pathetic careers advisors of the nineteen-sixties, and, for that matter, virtually every adult who clapped eyes on her.

"Ooh! You are a tall young girl," they would remark, "You should join the Police Force!" As if her height eliminated her from any other role in life.

He held his breath now, so that she couldn't hear him. They had always got on well, in that brother and sister kind of way, had David and Maggie - or Teragram Snosrap, as he always called her. At grammar school they had all written their names backwards at the start of one new term, and hers was unanimously voted the funniest. He'd never forgotten it.

It was time to pounce.

He shoved his banana into the small of her back and clasped his left hand over her mouth.

"Don't move, Teragram Snosrap," he barked, "or I'll drill you with my banana!"

What happened next was something of a blur, but he was acutely aware of an unbearable pain and a cracking noise as his banana arm was twisted forcefully up his back. This was followed swiftly by the sickening thud of hard, cold pavement coming up to meet his ear, which began to throb horribly. To add to his considerable discomfort, someone appeared to have dumped a two-hundred-weight sack of coal on top of him.

"You are under arrest for assaulting a police officer," said the sack of coal, which, like Queen Victoria, was not amused.

"Gnah!" moaned David.

His rapidly swelling left eye was about half an inch from a rather unpleasant cigarette butt, which had pink lipstick all over the tip and was still glowing red at the business end. It was funny how he could still be so observant, given the trying circumstances. Perhaps it was his artistic training coming into play.

A small crowd had now gathered to watch the arrest, and an old lady shouted, "Good on yer, love. Throttle the bastard!"

David struggled to articulate his feelings. His face was flushed red with the shame and embarrassment of it all.

"Snosrap! It's me, David. David Day," he whimpered.

"My name is WPC Kim Hobbins. I would be very surprised if anyone was actually called Snosrap. Are you on any medication, sir?"

"Yes I am, but I can't see what that's got to do with anything!" he protested.

"What are you on, sir?"

Realizing that she had the upper hand, he decided to help the police with their enquiries.

"It's called Benylin. I've had a bad cough. My mom says it's because I go to B.J.'s club to see rock bands, and everybody smokes there, apart from me of course."

"That's not what I meant," said the WPC, trying her hardest to be patient. "Why did you attack me with a banana, sir?"

"I thought you were Margaret," he replied feebly.

"If you thought I was Margaret, why did you call me Telegram Snogwop?"

"I didn't!"

"You bloody well did."

"No I didn't," insisted David. "I called you Teragram Snosrap; it's Margaret Parsons spelt backwards."

The officer stared at him critically. "Are you *sure* you're not on some form of medication?"

"No. I mean yes. I thought you were my friend Maggie, the policewoman. She's got hair three feet long. We went to school together. Not me and her hair you understand. Me and all of her, including her hair of course, if you…..."

"Not Maggie Evans?"

"Parsons."

"She used to be Parsons I think. She got married to Barry Evans, another officer."

"Oh! I didn't know that she was married. I haven't seen her for ages. This cigarette butt is burning my brow. I may have to scream any time now."

The officer seemed to soften a little. "Okay. I'm going to let you stand up. If you misbehave, I have a truncheon, remember?"

"Understood," he groaned.

"Have I hurt you?" she asked, concerned by his pitiful voice.

"No" he replied, "I'm okay, apart from my ear, which has been grated off, my arm, which is snapped in sixteen places and my eye, which may never see clearly enough for me to paint pictures again. I also have a third degree cigarette burn on my brow, so I'm scarred for life, CPW Mik Snibboh."

"What?"

"Mik Snibboh. That's your name spelt backwards."

"I see," she said, half smiling now. "Well, in future, make sure you know someone before you attack them with bananas in shopping precincts. You've got a fag-end stuck to your cheek."

"Thank you. I may leave it there."

"That's your choice, sir."

"And now," said David, dusting himself off, "if it's okay with you, WPC Snibboh, I intend to enter this café and partake of a large greasy sausage roll and a pot of tea. Would you care to join me?"

The WPC began to laugh out loud, and turned to the now substantial crowd.

"It's all over folks. Big misunderstanding. Nothing to see. Move along please!"

She waited till they had dispersed and returned her gaze to David.

"A friend of Maggie's eh? She never mentioned any lunatic acquaintances, but then again, she wouldn't, would she? Buy me that apple turn-over and we're quits. I'm starving!"

David grinned. "It's the least I can do after you've dislocated my arm and fractured my skull. I will buy you this cake, but I must warn you that I am liable to call in this favour at any time."

He flicked the dog-end from his cheek, retrieved it from the floor and deposited it in a nearby litter bin. He was damned if she was going to re-arrest him for littering. Affecting an air of nonchalance, he entered the café, and emerged seconds later with the apple turnover in a paper bag.

"Just out of interest, my dear Snibbs, how long *is* your hair?" he asked. WPC Hobbins appeared to blush, which David found very appealing. These hard-nut females always softened eventually. They seemed to respond favourably to his boyish charm, once the initial violence had concluded.

"Oh, not in the Maggie Parson's class I'm afraid," she smiled. "It was about two-foot-three inches, last time I measured."

"Well, from the back you and Maggie are identical, and you don't disappoint from the front either, if you don't mind my saying so. The good news is, I can stick my banana into the backs of two lovely police officers with impunity now that we've been introduced."

"I wouldn't count on it, buster," she warned. "You can't bribe me with an apple turn-over and think that gives you the right to prod me with your banana. I'm not a cheap date. Now, if you'll

5

excuse me, Divad Yad, I have a job to do, protecting the good folk of Wolverhampton from nutters." With a cheeky wink, she was on her way.

David stood dumbly watching her disappear around the corner. This had done his blossoming uniform fetish no good at all. He was just fantasizing about liberating her shining hair from its Victorian bun and watching it cascade down her back, prior to slowly unbuttoning her tunic, when he was rudely interrupted by a heavy slap on his back which brought him unceremoniously back into the real world - the one where police women he'd only just met didn't want to make love to penniless art students.

"Morning!" said Dylan cheerfully. "Day dreaming again? Mine's a bacon sandwich, well done, on brown, pot of tea, your turn to pay."

"I'm sure it's your turn!" protested David indignantly. "Tell you what. I'll ask you a simple artistic-type question. Get it right and I'll pay. Get it wrong and you do."

"Okay. Fair enough!" agreed Dylan. He had nothing to lose; he knew full well that David had paid on the previous day. Usually David was himself too vague to question his friend's selective amnesia. They wandered into the café and sat in the window where they could keep an eye on the Foundation course girls, as they strolled by in their skimpy outfits and multi-coloured hair-dos. It was the Monday morning ritual, just to ease them into the week.

"Right!" said David. "You're a good pencil artist. You know all about the old sticks of graphite, be they Mars, Staedtler, Venus, Faber Castell….."

"Caran d'Ache?" added Dylan helpfully.

"Exactly! So tell me, what do the letters H and B stand for?"

Dylan looked blank for around a minute, sighed and produced a wallet from the top pocket of his Levi's jacket. He strode up to the counter, his head still in obvious mental turmoil. How could he not know something so fundamental to his trade?

Olga, one of two sisters who ran the café, emerged from one of the two doors behind the counter. Her twin sister, Helga, usually emerged from the other, which always reminded David of ornamental Swiss weather houses. If it was rainy, a little figure popped out of a door, and if it was sunny, it went back in and the other one came out. It was rare that both sisters would emerge simultaneously, but when they did, they would invariably argue about everything and anything, loudly and tetchily, so that all the customers could hear. Olga would ask Dylan what he wanted to eat, whereupon Helga would volunteer to cook it. This would incense Olga, as she had rather hoped to cook it. Some mornings, however, Olga would take the order, berate her sister because she hadn't offered to do the cooking, and accuse her of slacking. Other days it would be the state of the work surfaces, or disagreements about how soft a jacket potato should be. Neither of them ever bothered to write down orders, relying instead on memory, which was suspect at the best of times, and in times of stress, when there were more than three customers to be fed, downright hopeless. David would order spaghetti on toast, and be given beans. Dylan would ask for bread and butter pudding, and be given an omelette. If either of them complained, the sisters would furiously blame each other. Words would be exchanged, which culminated in one or the other disappearing through their allocated door and sulking, to the backdrop of clattering pans and thrown spoons, while the other smiled sweetly at the amazed customers, as if all were well. In spite of this, Tweedledum's was David and Dylan's favourite café. The food, when the orders were correct, was basic but good, and in terms of entertainment value the place was second to none.

Dylan returned to the window seats with two doughnuts and a pot of coffee. Even by Olga's standards, this was stretching it, but the lads had long since accepted that it was easier all round to take what they were given. It was food after all, and there were people in Africa starving, according to David's dad, Len.

"H stands for Hard," suggested Dylan. "No, that can't be right. Otherwise, they'd print S on the soft ones."

"I'm saying nothing," said David, contradicting himself.

Mid-morning snacks concluded, they took the short-cut through the shopping precinct and under the multi-storey car park, heading for Wolverhampton College of Art, where they were currently third year Bachelor of Arts students on an illustration course. They had become firm friends after meeting at the Foundation course interview three years before.

"Chewing gum?" offered Dylan, folding the Wrigley's stick neatly in half and tearing it into two pieces.

"Couldn't you stretch to a whole one, just once?" asked David, disappointed.

"Half is enough for any reasonable person," insisted Dylan, pocketing the other half. "What's that mark on your head?"

"Ah!" replied David, wincing at the memory. "I tried to smoke a fag through my brow. Don't ask."

They paused at the window of the Dragonfly Boutique, a tiny jewel of a shop tucked away at the back of the precinct in the open air, wedged under four storeys of dismal concrete car-park. It was crammed full of crushed velvet dresses, Pre-Raphaelite prints, scented candles, Buddha statuettes, bangles, beads, and just about every form of hippy merchandise ever created. David had stopped to take a look at a large and rather gorgeous Tiffany lamp with a grapes and leaves design, which was in the centre of the window display. He was doing a project on Louis Comfort Tiffany at college, and by sheer coincidence, currently working on a watercolour of the exact same lamp. Dylan left him to gaze while he rolled up a cigarette in the sunshine. Suddenly, shielding his eyes to shade himself from the powerful glare of the sun, he became aware of something untoward under David's feet.

"Dave," he called, "Come here a second. Quick! Step away from there."

David nervously tripped out of the shade into the brilliant white light of a perfect spring day.

"What's up?"

Dylan didn't speak: he just pointed to where David had been standing. A neat white chalk mark had been drawn on the pavement in the shape of a body. The very spot where David had stood was splashed with crimson, which had turned brown at the edges. Either this was some fine art student's idea of a joke, or David had been standing on the spot where someone had recently shuffled off his mortal coil.

## CHAPTER 2

### Ménage à trois

David did what he had always dreamt of doing. He undid the bobble at the back of Kim Hobbins's head and watched her thick, shining mass of straight hair cascade down her back. She turned and smiled at him, before slowly and sensually putting her fulsome lips to his, and sliding her tongue into his mouth. David gently began to undo the buttons on her tunic with trembling fingers. Her hand slid down his chest, paused at his leather belt, and then devilishly continued its journey south.

"I never realized that the general public were allowed to carry truncheons," she whispered, as her beautifully manicured hand teasingly circled. She sighed heavily in his ear as the object of her affections responded with involuntary leaps and jerks within his tightening trousers. Now he had the white blouse to deal with. He could feel her gorgeous, pert breasts beneath the soft cotton, their centres erect and aching to be touched.

WPC Parsons, meanwhile, not content to sit and watch for a second longer, walked over to the over-heated young couple and stood behind David, rubbing his buttocks, whilst WPC Hobbins pressed herself into him, begging him to do a little breaking and entering. WPC Parsons had her hand under his bottom now, thrilling to the touch of her colleague's hand as they met. Variety, after all, was the spice of life.

"Do you know what time it is?" she whispered in his ear, her other hand stroking his neck.

"No," gasped David.

"It's nearly a quarter to eight. I've made you a cup of tea."

"What?" he asked, suddenly confused.

"A cup of tea, David. Come on. You'll miss your lift to the bus station if you don't hurry up."

"What? Eh? Oh!"

David's mother was shaking his shoulder gently. "You've overslept again. Your dad's got to go in ten minutes. You'll miss your lift."

David groaned and stretched. He quickly turned to one side when he realized that he was turning his duvet into a wigwam. There were some things you didn't show your mother, no matter how well you got on.

"Are you *sure* you're at an Art college?" she asked, once he had come round a little. "It sounds to me like you're doing an African languages course. Swahili or something!"

David stared at her. "What, if anything, are you on about, woman?"

"When I came in your bedroom you kept saying really strange things, like 'Snogmisnibbo, Snogmisnograp' or something. You're not taking drugs or anything are you, David? I've heard about what goes on in these art colleges. You were never the same after you went to that grammar school. You used to be a lovely little boy. I could take you anywhere. You had lovely manners, but when you went there, you started getting cheeky."

David couldn't cope with this first thing in the morning. His head was reeling. Five minutes ago he was having the best time of his life, and now his mother was giving him a going over for being cheeky, taking drugs and speaking Swahili, and it wasn't

11

even eight o'clock yet. He wouldn't have minded a bit of his mother's loony brand of scolding if his dream had concluded successfully, but it hadn't. In fact, they never did. He was constantly having dreams where he was in an erotic situation with some girl or other, but he never got to do the dirty deed. All manner of crazy barriers would be placed in his way, ensuring that he woke up well and truly frustrated. A psychologist would have gleaned enough material from David's sleep patterns alone to warrant a lecture tour of the United States, all expenses paid.

"I'm not cheeky anymore," he argued, hurt at this slight. "That was at school. I'm nearly twenty-two now."

Ruby backed down. "I have to admit that you've calmed down a bit. I suppose we've got to go through it all again with your brother next. Now hurry up and get out of bed, before your dad goes without you!"

David had an old Mini Clubman which he usually drove to college each day, but for the foreseeable future his dad was borrowing it until his Morris Marina came back from the body shop. A few weeks previously, Len had been parked in Brierley Bank High Street, reading the Sun and eating a packet of pork scratchings, when a bus had smashed into the back of him, wrecking the family car and giving him a nasty dose of whiplash into the bargain. The bus driver had tried to convince the police that Len had suddenly pulled out on him, which was an interesting line, considering the car's ignition was switched off and the keys were in Len's back pocket at the time. The ensuing argument had delayed the insurance payout, leaving Len without a car, which, as the breadwinner, he needed for transport to and from work.

David didn't mind catching the bus. He was a great people-watcher and daydreamer, and four bus rides per day gave him plenty of opportunity to do both. It also meant that he could renew his acquaintance with an old friend, the Jamaican bus driver whom he'd christened 'Jimmy Triplicate'. Jimmy was a nice man, but he had a terrible vocal affliction. He found it utterly impossible to say anything just once, or for that matter, twice - it needed to be said three times before he was satisfied. The strange thing was, it didn't happen with every phrase that he uttered; just selected ones, and the more he struggled to get the better of his problem, the worse it got. It was as if the resident demons in his mixed-up head were fighting tooth and nail.

The 'Say it Just Once' demon would urge poor Jimmy to say things singly, like everyone else, but the 'Say it Three Times' demon was stronger, and after a hotly-contested battle, he would usually come out on top. The 'Say it Two Times' demon had long since given up the ghost, and presumably moved on to another head. David had once hitched a ride on Jimmy's bus, and entered into a conversation with the driver which culminated in him saying, "I know what you mean!" followed promptly by the predictable repetition a few seconds later. Then a remarkable thing happened. There was no third rendition. David observed with fascination the man's tortured countenance as he drove through town after town in silence, wincing at the driver's every anguished facial tic and bead of sweat. The bus began to weave all over the road as Jimmy bravely fought his obsession, causing a good deal of consternation amongst the worried passengers. It seemed as if the fellow would literally explode at any moment; there was so much happening in his head. Then, as they swung round the final bend into the terminus, it all became too much, and the final "I know what you mean!" burst forth like molten lava from a volcano, leaving behind a defeated husk of a bus driver draped over his giant steering wheel, drained and sobbing gently.

Having managed to get a lift with his dad by the skin of his teeth, David was happy to see his repetitive friend behind the wheel once more. He asked him how he'd been.

"Not too bad, not too bad, not too bad!" replied Jimmy, apparently at ease with himself. Perhaps, mused David, the 'Say it Just Once' demon was taking a nap.

13

"It's going to be fun seeing all the old characters again," he laughed, settling down on the sideways bench seat just behind the driver. "Are they all still going strong, Jimmy? The Amorous Asian, The Complete Nutter, Masturbating Maurice, The Weird Woman, Arthur and Martha?"

"Absolutely. Absolutely Absolutely!" grinned Jimmy, totally unaware that David had tactfully missed out one important character from the 58 bus route loony list - namely Jimmy Triplicate himself.

The Amorous Asian was the first one that David encountered, an experience which still traumatized him to this day. Whilst on his Foundation course, (a preparatory year where students experiment with different areas of art before settling on a chosen subject to study at degree level) David had returned home one evening on a virtually empty bus, and had become aware of an Asian gentleman who had seated himself immediately behind him. Within seconds, the frisky little Asian was whispering sweet nothings in David's ear, while simultaneously feeling his bottom through the gap in the seat. David was a broad-minded young fellow, but this, he figured, was beyond the pale. The situation deteriorated when the gentleman gently kissed his ear, leaving David no alternative but to trick this persistent little pest into thinking that he was getting off the bus at the next stop. Beckoning the man and winking horribly, like Kenneth Williams in a Carry On film, he persuaded the Amorous Asian to follow him off the bus, whereupon he shoved him into a privet hedge and leapt back onto the vehicle, telling Jimmy to step on the gas and be quick about it.

To make matters worse, the self same gentleman showed up at a working men's club where David and his rock band were performing, which forced David to wear a disguise comprising 'Werewolf Eyebrows' and 'Icky Teeth' for the rest of the evening in an attempt to avoid further contact. This prompted several audience members to observe that the lead guitarist was talented, but physically unfortunate.

The Complete Nutter was also a regular traveller who had caused David the occasional sleepless night. He was a perfectly normal-looking man of around thirty-five, who would sit on the bus and mind his own business, thus lulling the other passengers into a false sense of security. Then, with no prior warning, he would scream at the top of his voice, "Bust it clean open!" causing passengers to bump their heads on the ceiling panels, choke on their pasties or, at worst, have life-threatening coronaries. Unaware of the impact he had had on his fellow travellers, the C.N. would then quietly resume reading his newspaper. David, who was plagued with a fertile imagination, suspected that he had probably just murdered his wife with a meat cleaver, and was describing to all and sundry what he'd done to her head, by way of exorcising his guilt.

Then there was Masturbating Maurice. It is best not to dwell on Maurice's particular penchant, but suffice it to say that the vibration of the bus as it travelled seemed to excite him more than somewhat; so much so that this outwardly respectable businessman of some fifty summers got carried away to the point where he never noticed the large circular mirrors that enabled Jimmy to keep an eye on the top deck.

Arthur and Martha were David's favourites, or perhaps it would be more grammatically correct to say 'was his favourite'. Mondays through to Thursdays, Arthur, a middle-aged bald-headed man with a trilby and a newspaper, would join the bus in Sedgley and travel to Dudley. However, on Fridays, Martha, a middle-aged woman in a frock and sporting a suspect and static-filled nylon blonde hairpiece, would travel the exact same route. The logical explanation was that Arthur had a twin sister, but somehow, David had his doubts, which were based on what is commonly referred to as five o'clock shadow.

This strange and rather wonderful collection of life's oddballs made bus travel a joy, with the exception of one passenger in particular, who scared David to death. She was the stuff of horror films, and every time he saw her, the hairs on the back of his neck stood to attention. He had heard all about The Exorcist, a film which was currently doing the rounds of the local fleapits and terrifying the wits out of everyone. He'd planned to take Dylan along to see it with him, for moral support, sometime that month. They had been told countless times how horrible the child star of the film was, how mortifying the grisly effects, the nasty voices, and the head that turned a full three-hundred and sixty degrees. It would have to be pretty damned scary to frighten him more than The Weird Woman.

It wasn't that she was obviously scary, like the Exorcist girl. So far, there had been no projectile vomit or speaking in tongues, and the head had so far only managed one hundred and eighty degree turns, but this woman chilled the blood in a far more subtle way. She was around thirty years old, and dressed in a school blazer of sorts, with a black skirt, under which stood a pair of incongruous black rubber Wellingtons. She always wore a strange, multi-coloured turban affair, with a mounted gemstone in the centre, just like Maharajas wore in old Rudyard Kipling films. All very eccentric, the casual observer would have to admit, but what of it? However, had this casual observer been of a nervous disposition, and paused to study the face below the turban, it would have guaranteed sleepless nights for at least the next year.

It was hard to describe that face. Perhaps Pixie-like was as good as anything, but certainly not the cute, good-natured pixies of the Enid Blyton stories, or even her more mischievous ones. This was an evil, God-forsaken pixie from Tolkien, or something featured in a painting by Richard Dadd, the Victorian artist who went completely insane, murdered his father and spent the rest of his life in a mental institution, painting unnervingly strange fairy folk.

Her features were not of this earth. She was humanoid, but not human, with incredibly sharp cheekbones, piercing cold black eyes and ferret teeth. The eyes, in particular, were the stuff of nightmares. They were heavily angled, which gave her an oriental look, and jet-black like a bird's, with no discernable pupils. She wore a heavy foundation which allowed none of her natural skin to show through, but unlike most foundation powders and creams, which attempt to simulate a healthy tan, this was white, like the skin of a corpse. She was a creature, (and creature is the right word) of habit. She would stand at the bus stop by the Polytechnic every Friday, carrying a Mary Poppins-style crocodile skin bag, big enough to hold several dead babies. The stance was always motionless, unaware of her surroundings, aloof. She would glide into position, as if from nowhere, at precisely ten minutes to six, in time for the six o'clock bus. No one spoke to her, and she spoke to no one.

Once, out of sheer curiosity, David had dared to ask her the time, just to hear her speak. It had taken enormous courage because she frightened him rigid. He would never forget what happened next. She turned her head very slowly - so slowly that it gave an audible creak - and stared at him. There was no vomit, no unearthly voice, and no evil cackle; nothing. She studied him with her impenetrable eyes for what seemed an eternity, and then slowly reverted to her original position. The effect was so chilling that David continually saw her face in his rear view mirror as he drove home through dark country lanes. She would also pop up when he was in the shower, or trying to sleep in his dark bedroom, too scared to get up and close the wardrobe door.

After her, The Exorcist held no fear.

That day, however, was a quiet one. Just David, Jimmy, and a few old ladies moaning about the weather and comparing notes on which of their circle had died that month. He desperately needed to lighten his mood. The thought of The Weird Woman had given him the willies. He tried to think of more pleasant things, such as the promise of a snooker match with Dylan that lunchtime, his Tiffany glass project and, when that didn't work, WPC Hobbins's breasts. A pang of guilt struck him, as he remembered his beautiful girlfriend, Suzanne, and their enforced separation due to her enrolment at the rival Birmingham College of Art, to study Graphic Design. What with the physical distance

17

they needed to travel just to see each other, and the busy final year of their courses, they had rather let things slide on the romance front, and already he was fancying policewomen.

Suzanne and David had first met on the Foundation course, three years earlier, but she had moved to a different college afterwards, leaving David to seek solace in marathon snooker sessions with Dylan, most of which Dylan won. She lived with her parents in Sutton Coldfield, on the other side of Birmingham, and tried to keep in touch with him at weekends, when she wasn't too busy with project work, and when he wasn't busy rehearsing with his band. David also lived at home, unless there was an event to attend after college, in which case he slept at Dylan's flat, in the spare bedroom. The other third year students were constantly ribbing him about being a mommy's boy, and warned him that he was missing out on the college nightlife. This consisted of meeting each evening at the Castle pub in Dunsinane Street at the back of the college building, playing darts and dominoes, smoking cigarettes, eating awful food and getting blind drunk. Occasionally, to relieve the monotony, they would decamp to The Crypt, a seedy nightclub which had live bands on Fridays and Saturdays, where they would smoke cigarettes, eat awful food, and get blind drunk. If they were very lucky, they would stagger back to the halls of residence and have sex with someone. It didn't matter who, as long as their victims were still breathing. Some students weren't even that choosy, and as to gender, the old adage, 'Any port in a storm' about summed it up.

Meanwhile, David was busy rehearsing with his new band, having his dinner made for him each night, lying in a comfortable warm bed and seeing a rather beautiful girl for quiet dinners when he could fit her in. Some nights he couldn't sleep for worrying about all the college nightlife he was missing.

David had been in rock bands since he was seventeen. He learnt lead guitar by sitting in his bedroom virtually every night for a year, playing to his records over and over again, and picking up tips from his best friend, Laz, who had played guitar and

18

keyboards since he was a small boy. They say that opposites attract, and so it was with David and Laz. David was a grammar school-educated goody-two-shoes who had been suffering private clarinet lessons for years, and now wanted to learn an instrument that would make young women desire him carnally. Laz, on the other hand, was born a hippy. He had a mass of tightly curled hair, which, left untouched, formed into a triangle of frizz, causing him to resemble a reincarnated ancient Egyptian prince, or as Nick, the plain-speaking Brummie drummer of the band would have it, a 'weird looking twat'.

Frank Zappa always claimed that the lead guitarist in a band attracted the most groupies, especially if he could sing as well. His theory was that their guitar solos echoed the sexual act itself in construction. First there would be a lumbering guitar riff as the musician tried to feel his way, followed by some slightly more confident middle-of-the-guitar stuff, before fingering the top ends of their fret boards and indulging in lots of orgasmic twiddling with their Fuzz Boxes turned on. If guitarists were particularly aroused, they had been known to throw in a bit of Wah Wah right at the end. Before you could say 'Clapton', women were queuing up outside the dressing room. David couldn't imagine any women getting quite as worked up about 'Stranger on the Shore', so he abandoned the Boosey & Hawkes B flat, and got himself a Gibson 'Les Paul'.

When he wasn't in his bedroom, perfecting his technique, he was in Laz's bedroom doing exactly the same thing. Their first band had been a covers outfit, playing charts songs and the Beatles, working in smoky labour clubs and pubs around the Midlands. Eventually, their singer, George, had left, and been replaced by Duncan Lake, who had far greater ambitions for them. Their goal now was to play their own material at colleges and universities, which meant ditching their old name, The Stubbles, (one of many doomed names) and starting afresh.

Duncan, who loved nothing better than to stare nobly at himself in mirrors and toss his lion-like mane occasionally, suggested the name 'Epitaph', which he felt had sufficient gravitas to suit their brand of 'orchestral' progressive pomp rock. David countered with the name Gravitas, which he argued had sufficient epitaph. Duncan did not seem overly amused. He was a very single-minded and serious character. Inspired by his heroes, Peter Hammill, of Van Der Graaf Generator, and Peter Gabriel of Genesis, he had recently penned a concept album, possibly even a double, which he confidently expected the record companies to snap up, as soon as he could get his new band tightly rehearsed enough to complete some demo recordings. This was proving frustrating, as everyone's time, other than his, was limited for various reasons.

Laz had been working at British Leyland on the production line, a soul-destroying job which he hated. He had recently teamed up with a Brummie barrow boy by the name of Sammie Chinn, who came complete with the regulation sheepskin coat and sovereign ring combination, and they were making decent money in their spare time, ripping off old ladies with their house clearance business. The money was so good, in fact, that they decided to hand in their notices, and become self-employed. This had seriously impacted on Laz's free time at weekends. David too was struggling to fit in the rehearsals, what with his final year college work and Suzanne, who preferred to spend Saturdays trying to buy every pair of shoes in Sutton Coldfield.

Nick Chinn, (Sammy's cousin) a superb drummer with a mouth slightly louder than his drum kit, still worked at British Leyland and loved the camaraderie of being in a band, but the round trip from his home to Laz's father's factory, where they rehearsed, was a long one, and sometimes he would fail to show. That just left Ken, the bass player, who would always turn up, providing he wasn't lying drunk in a gutter somewhere, and of course Duncan, who was a full-time musician and poet, currently drawing his dole and spending most of it on cheap cider and pretentious concept albums.

Regardless of everyone's personal problems, however, they had all solemnly sworn to attend the weekend's rehearsal, because their first gig had been arranged at none other than the art college's favourite nightclub, The Crypt. Duncan was keen to get 'his' band nice and professional by then, and the date was only a month away.

* * *

David spent the final minutes of his uneventful bus ride imagining how Jimmy Triplicate would deal with the Beatles' song, 'She Loves You.' He envisaged the driver trying to explain to a friend what the song was called.

"C'mon man. Surely you know it! It's called 'She loves you, yeah yeah yeah yeah yeah yeah yeah yeah yeah.'"

David hoped and prayed that this unlikely scenario would never occur. The resulting fiasco could send his Jamaican friend over the edge, into some kind of psychotic state. Any more or less than nine 'yeahs' and he'd have to do it all over again. The 'Say It Three Times' devil would be demanding a re-count. The resulting confusion didn't bear thinking about.

The filthy bus ground to a halt and the double doors hissed open. David bade his driver farewell and was much amused to see him respond, not with words, but with three casual waves of the hand. Alighting from the bus, David strode purposefully towards the college, large black portfolio under his arm, past the stop where The Weird Woman stood on Friday evenings.

Wolverhampton College of Art was and still is an ugly seven-storey block of flats on the ring road, immediately next to Wolverhampton Wanderers Football Club, and just up the street from the headquarters of Tarmac. It was constructed entirely from ghastly grey concrete, and had around three hundred assorted aerials attached to its flat roof, the purpose of which had eluded everyone who had ever studied there. The building housed not only the illustration and graphic design departments where David and Dylan worked, but also Printmaking, Bookbinding, Photography, Textiles, Three Dimensional Design, Sculpture and Fine Art. There was a refectory where a starving artist could grab a meat pie and a cup of tea, though only the unfortunate ones who *were* actually starving ate there. The rest risked their lives each day to cross the ring road in search of sustenance at the larger Polytechnic refectory. The choice of food was slightly better and there were more pretty women to ogle at.

The Foundation department was situated just across town in the same building as the town's art gallery. It was a much nicer, Victorian labyrinth of lived-in, paint-spattered studios, and a place where David had been idyllically happy. The uglier main building did have its advantages, however. From the seventh floor it was possible to follow the football match on Saturday afternoons, which meant that the normally work-shy fine art students would suddenly be eager to catch up on a bit of painting.

The college was laid out in such a way that each discipline had a floor to itself. The lower ground floor housed the photographic students. It had large, drive-in studios and a communal darkroom - a huge room where up to twenty students could develop and print their pictures at the same time. David loved working there, because he could think better in the dark, away from the mad hustle and bustle of the rest of the college. There was something quite magical about signing a camera out, taking pictures around the town, and then coming back into the college to develop the negatives in total darkness. When the negatives were washed and dried, he would book an enlarger for the afternoon and make test strips, which showed him the correct exposure times for his prints. Once these had been ascertained, a full sheet of light-sensitive paper was slid out of its light-fast black bag and positioned on the base of the enlarger under safe red lighting. The enlarger lamp was turned on for the required time, before the paper was slipped into the first dish of chemical. This was where the real magic occurred. Slowly, over the course of a minute or two, an image would appear in beautiful, elegant black and white. Once fully developed, the paper was removed, placed into another dish to fix the image, and finally washed and dried. The ambiance of the darkroom reminded David of the hushed reverence of a church, but with far more miraculous visions on offer. It was also an excellent place for a frisky couple to have a snog.

The ground floor was home to the bookbinding and typography department, where students learnt to set lead type in galley form, as used in newspaper production. The tiny lead letters were kept in racks, with the capital letters at the top and the small letters beneath, hence the expressions, 'upper and lower case'. Students were also taught how to make a leather-bound book from scratch, and print proofs of their design work. As one climbed the building, the air became more rarefied. The middle floors housed the product designers, illustrators and graphic artists, who were looked down upon, in both senses of the expression, by the fine artists, who occupied the seventh floor, or The Astral Plane, as David called it. They despised the artistic prostitutes below, who would one day be selling their souls by painting commercial work, in return for the promise of considerable sums of money. Fine art students were purists. They splashed paint onto canvases with bike pumps, rolled over them naked, and hung the entrails of dead road-kill badgers down the stairwells in the name of art. They never smiled. They were intense, scruffily dressed, paint-stained, shaven-headed, earring-wearing intellectuals. Few had bothered to master the traditional drawing and painting skills, because that was so 'yesterday'. Expression was all, and if the art came with a forty page printed dossier to explain why it was a work of genius, so much the better. These people were the purest of the pure. They lived in squalor and poverty, just as Van Gogh had done, and they engaged in violent discussions at The Castle Pub about the comparative merits of post-modernism and abstract expressionism, in between darts matches.

23

When it was all over, and they'd gained their worthless bit of paper with Bachelor of Arts printed on it, they inevitably did a teaching degree with a view to spending their lives teaching others how to do what they'd done, so that the art school dance could go on forever. Those that didn't survive got themselves real jobs, in factories, supermarkets and bicycle repair shops, and never painted again. In fact, they hardly ever spoke about art again, except when they were deriding the ones who were earning too much money, painting for a living, but doing what they were told. Occasionally though, one of their number would do well, and become London's next big thing, subsequently returning to the college to give self-important lectures in the amphitheatre. They invariably had intense-sounding eastern-European names, and their 'installation' art; typically a pile of bricks or a box full of coloured rags, was being snapped up by the Tate for many thousands of pounds. This would inspire the seventh floor zealots no end, and they would begin splashing the paint about with renewed vigour, once they'd returned from their bohemian-style three hour lunch sessions at The Castle.

\* \* \*

David walked up the front steps and towards the automatic glass doors. They politely opened as they sensed his presence, allowing him into the depressing concrete entrance hall, with its wood textured finish. Some bright seventies' architect, he mused, had actually designed this place on purpose. He must have used a condemned Ukrainian tower block as inspiration. Pushing planks of rough-hewn wood into the still-wet concrete to create texture was a nice touch. It reminded the visitor of all the beautiful, natural materials the place *could* have been constructed with, had the architect not been a complete turd.

Dylan followed him through the glass doors and said hello. They decided to be lazy and catch the lift, as Dylan was tired from doing his bit for conservation on Monday night. He'd been busy culling bottles of Guinness, which had been breeding profusely in his local pub, resulting in the shelves being overrun with the stuff. Every now and then, Dylan and his girlfriend, a spirited redhead called Kathleen, would be called in, like pest control officers, to keep the numbers down. Both of them were tireless in their enthusiasm for this important ecological labour of love, but it tended to leave them feeling a tad delicate the following day, and three flights of cruelly steep stairs can quickly bring on a throbbing head.

After keeping the two friends waiting for at least an hour longer than it would have taken them to tackle the stairs, the lift finally creaked open, giving the pair a nasty start. The interior of the lift had been wallpapered and carpeted, and there was even skirting board. A small television stood in the left hand corner, and on the right, a two-seater nineteen-fifties settee with a small coffee table in front of it. Cosily ensconced on the settee were two straight-faced characters, a lady with a pinafore and curlers and a man with slippers, a maroon cardigan and a pipe. They both appeared to be engrossed in their reading matter: Woman's Realm for her, and the Daily Mirror for him.

The effect this had on David and Dylan was quite interesting. Neither seemed to know whether to let this particular lift go and wait for the next, or invade this couple's private space by strolling in. The couple weren't paying them any attention whatsoever, which didn't help matters. They just carried on reading. Eventually, David plucked up the courage to step inside. Dylan followed sheepishly, narrowly avoiding the closing doors.

Juddering violently as it always did, the lift began its laborious haul up to the third floor. David had needed to reach across the lady in curlers to reach the buttons, causing her to 'tut' under her breath and lay down her Woman's Realm for a second. Dylan, in an attempt to appear nonchalant, asked the pipe and slippers man if the snooker was on telly that evening, but he didn't reply. As lift jokes went, this bogus living room was as elaborate as it was unnerving, and obviously a seventh floor stunt. At least, he mused, it was a touch more creative than their usual efforts, but was it art?

David was no stranger to lift humour himself, having printed a formal-looking sign a few weeks earlier stating that 'Talking in the Lift is Expressly Forbidden.' and signing it Claude Beardsley, Head of Department. Disappointed with the lack of public reaction, he had printed another sign the week after, which read:

'Due to the increased number of students now using this building, it will now be necessary to book cubicle toilets at the office on the ground floor', again signed by Mr Beardsley. As yet, there had been no response to this latest ruse. In his heart of hearts, he didn't really believe that anyone could be so stupid as to swallow the bait, but he lived in hope.

After what seemed like an eternity, the lift rumbled to a halt, and the doors opened on floor three. Dylan pressed the seventh floor button, and the doors closed again.

"Where are we going?" asked David, puzzled.

"I forgot," explained Dylan. "There's an art exhibition up on the seventh floor. I thought we might take a look at what the Astral Plane mob is up to."

The pipe and slippers man gave him a mean look.

"Do you actually mean to tell me that they paint pictures?" grinned David devilishly, warming to the theme. "I thought *real* art was a thing of the past with that lot. Don't they mainly just do performance art nowadays, because none of them know how to draw?"

"Well," said Dylan, "here we are. Let's find out!" They strode bravely onto the alien corridor, David trying desperately to stifle a giggling fit. The doors closed behind them, and once more the couple on the settee were alone. The pipe and slippers man lowered his newspaper and addressed the curlers lady.

"Pair of tossers!" he snarled, and resumed his crossword.

The corridors of the seventh floor had been turned into an exhibition space for the third year Fine Art degree students. Most of the work was on huge unframed canvases, and virtually all of it was abstract. David paused at the first picture, which was called 'Black Spot on Black Canvas', by Chui Placenta.

"Have you noticed," observed Dylan, "That they all have bloody funny names up here? Why is that? On our floor, we've got normal sounding names like Ted Jennings, Nigel Sutherland and what have you. Look at this one, for example!"

He directed David to a canvas that looked as if random strips of masking tape had been daubed over, and then the tapes removed. The word MOOD was roughly stencilled in the bottom right corner.

"Ah!" smiled David. "This is 'Mood 4 in Grey', by Fanny Needham-Trimmer. I see what you mean. And here's one by Heston Ching."

A series of paintings at the far end of the corridor stood out from the rest, because they were quite well painted, figurative pictures of the old school. From a distance, they resembled the work of Caravaggio, with lots of writhing naked figures set against dark backgrounds.

"Let's take a look at those," suggested Dylan. "They look interesting."

As they approached, they realized that here was a painter who wasn't content with superficial likenesses, but an artist who tried to paint the inner person, in a quite literal sense. The subjects were naked, or semi-naked, men and women interlinked in various pseudo-classical poses, presumably seconds after Jack the Ripper had experimented on them with a kitchen knife or potato peeler. Huge dollops of intestine and gore were protruding from nasty gashes, cascading down onto the floor or onto the backs of anyone unfortunate enough to be just underneath. The painter's subjects, however, seemed largely unperturbed by the fact that their spleens had been vented, and appeared to be carrying on regardless and chatting nonchalantly about this and that.

"This bloke is *seriously* deranged!" gasped Dylan, shocked. "He should be in a psychiatric unit, not an art college. What's his name?"

"Laurence Fuchs," laughed David. "You couldn't make it up, could you?"

"It's pronounced Fooks," added Dylan helpfully. "It's German, like Fokker."

David shuddered. "I'd hate to be inside that bloke's head. I wonder if he knows The Weird Woman. They'd make a great couple. This stuff gives me the creeps, let's go."

Kieron Hastings, the diminutive Head of Fine Art, strutted down the corridor towards the two long-haired characters in denim jackets whom he'd observed falling about laughing at his protégés' work. He was not overly amused.

"Can I remind you two that your presence is required in the Lecture Theatre in five minutes, along with every other student currently studying at this college?" he said, rather stiffly. This came as a surprise to both of them. Presumably, because they'd taken a detour to the Astral Plane, they'd missed out on hearing this information from their own Head of Department, Claude Beardsley.

"The whole college?" asked Dylan. "I've never known it. What's so important?"

"I suggest you get down there and find out, instead of ridiculing work that you don't have the brains to understand," snapped Mr Hastings, plainly wounded. "And right away please. It's essential that we are on time. I'm only guessing, but it may well be to do with the spate of art thefts at the college. Were you aware, gentlemen, that several paintings, prints, etchings and drawings have disappeared; a lot of it important degree show work?"

Dylan had not only heard about it, he was a victim himself. One of his best pencil drawings of a pair of bell peppers had gone missing from his drawer the previous week, and his friend Tony Lockley, who had won the prestigious Tarmac Printmaking Prize that year, had lost several silk-screen prints, including his winning entry. David, who always kept his work at home or in his closely-guarded portfolio, told Kieron that he had been more fortunate.

"That's because they seem to be targeting only the most talented students," added Dylan cattishly.

The three commandeered the next lift, which was thankfully devoid of fine art pranksters, and headed, in even more stony silence than usual, for the ground floor. In an attempt to build bridges, David coughed a polite cough, and asked Kieron a question.

"Erm, I hope you don't mind my asking, but do you know what H and B stand for on pencils?"

"I, erm, do, of course!" stuttered the Head of Department, saved by the lift bell announcing that the first floor was awaiting them. "Come on now, we're late!"

They filed into an already packed lecture theatre and squeezed onto the end of an aisle near the back. Claude Beardsley, an Oliver Reed look-alike with a heavy black leather flying jacket worn over his shoulders, Gestapo-style, strode purposefully across the stage, followed by a young woman police officer with her long, shiny hair done up in a bun.

"That's WPC Snibboh!" exclaimed David excitedly. "What's she doing here?"

"Is everyone in this town blessed with a stupid bloody name?" asked Dylan, not unreasonably.

Claude Beardsley called for order, which, as usual, took far too long coming. Eventually, the expectant chatter of some two hundred students and staff subsided.

He spoke.

"Okay ladies and gentlemen. I have called you all together today to announce the sad news that one of our second year Photography students, Jack Hamphlett, died tragically on Friday evening at around six o'clock. It appears that he may have committed suicide."

Many of the students turned to each other with shocked expressions at this point, and several girls began to cry. David did not recognize the student's name; nor, it transpired, did Dylan. Claude Beardsley continued.

"I am very sorry to break this awful news to you. I know many of you were friends of Jack's, and this must have come as a huge shock. I would like to pass you over to WPC Hobbins of the Wolverhampton Police, who is looking for information regarding this terrible tragedy."

The policewoman stepped up to the microphone.

"Folks, as Mr Beardsley just said, this is a tragic end to a young man's life, and we need to determine what happened. I'm informed that Jack was the son of your previous Head of Department, who also died tragically last year due to an allergic reaction whilst having his lunch in West Park. His widow - Jack's mother, Mrs Gertrude Hamphlett - is understandably distraught at the moment, and under sedation at home. It must be an incredible shock to lose not only a husband but also her only son in the same year. We understand from our initial enquiries that Jack was extremely depressed about his beloved father's death, and this may well have triggered events on Friday. We know that he'd been seeing his doctor about his troubles, and he was on anti-depressants. It is essential that we get a full picture of Jack's whereabouts and general state of mind last week. Can I ask those who knew him, if you have anything you can tell us, no matter how trivial or inconsequential it seems, would you please talk to me afterwards? I'll be around the college for the rest of the morning in the third floor tutorial room if you need me, and you can be assured of total confidentiality. May I also take this opportunity to offer my sincere condolences to Jack's family and friends? By all accounts, he was a very likeable, serious-minded and talented young man, with a beautiful girlfriend, the promise of a first class degree, and everything to live for. Please help us to try and fathom out what drove him to do this. Thank you."

The room broke out into a flurry of animated conversation, and some of the students, clearly very distressed by the news, headed for the exits, comforted by friends. David held his hand over his mouth as he looked at Dylan.

"The chalk line by the Dragonfly Boutique. It was no fine art stunt. I was standing on the very spot where this lad fell."

The students began to file out of the room, past WPC Hobbins, who stood near the exit, thanking them for their cooperation.

"Snibboh, we meet again!" whispered David as he passed by.

"Ah!" she smiled. "Do you mind if I take you somewhere quiet to frisk you? I suspect that you may have a banana on your person, and I'm starving."

"What is it with you?" asked David, once he'd politely introduced her to Dylan. "You're always hungry. We usually pop up to the refectory about now for a cup of tea and a blueberry muffin. Care to join us?"

"I'd love to," she said. "I like a good muffin, when the mood takes me…"

"My kind of woman," enthused David, drooling visibly.

"…but I'm needed in the tutorial room. Tell you what, here's some money. Be a darling and get me something and drop it in for me, would you?"

David pushed her hand away. "Keep your money. It will be my pleasure to supply my favourite policewoman with a muffin and a tea out of my meagre student funds. Dyl, lend me two quid."

Dylan, who obviously didn't wish to be seen as mean by those present, coughed up without a murmur. He also offered the WPC a whole stick of chewing gum, a gesture that didn't go unnoticed by his friend. David bit his lip and resolved to use it as evidence against him on some future occasion. Five minutes later, he was politely knocking on the tutorial room door. No one had been to give evidence so far, so he sat down for a minute to drink his tea.

"Just after you beat me up," he began, "I inadvertently stood on that blasted chalk line by the Dragonfly. It's been playing on my mind ever since."

WPC Hobbins apologized, and asked if he'd ever met the deceased.

"No." David replied, "Not as such, but I recognized that photo you were circulating earlier, and it dawned on me that he was the lad I used to see in the darkrooms all the time. He'd just smile and say hello as we passed, but other than that, we never spoke. He was a year below me, and you know how it is. We tend not to mix with them as much as our own year. I never realized that he was Mr Hamphlett's son either."

WPC Hobbins wolfed down her cake. "Well, as no one else has arrived yet, I'll talk to you, David. Did you know his dad well?"

"Yes," said David. It seemed strange being alone in a room with the woman he had recently seduced in his dream. He was struggling to stay focussed on her questions, as he re-lived the juicier bits.

"Yes, Kingsley Hamphlett was a lovely bloke. He was my Head of Department for nearly two years, so I knew him quite well. It's just horrible what's happened to his family. I saw him the day he died; I had a tutorial with him, in this very room, till about ten to one. As he wrapped it up, he mentioned that he was going to take his sandwiches down to the boating lake and relax in the sun for an hour. He was always down there. I know, because we sometimes took a football and had a game of five-a-side, and we'd see him. He used to hire a boat, row into the middle of the lake and sit there, eating his dinner and sipping his tea - a creature of habit. He always brought a flask to work because he liked Earl Grey, and you can't get it in our canteen."

WPC Hobbins took a sip of her own tea and grimaced. "Christ! This tastes like camel piss. I don't blame him."

"Anyway, this particular day, after my tutorial, he grabbed his dinner and his coat, and said that he'd see me afterwards, but I never saw him again. Dead at fifty and killed by a peanut. How ridiculous is that? There was a man in the paper last week who had a huge wooden stake enter his lorry cab and pierce his body. Another chap had a javelin go through his neck and come out through his leg. Both of 'em lived to tell the tale. Kids get impaled on spiked railings in parks, and they survive. You get an allergic reaction to a peanut, or a wasp sting, and you're a goner. It's a funny old world."

The policewoman stood, removed her jacket and sat down again. The crisp white blouse brought the memories flooding back. David had misled her earlier. He had what felt like a banana in his trouser pocket after all. He should really have been back in the studio, completing his Tiffany drawing, but he deemed it best to stay seated for the time being, until his ardour subsided a little.

"How come he had a peanut in his lunch?" she asked. "Surely he knew how careful he had to be, or didn't he realize that he had this allergy?"

"No, he knew. He always used to tell us a story about a fellow peanut allergy sufferer who died on a plane. He'd sat himself down in a place where the previous occupant had eaten his complimentary nuts and wiped his greasy hands on the seat. The victim had literally just brushed his hand against the area and started biting his nails, and that was it. His throat swelled up and he couldn't breathe. Dead in ten minutes. No, he was careful, and he kept some sort of syringe with him. I know, because he showed me. Adrenalin is it? Anyway, he'd picked up his sandwiches from the little corner shop as usual, you know the sort of thing, in a see-through plastic triangular box, and his apple, and his Mister Kipling cake, before he arrived for work. We both frequented the same place, and he trusted Mrs Timmins to be careful, as she was aware of his problem. She made it her business to check with the sandwich makers that nothing dodgy was ever placed near his ingredients. She told me. You can imagine how upset she was when she heard about his death. She felt responsible."

"What happened, then?" asked WPC Hobbins. "How did the peanut find its way into the box?"

"They reckon there was a new chap started work that week, and the likelihood was that it was his fault. He admitted that he'd been eating peanuts himself in his own lunch break, and maybe he hadn't been as hygienic as the rest of them were trained to be. The forensic people discovered a few minute scraps of peanut in the sandwich, but it was enough. The employee got the sack, and by all accounts felt equally as shitty as poor Mrs Timmins did about it all, but it's no good castigating the chap and making him feel wretched. It was an innocent mistake after all."

"What about Kingsley's syringe then? Why didn't he use it?" asked WPC Hobbins.

"I don't know, to be honest," admitted David. "Perhaps he dropped it in the lake, struggling to inject himself. It wasn't here at college, because I remember the police looking for it. Anyway, I have to go. Unless I'm very much mistaken, your first customer has arrived."

He stood up, holding the drinks tray strategically over his enhanced member, and sidled self-consciously over to the door.

"See you around!" he said sheepishly, his face flushed with embarrassment.

"I hope so!" she smiled. "You know where to find me."

David opened the door to find three first year girls, who obviously had a few snippets of information for the police. He ushered them in and limped back to the studio.

# CHAPTER 3

## Introducing Mrs M

It was one-fifteen, and Dylan was late. David walked into Tweedledum's Café, which was, unusually for the time of day, almost empty. There were just two customers sitting near the door; a slight, hen-pecked middle-aged man and his robust, loud wife. When Olga asked them what they wanted, he asked for a bacon sandwich, whereupon the wife began to berate him loudly, reminding him that bacon was not good for him. He accepted her judgment with a sad, tired look, and resigned himself to a round of dry toast. David made a mental note to add them to his list of characters, and gave them a working title of Dry Toast and The Dragon, until he could come up with something more inspired.

After ordering a tea, he headed for the back of the café, which was long and narrow like a galley, with the tables laid out with two chairs either side, and partitions separating each block of four seats. These booths gave the place a feeling of privacy, like the old Regency London coffee houses, which David liked. Being a thoughtful soul, he always headed for the furthest booth because it was the only one that housed just two people, due to an old chimney breast that took the place of the two inner seats. This way, he wouldn't be selfishly taking up a four-seater table if the café got crowded.

He ordered a tea and sat down. He was meeting Dylan for a quick snack, prior to walking over the road to Glass Eye's

Snooker Joint. This, of course, wasn't the real name of the place, but Dylan had christened it so because the proprietor, a seedy looking character who always seemed to be studying the Racing Post and smoking a cigarette, appeared to have a glass eye. Glass eye or no glass eye, he could knock up breaks of over a hundred when push came to shove, so it was obviously not a terrible problem for him.

David was pondering the frailty of human life, interspersed with the occasional fantasy about lying the WPC face down on the edge of a silken bed and slipping off her black skirt, when his deep thoughts were interrupted, not by Dylan, but by a small man of about thirty with unkempt hair, pebble glasses and a huge and hideous red, knitted cardigan with a repeat pattern of white puppies all over it.

"Can I sit here?" asked the man.

David scanned the café. It was still virtually empty. This man with a coffee in his hand wanted to sit opposite him in the two-seater booth. David was masterful at witty banter and the Oscar Wilde-style put down when the mood took him. He could be sarcastic and even forceful on occasion, when he needed to be, but he had absolutely no ammunition for situations like this. Perhaps the man simply liked company while he got his caffeine fix. Somehow, he didn't strike David as your typical gay predator.

"Help yourself," replied David, unsurely.

The man sat down and tried to open his sugar sachets, without success.

"Can you open this for me?" he asked David, without a hint of shame or embarrassment. David obliged.

Two more people appeared at the two-seater booth. Another man of around twenty, and a chubby lady wearing a pink Donny Osmond T shirt.

"Hello," they said. "Can we sit with you please?"

"There's only two seats," David pointed out.

"I'll move up," said the Puppy Cardigan. "Sit by me."

He crammed himself tightly against the chimney breast, and they somehow managed to fit into the space, with the chubby girl's right bottom cheek hanging in mid-air. David busied himself opening the Puppy Cardigan's sugar, his agile mind in overdrive.

"Hello!" said two new faces, in unison. A man of around forty-five with only one tooth - just off-centre, long and yellow - and a woman with enormous breasts, which were swinging bra-less in a grubby lime green T shirt.

"Can we sit by you?"

"Feel free!" sighed David. "There's loads of room yet." His defence mechanism was at last kicking in.

"Move up," ordered the Lime Green Breasts. Before David could get out of the way, she had rammed him sideways into the chimney breast, nearly dislocating his shoulder.

"Where can I go?" moaned Central Eating. He began to sob uncontrollably.

"Sit on my lap!" suggested Lime Green Breasts. Heartened by this, he ceased the waterworks and tried to fit himself onto her lap, but the low table and her giant bosom conspired against him. He began to weep again.

"Look, I'll tell you what," suggested David. "Shall I get out, and then you can all fit in?"

"Ooh! Thank you!" said Puppy Cardigan. "Thank you very much!" added the other four.

David grabbed his teacup and squeezed out, just as Dylan entered the café.

"Having a party?" he asked.

"Why does it always happen to me?" asked David.

"It doesn't!" replied Dylan. "They all sat by me last week. It drives Olga mad. They're from the home across the road. It's nice to let them have a bit of freedom, don't you think? They're harmless, most of them, but watch out for the civil war bloke and the one in a dinner suit with a pipe and cravat."

"Why?"

"Well, the civil war chap's apparently very intelligent, and used to go to university, but he flipped. If he ever starts talking to you, you've had it. You'll never get away. Some days, he thinks he's Elmer Johnson, an American Civil War soldier, and he keeps on about fighting the Confederates, and stuff. He asked me to help him flush them out, but I told him there weren't any, as this was the Mander Centre. I thought maybe a bit of a reality check might jolt him out of it, but it didn't.

The pipe man is worse though. Olga banned him for shouting at an imaginary snake, and he returned the next day, stark-bollock-naked and stood across the front door, refusing to let folks in. Two burly coppers led him away, and Olga lent them a tea towel to cover his todger up with."

"Jesus! It's enough to put you off your sausage roll. Shall we eat?"

"Yes. You're paying. I'll have the soup," said Dylan, hopefully.

"So will I. That's two soups then. We'll sit in the window seats." David was too traumatized to argue about whose turn it was. He stumped up without a whimper.

Fifteen minutes later, they were pushing their plates away and getting ready to leave.

"How was your omelette?" asked David.

"Excellent!" smiled Dylan. "How was yours?"

"Perfect!" agreed David. They said farewell to Olga, who looked weary, and made their way across the road to the snooker club.

"Did I tell you about the Hand Grenade Thrower?" asked Dylan. "He wanders around town pretending to throw grenades, and occasionally he'll duck to avoid one himself. Sad really. He's shell-shocked, due to the war. Completely harmless of course!"

"Till he kills somebody," added David, a tad unsympathetically. "We'd better only play two frames today. I've got to see Mrs M this afternoon."

"Talking of mad people!" grinned Dylan.

"A bit unfair, if you don't mind my saying so," argued David, frowning. "I admit that her tale is a strange one, but she's a perfectly normal person who became part of an abnormal situation, if you see what I mean. A bit like me. I attract strangeness, but I'm not strange myself am I?"

"Can I take the fifth amendment?" asked Dylan, rather obliquely.

After two rushed frames of sub-standard snooker, which were dominated by talk of Jack Hamphlett's suicide, they walked back to college, honours even. Dylan was a little miffed because he thought that David had fluked the final pink, robbing him of a two-nil victory and prize money of over three pounds, but David was adamant that he'd purposely intended to go off eight cushions in order to leave himself on the black. When Dylan asked, somewhat bitterly, why he was still eleven feet away from the black after the pot, David changed the subject back to the suicide.

"Do you know, Dyl, I'm getting obsessed with this. I think it's because I was standing on the exact spot where this poor chap hit the deck. It's made me feel part of it, somehow. Does that sound stupid?"

"Yes."

"And I know this'll make me sound like Columbo, but there's something I don't get. People I've been speaking to reckon he was up on the multi-storey roof taking photographs for his project on townscapes, and that the police found his Pentax unharmed. Nigel Reed, a chap I know in third year photography, said the policewoman that I introduced you to this morning has asked Mike, the photography technician to develop Jack's film to see if there are any clues to be had."

"So?"

"Look! If I admit the pink was a fluke, will you stop being monosyllabic?"

"Yeah!"

"Okay, I fluked it, but they still count, so tough shit. What I'm getting at is this; if you were depressed out of your mind, would you be taking pictures for your B.A. show?"

Dylan pondered. "Maybe he wasn't taking pictures for his project. Maybe he'd gone to toss himself off."

"Did I really just hear you say that?"

"Not the best way of putting it. What I mean is, just 'cause he had his camera with him, it doesn't mean he was going there to take pictures does it?"

David had to agree. "Maybe I've seen too many thrillers. It would be interesting to see the contents of that camera though, but obviously the coppers will keep that closely guarded, just in case. The rumours are already flying around. Katie in our studio reckons that Jack had been in the Castle every night, drinking heavily. He hadn't been looking after himself either. You know, not eating and so on. It couldn't have been easy losing his dad like that, and he seemed to be beating himself up over it. She said he'd had a stand-up drunken row with his girlfriend not long ago, as a result of which she'd walked out on him. I suppose he just

41

flipped. It'll be interesting to see if he was pissed up when he jumped."

They approached the college steps and shelved the suicide debate for the time being. They summoned the lift, which was mercifully free of settees, televisions and tossers, and pressed floors three and five. David said goodbye to Dylan and stayed in the lift. He was going straight to the soft materials room to see Mrs M. Having completed a series of drawings and paintings on Tiffany glass, he now wanted to make one of the designs in soft materials, using blue and purple satins for the grapes, and juxtaposing them against coarser canvases and corduroys in shades of green.

He always looked forward to seeing Mrs Meriden, and deliberately tried to steer his projects so that he could spend the odd afternoon with her. Hers was a cosy room, which normally housed no more than three or four favourite students. The banter was always fun, and there was never a shortage of tea and cakes.

Dylan's earlier reference to Mrs M had caused David to become defensive. Usually, he had no time for the supernatural whatsoever, but Mrs M was a special case. He believed her to be a genuine psychic, and any cynicism he once had was washed away instantly by the events of the previous summer.

Mrs M had not always been gifted in that way. She was a perfectly normal sewing teacher, who lived with her husband, Norman, in nearby Tettenhall. Around ten years before David arrived at the college, she had been having a restless night, and awoke at three in the morning to witness a remarkable red glow in the sky, which she attributed to the sunrise. Having double-checked her alarm clock, she realized that sunrise was not due for a considerable time, and walked over to the open window to see what was going on.

The sky became alive with whizzing lights, which suddenly orchestrated into one huge ball and catapulted heavenwards at an incredible rate. Then the red glow subsided and was gone in seconds.

Thinking that she had been dreaming, she crawled back to bed and awoke at nine to make her husband a cup of tea, as was her habit on Saturdays. Whilst in the kitchen, she became aware of a slight itching sensation on her face, which gradually became worse and worse as the week progressed. Her hair began to fall out in handfuls and the itching became unbearable, so she went to her doctor, who sent her for tests. In three weeks, she had lost most of her hair, and was having to wear a wig. She also noticed that she was saying strange things, for no apparent reason. One morning, when her husband was about to set off for work, she suddenly warned him to careful on the ring road, as a young boy was going to run in front of his car. Thinking she'd been at the sherry, he waved, thanked her politely, and ten minutes later hit a ten year old boy, who 'luckily' suffered only a broken leg and a black eye. Obviously shocked by this sudden bout of psychic power, he began to listen more carefully to his wife's occasional odd comments.

One day, she casually informed him that she fancied a trip to West Bromwich so that she could see the town hall burn down. He decided to take her, just for the hell of it, and was stunned when they were turned back by police as they tried to enter the high street, in order that the fire engines would not be hampered in their duty.

David had seen Mrs M's awesome talent at work himself in his second year, when she told him, apropos of nothing, not to take the bus home that evening as it was going to hit a tree. He ignored her warning, because there was no easy alternative to the bus for getting back to Brierley Bank, and also because he didn't believe in such nonsense. He travelled unscathed, but as his bus pulled into Dudley, he saw a bus travelling in the opposite direction smash into a huge tree, killing the driver and two passengers. Sometimes, Mrs M got it slightly wrong, and occasionally completely wrong, but David knew there was something going on in that mind of hers which didn't happen with other people. What also convinced him were the results of her doctor's tests, which Mrs M still carried in her handbag, years afterwards.

The report said:

*'The skin irritation appears to have been caused by radiation of some sort, but I am both disappointed to have let you down, and perplexed, because it is a form of radiation that we have never encountered before, and as such, we find it difficult to advise your patient on a cure for her problem.'*

Though much better than it had been, Mrs M's itching and redness never went away, and she still wore a wig.

David burst into the soft materials room singing, "I'm putting on my top hat, fastening my bow-tie, shining up my shoes." and tap-dancing like Fred Astaire. He loved to make Mrs M laugh because she, like himself, was a great giggler. She responded by dashing into her storeroom and emerging seconds later, swathed in a huge roll of fake leopard skin and growling.

"Well!" she exclaimed, once the inevitable laughter had subsided. "If it isn't our David, and if it isn't, I haven't got a clue who it is. What are you here for this time? Another jacket?"

The previous term he had made himself a fake tiger-skin bomber jacket with a stand-up collar so that he could be Bryan Ferry from Roxy Music at the end of term fancy dress bash. He'd never had the courage to wear it again after a visiting lecturer called Gerald had tried to seduce him, and had given him a lowly sixty percent for his project when David told him to sod off.

David showed her the design, and she scurried off into her storeroom looking for samples while he put the kettle on. They sat down on a mountain of foam rubber to discuss the options, which he loved doing, because it reminded him of being at his infants' school. Mrs M's room was a kind of soft play area for adults; the fifth floor creatives' crèche.

She began to lay out small samples of material, so that they could see which ones looked good together. David asked her if she had ever met Jack Hamphlett.

"Yes," she replied, her beaming, benign old face suddenly turning sad. "I knew him since he was a little boy of fifteen, because I was a friend of his mother and father. He was a lovely young man, if a little serious, and very deep. I cried my eyes out when I heard the news, but I wasn't surprised. He was never the same after his dad died, you know, and what with his mother having an affair, and his girl friend falling out with him, it must have turned his mind."

David looked puzzled. "I didn't know about the affair. Who with?"

"I'm surprised you haven't heard. It's been circulating the college. Gertie - that's Kingsley Hamphlett's widow, was having a bit of a fling with your head of department, Claude Beardsley. She was attracted to his tough guy Oliver Reed looks and his posh London accent, plus the fact that he knew loads of famous people. I suppose he *is* a bit glamorous, the way he swaggers around with that leather flying-jacket draped over his shoulders. He lives in one of those typical big London terraced four-storey houses, and mixes with actors like Terence Stamp and artists such as Peter Blake and David Hockney. That little place down the road is just his weekday pad to save him commuting. He's got another place in Cornwall too, apparently. It's enough to turn a lady's head, if she's been used to someone like Kingsley."

"I thought Kingsley was a nice man," said David, surprised.

"Oh, he was. He was lovely," replied Mrs M. "He was a gentle, lovable type, and excellent at his job, but a bit of a creature of habit, a safe pair of hands if you will. He adored his wife and son, but perhaps he wasn't exciting enough for her. Some women like exciting men don't they? I'm not being uncharitable, because I like Gertie too, but she's one of those strange women that love it when they're treated like dirt, stood up and two-timed. I've never seen the percentage in it myself. Give me my safe old dependable Norman any time!"

"Are you saying that Claude is like that, a bit of a devil with the women?"

David didn't know much about his new head of department, having only met him briefly for tutorials.

"Well," whispered Mrs M. "I shouldn't be telling you things, as I'm a lecturer and you're a student, but he thinks a lot of himself. I know which of the two I preferred as a person, and I thought Kingsley was a better head of department too. Old Claude is about as similar to Kingsley as I am to Clint Eastwood. Kingsley fretted and cared about his students, and he was the same with Gertie. *Too* caring really, I suppose. She'd only have to have a cold and he was fussing around like a mother hen, asking if she was okay and getting her hot water bottles and Beecham's powders. She repaid him by dropping her drawers for old Oliver Reed every time her husband was out train spotting or walking the fells. He never found out that his own deputy head was at it with his beloved wife, as far as I know. At least he was spared that. I found it hard to be friendly with Gertie when Kingsley died, but in fairness, she was beside herself with grief at the time. It's the same old story, David. Joni Mitchell sang about it."

"What, Woodstock?"

"No, stupid, 'You don't know what you've got till it's gone.' Big Yellow Taxi."

"So what's the situation now?" asked David. "Is she still with old Claude?"

"'Fraid so. There was an all too brief period of mourning and before long she was 'being comforted', as they say in the gossip columns, by family friend and colleague Claude. Young Jack was doubly incensed, of course. There was no love lost between him and Claude, so Jack used to come up here and get things off his chest over a coffee. One day I asked him about how he was, now that his dad's funeral was out of the way. He replied that Claude and his mother should get married straight away to save on the catering bill. When I asked him what he meant, he said that they could use the left-over funeral food as a cold buffet for their wedding. He was understandably bitter. He kept asking his mother how she could be so callous and dismissive of the person she was married to for twenty years. They had blazing rows, especially when he told her that he reckoned their dog had mourned him longer than she did."

"When did you last see Jack?" asked David. "Did he keep in touch?"

"Not so much recently," admitted Mrs M sadly. "He began to drink a lot, and he was skipping college. That wasn't typical of him. He used to be so conscientious. I was very upset when he fell out with his girlfriend Leonora Willowbrook. She was a lovely, dreamy, Pre-Raphaelite beauty from the Foundation course, who adored him, but she didn't like how the booze changed his personality and made him argumentative. Then she had a tragedy of her own to cope with; her father was killed by a hit-and-run driver, which devastated her. They were two people who should have found strength in each other to overcome similar family disasters, but instead he started to self-destruct, and you know what happened next of course. I saw him on the Thursday before he died. He popped in briefly to collect the bobble hat he'd left here, and we had a chat. He said he was going across town to the car park, because there was a fantastic panoramic view of town from there. He wanted to take shots and paste them together inside a circular frame to create a complete three hundred and sixty degree continual view. He was always coming up with novel ideas like that. He needed his hat because he said it was always freezing on top of the car park, and he felt the cold, with his short blond hair. Then he said goodbye and he was gone forever. He never even took his hat. It's still over there, look!"

David walked over to the window and picked it up. "It looks like one of yours, Mrs M."

"It was. I knitted it when he was a first year because he lived in miserable student digs with no heating and I felt sorry for him."

Her lip began to quiver uncontrollably and she began to cry. "Sorry David, but it's such a waste of life. Let me see his hat."

David handed it to her. She looked inside it and ran her fingers along the lines of knitting.

"Isn't that funny?" she said suddenly, dabbing her eyes on her sleeve. "I've just had a picture of a Kodak film canister come into my mind!"

## CHAPTER 4

### Dark Secrets

David stayed with Mrs M until just after four and then caught the lift down to the Photography department. Talking to her had reinforced his belief that Jack hadn't intended to end his life when he set off for the car park. Of course, this didn't mean much. It was quite conceivable that his dark mood had turned black by the time he got to the top floor, where perhaps the lure of the sheer drop had proved too much for him to resist. Maybe the image of his mother being 'comforted' by Claude had popped into his disturbed mind, just at the wrong time. It was pointless trying to guess what went on in another person's head.

David tapped on Mike Sandbroke's door and waited. He knew that he was in, because the red light above the door was switched on. If students barged in unannounced, they ran the risk of fogging hundreds of pounds worth of paper, so the red light meant 'wait'. Mike was the college's colour printing technician, a very gentle-natured, quiet and accommodating man.

Students were allowed to print in black and white, but colour printing was more expensive and complex, which meant that Mike did most of it. He must have spent most of his working life in darkness, which gave him lots of time to think. Perhaps that was Jack's problem. David was convinced that too much deep thinking was detrimental to a person's happiness, which explained why Radio One disc jockeys like Noel Edmonds and Peter Powell always seemed so cheerful.

A voice from inside muttered "I'm coming, hang on!" and a few seconds later, Mike emerged dazed and blinking into the light. David often wondered to himself if Mike slept hanging upside down and lived on insects.

"Ah, Dylan! To what do I owe the pleasure? Do come in."

"Actually, it's David!"

"Sorry David. I always get you two confused. It's probably because you hang around together. Come in; come in, whoever you are!"

David followed him through a dark storage room into the darkroom. At first, he stumbled into desks and chairs, effing and blinding as they came into contact with his shins, but eventually his eyes adjusted to the dim red lights, and he could see where everything was. He noticed Mike's lunchbox, and smiled a wry smile as he spotted the Kit Kat lurking within. Perhaps it was to take away the nasty taste of all those insects.

"Sorry to disturb you Mike," he began. "You'll probably think I'm barmy, but I came down to see you because of something Mrs M said just now. We were talking about Jack Hamphlett, you see."

Mike sighed a huge sigh. "Ah yes, Jack. We're all very upset about that down here, as you can imagine. I saw a lot of him these last few weeks, because I was printing all his degree show photos. Those are some of them on the wall over there. I reckon we should put on an exhibition of his work or something, to commemorate his life, don't you?"

David owned up to not knowing the student personally, but agreed that this was a fitting tribute.

"I've had the police here this morning," Mike continued. "They wanted me to develop his last film, just in case it gave them any clues. I've printed the entire roll, but I can't see how that's going to help. They were just panoramic views of the town. Still, they have to be thorough, don't they?"

"That's why I came," said David. "You know how Mrs M is psychic. She just handled Jack's bobble hat and had one of her turns. She saw a roll of film in her mind, so I wondered if you've discovered anything remarkable on it. Obviously not!"

"Sorry to disappoint you, Dave. No blurred shots of the villain pushing him off the balcony if that's what you mean."

"Well, I knew it was asking a bit much, but you must admit, she's usually pretty accurate, our Mrs M."

Mike had to agree. He recalled the time that she had casually mentioned to him that he should take his camera to the Wolves game on a certain Saturday, as it might earn him some money. He duly took his Nikon to the game, equipped with a telephoto lens, and snapped a lady streaker who had run onto the pitch and pulled the goal-keeper's shorts off as he stood idly watching the action in the opposite goalmouth. Miraculously, Mike was the only photographer to capture the moment, and he was able to sell the image to several national newspapers, which had to 'pixilate' not only the streaker's assets but also the keeper's pride and joy in order to uphold public decency. The goalie in question was mightily relieved by this decision, as it had been a bitterly cold day, and he wasn't looking his best.

On another occasion, Mrs M had suddenly called out the words 'Croquet Boy' in the staff room as she made herself a pot of tea, which made Mike jump, as he had been reading those exact words at exactly the same time in the Express and Star. He decided to invest a few pounds on the aforementioned horse, which was a twenty to one no-hoper in the Grand National, and lo and behold, it won. Mike, like David, never underestimated Mrs M after that.

"I wonder," asked David cheekily, "Erm, would you mind if I had a look at the pictures in Jack's camera, just out of curiosity?"

"Sorry Dave," said Mike. "I trust you, you know that, but I was under strict instruction not to show anyone. The policewoman collected the shots and the negs, and I had to sign a form saying that no other prints were made. It's evidence, after all!"

David apologized. "No problem. I only asked because of Mrs M's comment, but if you've seen them and couldn't spot anything obvious, I'm sure I won't either."

He said goodbye to Mike, who asked David to let himself out, as he needed to get back to an urgent printing job. The darkroom had a middle door, almost like an airlock on a submarine, so that anyone who unwittingly stumbled through the first door wouldn't immediately fog the light-sensitive materials. Mike locked himself in the bat cave once more, leaving David to walk through the outer area, which served as a storage room for chemical bottles and photographic paper boxes. As he approached the outer door that led onto the main corridor, he fell over a black, knee-high waste-paper bin and bashed his head on the door, causing the previously black air to turn blue. Mike called from his lair to ask if he was okay, and David said that he would be, more or less, once the cartoon birds had stopped twittering in circles above his head. He bent down to gather up the screwed up papers from the upturned bin and replace them, but the light was so poor that it was impossible to see what sort of mess he'd made.

He called back to Mike to ask if he could open the outer door, and Mike said it was okay, as all the paper boxes were closed. After scrambling around on his hands and knees for a few moments, scooping up the vile smelling, chemical-soaked reject prints, he came across some test strips. These were not complete photographs, just narrow strips of paper showing a random section of the negative, onto which Mike printed a range of timed exposures to light. This strip would then have been examined, and the perfect exposure time noted. A few seconds either way and the print would be too light or dark, meaning that an expensive whole sheet of paper would have been wasted. David immediately recognized the subject matter. These were pictures of Wolverhampton taken from a high viewpoint with a wide-angle lens. He grabbed them and stuffed them into his pockets, before placing the remaining reject work back into the bin. He shouted goodbye to Mike, closed the outer door, and was gone.

\* \* \*

David showed the bus driver his student pass and climbed the stairs to the top deck. For the last two years, he had been carrying around a pass that featured a picture of a gorilla, plastic-encapsulated over the spot where his identity photograph should have been. He had been telling his friend Laz about how the drivers never bothered to examine the passes, so Laz had bet him ten pounds that he couldn't get away with the gorilla photograph for two full years. Laz had a habit of laying unusual wagers, but it looked as if he'd lost his money on this particular one. One more week as King Kong and the money was David's.

He thoroughly inspected his chosen seat, looking for any small clues that pointed to the previous occupant being Masturbating Maurice. One couldn't be too careful. Only when he was completely satisfied did he sit down and eagerly pull out the chemical soaked scraps of paper, which he began to study carefully. He didn't have the foggiest idea what he was expecting to see, but the feeling of excitement caused by his purloining important police evidence, made even more intense by Mrs M's comment, was making his hands tremble.

The reality, however, was far more prosaic. Firstly, these were narrow strips, with at least seventy percent of the image missing. Secondly, the exposure tests meant that one side of the paper was almost bleached out, whilst the other side was virtually black. Only the middle section of what in itself was just a narrow sliver was of any use.

In total, there were fifteen test strips, which looked as if they'd been taken at two distinctly different times. The first batch showed a bright, summer's day, with strong shadows and a clear blue sky, whilst the second and smaller batch of five showed evidence of the beautiful orange glow that comes as the afternoon is drawing to a close, when the sun is golden and low in the sky. David could see what Jack was trying to achieve. By waiting for an hour or two, he had injected a touch of magic into the scenes, courtesy of the imminent sunset. It seemed ironic that someone watching these stunningly beautiful townscapes should choose to deliberately end his life, thus denying himself the chance to see such views ever again.

It was easy for David to pontificate on such matters. He hadn't had any real tragedies in his young life, other than the death of a beloved grandfather, whereas poor Jack had been subjected to more than enough. Maybe he simply didn't see the world in the same way that David did. One man's magical cloud formation was another's foul and pestilent congregation of vapours. It all depended on the viewer's state of mind.

One of the sunset shots was of particular interest to David, but only for personal reasons. He could just about make out the very bus stop that he stood at each night, with a couple of people in the queue, silhouetted against a passing bright yellow van. He screwed up his eyes to try and make out more detail, but without success. He would need a very much bigger enlargement to have any chance of seeing them clearly, and this was impossible, now that the police had the negatives.

David got home around six thirty, tired and hungry from his bus rides and the final one mile walk to his parents' home in Brierley Bank. He crawled into the living room and threw his portfolio onto the settee, flopping down alongside it with a heavy theatrical sigh. His dad, Len, also exhausted from a hard day's tool-making in the factory, was slumped in his favourite armchair fast asleep. David's ten year old brother Paul, who had heard him arrive, abandoned his solo game of Subbuteo and came rushing down from his bedroom to welcome him home by leaping onto his stomach. Their mother, Ruby, entered the room shortly afterwards to give him an approximate E.T.A. on the dinner arrangements.

"Sorry it's a bit cold," she called, as she returned to the kitchen. "The gas fire seems to have stopped working. I've had to ring Graves Brothers to come and fix it, but they're stacked out, so it could be a while. It's a good job it's spring time, and not the winter!"

David decided to retire to his bedroom until the dinner was done, as it had a small electric heater. He also wanted to examine the test strips more closely. His bedroom doubled as a workroom, and had a desk with a drawing board with a draughtsman's angle-poise lamp, which his dad had acquired from the offices at work.

Len was one of those dads who always came home with unusual things. Since Christmas, he'd handed his bemused sons a Victorian electric shock therapy machine, an ornately decorated zither and a submarine periscope, to name but three. Quite how a foreman at a tool-making shop came by these wonderful items was another matter, but as a child, David would eagerly run down to the garage as his tired father parked the car, to ask what he'd got for him. One evening, he arrived with a hamster in a cage, which David christened Jennings, after a character in his favourite books, but the friendship was a short-lived one.

Finding the poor creature stiff and lifeless one cold autumn morning, Len had ignored David's request for a large state funeral attended by the whole family, and gone for the simpler pedal bin option, comforting his tearful eleven-year-old son with the usual old flannel about it being what Jennings would have wanted. A chance encounter with the Observer Book of Small Mammals an hour later convinced the Day family that the reports of Jennings's death were premature. The advertisement in the Times Obituary column was immediately cancelled, and the pedal bin, since topped up with cold baked beans and carrot scrapings, was searched for stiff little rodents. It appeared that the hapless little bundle of fur was just hibernating, meaning that a lie-down by the fire and a drop of brandy would soon see it restored as the Day family's pet in residence.

Covered in Heinz tomato sauce and looking the worse for wear, Jennings was wrapped in a sock by the gas fire whilst David ate his breakfast. However, the results of this remedial action were swifter than anyone could have bargained for, and this Jesus of the rodent world was resurrected and making for the cavity behind the gas fire before anyone could say 'Hallelujah!' More bitter tears ensued, which Len could only quell with promises of another hamster. Jennings was never glimpsed again, and his whereabouts remained a mystery.

A letter from David to both Scotland Yard and Interpol failed to produce results, so Len sprang into action. Darbyshire, Jennings's replacement, arrived the following week, only, alas, to meet his maker prematurely after a discussion with a vintage steam roller that was trundling towards a country fair In nearby Stourbridge. From then on, Len only brought home inanimate objects, as David's track record with pets was abysmal.

One such inanimate object had remained in its box for ten years, waiting for its 'raison d'être', and tonight was the night. David rummaged around in his wardrobe and eventually found what he was looking for; a large, illuminated magnifying glass on a stand - the type that model makers use when they are trying to paint the eyebrows on a one-hundredth scale grenadier guardsman. He plugged it in and placed it on the corner of his drawing board. Then he selected the test strip showing the bus stop and placed it beneath the powerful glass.

Voila! There was a surprising amount of detail in the negative, thanks to the superior Pentax lens, and David could clearly see two figures silhouetted against a passing sunflower yellow delivery van. He could even make out the sign writing, in spite of a slight blur caused by the van's movement. It read:

VINCENT GOUGH - FLORIST

His attention now shifted to the two figures in front of the van. One was an elderly man with a trilby hat. It was impossible to discern facial detail, but the gentleman's posture indicated that he was of a certain age. Next to him was someone that David recognized immediately. The school blazer and the turban were unmistakable. It was The Weird Woman, standing bolt upright with her large crocodile skin bag, staring into space, as silent as the grave.

## CHAPTER 5

### Laz, the Artful Dodger

"I don't wanna talk about it, alright?"

Nick the drummer was an hour late for the rehearsal. Duncan was not amused, but then again, it didn't take much to not amuse Duncan. That said, Nick was definitely trying it on, and Laz told him so.

"Nick, that 'I don't wanna talk about it, right?' routine was brilliant the first time. You came in looking like you'd had the worst imaginable time, like your parents had been killed in a car crash, your house had burnt down while you were out at the morgue identifying them, during which time your car was stolen and used to run over your cat. We all bought it, and none of us dared pry into what had happened to you, because it was obvious to the meanest intelligence that a tragedy of Shakespearian proportions had rocked your world. However, it does tend to dilute the impact a bit when you turn up late every week for a year and say, 'I don't wanna talk about it, right', just because it worked the bloody first time."

Nick threw his sheepskin over an amplifier and guffawed with laughter. "Nothin' gets past you does it, Laz?"

"Anyway," continued Duncan, clapping his hands like a headmaster addressing a bunch of unruly eleven-year-olds. "Let's not waste any more time shall we? This gig's only a month away."

"Right with you," replied Nick. "Once I've blagged a cup of tea from Kenny boy."

"You may not be familiar with this invention, Latecomer," said Ken, pouring himself a cup of hot, steaming tea, "but this plastic cylinder that I'm holding is called a thermos flask. It's used for keeping hot drinks hot, and conversely, cold drinks cold, if you can believe that. The real beauty of this apparatus though, is its low cost. I daresay, when they were first invented, they were hundreds of pounds each, but now, with the benefits of mass production and cheap raw materials, it is possible to procure one in a range of finishes, from plain blue, red or green to even tartan. The one I'm using today is the aforementioned tartan variety, which only cost me a few pounds from Woolworths, and, joy of joys, O Latecomer, the contents are even cheaper. It's simply boiling water which has had a tea bag immersed in it for a few minutes. I would estimate that a few pence is all that I've spent on the contents, plus of course a small plastic bottle to hold the drop of milk I require to prevent the tea gnawing at my stomach. All in all, a sound investment. You should get one."

"Does that mean you're not going to give me a cup of your tea," asked Nick, "after I've travelled halfway across England to attend this rehearsal, for which none of us are paid?"

"You have grasped the essence of my diatribe. Well done," smiled Ken, provocatively sipping at his private property.

"Just give me a swig of that then," begged the parched Brummie drummer. "It's the least you can do, man!"

Ken allowed him a small sip, keeping a watchful eye in case it evolved, as had happened in the past, into a huge gulp.

"Christ!" groaned Nick, wrinkling his nose up. "There's no sugar in it. Have you packed in taking sugar now?"

"Au contraire!" replied Ken. "I left the sugar out because I know you can't stand tea without sugar, which means that you won't keep stealing my tea at rehearsals. All of you might just remember to take the trouble and bring your own one day, just like I do."

Nick considered this. "But hang on Ken. You take sugar as well, so are you telling me you've deliberately made tea the way *you* don't like it, just to spite us?"

"Correct!" grinned Ken. "But I can just about cope without adding sugar, and you obviously can't."

"Can we actually play a song or two before my bus comes to take me home from this mad house?" asked Duncan, exasperated.

They sauntered over to the equipment and began the inevitable musician's ritual, (which Laz referred to as 'noodling') whereby everyone showed off their dexterity and played whatever they wanted to play, without showing the least interest in what the others were up to. This created a cacophony of sound which infuriated the singer, who could only show off himself when the rest of them were performing as a unit. Eventually, once their musical urges were satisfied, order was restored, and it was time to trawl through the set list.

"Okay!" said Duncan, irritatingly clapping his hands once more, "We need to run through the opening song, which I think should be 'Maelstrom'. I've taped a passage from Debussy, which would be great as our opening music. Mo could play that from the mixing deck as you come on in the dark and strap on the guitars and so on. We'll get a dry ice machine to make the stage look all ethereal, and perhaps we could all wear white, which looks spiritual, don't you think? Anyway, the tape builds to this fantastic crescendo of orchestral music. It's in C minor, so Laz can play the final chord along with the tape on synthesized strings and segue into 'Maelstrom', which is also in C minor. Clever, eh? The lights will then go up dramatically to reveal the band already playing live. I'll come out and reach the microphone just in time to sing the opening line."

"Dramatic!" agreed Nick, who liked that kind of thing.

"And you arrive on stage after the plebs, which is only right and proper," frowned Laz.

"It's just to give the show some drama," insisted Duncan, hurt by the barbed comment. "It's not about me being the leader of the band."

"Because you're not," added David.

"No, I'm not," agreed Duncan frostily.

"So why have you written Duncan Lake's Epitaph on your notepad?" asked Laz.

"Good God!" said Ken, firmly screwing down the stopper on his beloved flask. "I didn't realize he'd died!"

"Can we begin?" shouted Mo, their powerfully-built Indian road manager-cum-sound engineer. "Or do I have to come up there and sort out your egos?"

Laz played the opening chords to 'Maelstrom'. The song lasted fifteen minutes and was full of complex time changes, which tested their musicianship to the full. The band's previous incarnation had played rock and roll standards at clubs and pubs, until after a while they could do it standing on their heads and half-drunk, or considerably more so in Ken's case. Their self-penned music was far more demanding, and required considerable concentration and expertise. They were trying to punch above their weight, and none of them possessed the virtuosity to breeze through the difficult pieces they had constructed. When it worked, it was magnificent. When it didn't, it was disastrous.

Secretly, David yearned for the simpler times, when, fronted by George, they blasted their way through Beatles classics in small, intimate clubs. The new songs were so difficult to play that there was no time for the band members to enjoy themselves. He was also facing a crisis of conscience. For Laz, Ken, Duncan and Nick, the band was a lifeline, an escape from their boring dead-end jobs. Their sights were set on turning professional as soon as possible, but David knew in his heart of hearts that he wouldn't be joining them. It was beginning to dawn on him that he wasn't comfortable in the framework of a band, with its raging egos, petty squabbles and late nights. The thought of living in each others' pockets appalled him, and his enthusiasm for being a musician was diminishing, as his interest in being an artist increased. An artist was his own boss, who stood or fell by his own efforts, and that was precisely how he liked it. He was not by nature a team player and, though a gregarious person, he was nevertheless also a very private person who loved to escape when he had had enough. The very idea of sharing a cramped van with his comrades filled him with a nameless fear.

It was a reasonable rehearsal, and the lads seemed heartened by their progress. A few more sessions, argued Laz, and they wouldn't be far off the standard required. Nick began to pack away his drums whilst Duncan explained the opening tape to Mo, and Ken finished off the contents of his flask. His addiction to tea was interesting, in that he was also addicted to alcohol, but both beverages knew their place and never tried to take over the other's territory. Tea was nine till six. Lager was seven till comatose, with no crossover at all. Alcoholic he may have been, but at least he was a very disciplined one. It was now six-thirty, Ken's no-man's land; the unhappy hour he gave his body to recover from the caffeine before the alcohol took over. He seemed restless packing away his equipment, as the lure of the Waggon and Horses began to tighten its deadly grip on his mind.

Laz sidled over to David who was sitting on his amplifier staring into space, sensing that he seemed troubled.

"What's up, old pal?"

"Oh, just thinking about that lad who committed suicide," lied David, as he placed his beloved Les Paul into its case.

"And worrying about your commitment to the band too, I bet."

Laz could read his old friend like a book. David was cursed with the kind of face that couldn't hide emotions. Even if he had burst into the room grinning broadly and tap-dancing, Laz would have known that things weren't right.

"Yeah!" agreed David. "The problem is, I'm doing this Bachelor of Arts degree because I've wanted to be an artist since I was four years old. I also love playing music, and you'll think this is crazy. I'm in turmoil because I'm good at two things…."

"I wouldn't say that."

"…and I can't work out in my mind which path to take. What?"

"Nothing, go on."

"Most people would give their right arm to be a good artist *and* a good guitarist," he continued.

"No they wouldn't, because then they wouldn't be able to play or draw would they?"

"Okay, their right bollock then. Shut up and listen. And here am I worrying because I can do both. You're all doing crap jobs and you want out. I'm not. My mom and dad are paying a fortune they haven't got to put me through art college, and I hear all you lot going on about turning pro, and I know in my heart that I can't. There, I said it!"

Laz put his arm around him. "Dave, I've known that for ages. It doesn't matter. Just enjoy it for now, and if - and it's a big if - we get a deal, *then's* the time to worry about it. One gig at The Crypt is hardly a world tour is it? Besides, I'm thinking of going to art college myself, so I know what you're going through."

David looked at him quizzically.

"There's just one small obstruction in your way, Laz. I don't know how I can break this to you gently. You can't draw, or for that matter, paint."

"So?"

"You did say art college didn't you? Not woodwork or plumbing or astro physics?"

"Art college. You heard me correctly. I have an appointment with Kieron Hastings on Monday at eleven. I need to ask you a few tips for passing the interview, if you don't mind. I've heard they're a bit strange."

David's quizzical expression had now modulated into something more akin to stark disbelief.

"YOU are having an interview for the B.A. Course in Fine Art?"

"Absolutely!"

"But you don't know the first bloody thing about art. You know you don't. You haven't done a foundation course, so how could you be considered for a B.A.? You're pulling my leg."

"There's a lot you don't know about me, old son," smiled Laz, tapping the side of his nose in a jaunty manner, like an East-End purveyor of blood oranges on a market stall. "Tell you what. I'll wager you fifty quid that I get accepted on that B.A. course on the strength of my work, which I've been beavering away at in secret for over a year now. As to the foundation course, I'm well aware of that, but did you know that you can achieve the necessary foundation certificate by doing an approved correspondence course? No you didn't! As I said, there's a lot about me that you don't know."

David was reeling. "So, for the past year or so, you have been signed up to a correspondence course in art, which you've now successfully completed, and you've got a fine art degree course interview on Monday, even though you've never once mentioned an interest in art in the five years I've known you, nor have I ever seen one single piece of evidence of any artistic talent whatsoever. Pull the other one. This is late April. Not the first of the month."

"I am both stunned and hurt," protested Laz, doing his best to look both stunned and hurt simultaneously, "that you have reacted thus. Press your bony effete little hand into mine and bet me fifty quid then."

David proffered the aforementioned B.E.L.H, whisking it away at the last moment.

"Hang on. There's a scam here. Run it past me again. You're betting me that you can't get accepted onto the fine art degree course?"

"Correctamundo."

"Does the bet hold if you fail the degree?"

"I can't promise that I'll pass in three years time, obviously. Just bet me that I won't be accepted."

The hand was proffered once more, only to be withdrawn again at the eleventh hour.

"Why are you doing this?"

"Simple!" said Laz "I was fed up with my humdrum existence. The house clearance business is better than working on the track at Leyland, but what I really wanted was the academic life, like you. Is there anything so wrong with wanting to better myself?"

David pocketed his hand. "In that case, I'd be foolish to bet against you, as you seem so confident. I merely applaud your efforts and wish you well."

This latest development seemed to rattle Laz somewhat.

"Okay, I'll come clean," he sighed. "I can't draw to save my life. The correspondence course was all about conceptual art, with no emphasis at all on traditional drawing skills. It's like the Emperor's New Clothes. All I've done is splash paint about on canvas and write pretentious essays which explain my concepts. I'm doing it for a joke, to see whether I can fool a degree course into thinking I'm talented. Now are you willing to bet me?"

David still seemed unconvinced. "Hang on! You fooled a correspondence course into thinking you had talent, and they granted you the certificate which enables you to apply for a B.A. That doesn't ring true. Who are these people? Are they bona-fide? Surely they wouldn't be suckered into giving you a certificate on the evidence of a load of abstract splashes and a few pretentious essays. And that's another point. It may be a load of bollocks, but you still have to use all the right phraseology and artistic bullshit, and, no offence, but you're not au fait with all that. You'd be spotted as a fraudster in about ten seconds."

Laz smiled a knowing smile. "I agree, but this particular correspondence course isn't too fussy about talent, as long as they get their cheque in the post, know what I mean?"

David was beginning to cotton on. "Ah! So they are a bogus outfit that'll hand over a meaningless certificate willy-nilly to any silly bugger as long as the price is right?"

"Correct."

"I've never heard of a correspondence course that was the equivalent to a foundation certificate for a start, let alone a fraudulent one." In short, David wasn't having any of it.

"Well," countered Laz, "That's because you're a little mommy's boy who hasn't got a clue about the corrupt underbelly of society. Is the bet on or off? Will I get away with it at B.A. interview level? Yes or no?"

"No!" insisted David, confident now. "They may be a load of pretentious twats on the seventh floor, but you still need to speak the jargon, and I don't think you could. You'll be sussed out right away by someone as astute as old Kieron Hastings. The bet's on. Final answer!"

David shook hands.

"Great!" grinned Laz. "Now give me a clue what they'll be asking me, and some idea of what I should say."

David looked at him incredulously. "WHAT? You honestly think I'm going to help you pass an interview by priming you on the correct responses to a load of artistic questions, when I stand to lose fifty quid? And another thing. You owe me a tenner for the gorilla on the bus pass bet."

Laz had to admit that his friend had a point. He needed a concession, or he was going to fall at the first hurdle.

"Okay. The bet is, I have to survive the course for a month. How's that? I'll deduct what I owe you for the bus pass wager from my winnings. How's that?"

David was now convinced that the money was his. He had no time for the seventh floor brigade, but he felt sure that a complete novice couldn't pass himself off as an art student for a month, without any knowledge of the correct terminology, let alone drawing or painting. Laz didn't know the difference between Caravaggio and Rolf Harris. He probably thought that Chiaroscuro and Impasto were Italian strikers, and he definitely didn't know what H and B stood for on pencils. No, the money was as good as his. He felt guilty accepting it, but he persuaded himself that, had the boot been on the other hand, Laz would definitely have taken it from him. The bet was on. So benevolent was he feeling at this point, that he freely volunteered valuable inside information about what his own interview had been like. It had taken place in the third floor interview room, where not long ago he had been alone with WPC Hobbins, trying to hold back the forces of nature as they were busy pumping copious quantities of blood into his excited member. The interview panel had consisted of Kingsley Hamphlett and his deputy, Claude Beardsley, and, coincidentally, Kieron Hastings, Head of Fine Art, deputizing for Jim Weston from Printmaking who'd had to cry off to tend to one of his many business interests, somewhere in Devon.

The panel had welcomed David in and asked him to open his portfolio. He placed it in front of them on the table, where two of them studied his work while Kieron asked a few questions.

His opening gambit was "Hello David. How would you make a hole in the river Thames?"

At first nonplussed, David gave it some thought before answering. "I would shove you in."

This amused Kieron no end. "Why shove me in, David? Why not jump in yourself?"

"Because," explained David, "I can't swim."

Claude looked up from perusing David's work.

"You can't swim? I'd learn if I were you, love. You never know when you're going to need it. It could save your life."

David agreed, but told them he was 'aquaphobic'.

"Shouldn't that word be 'Hydrophobic?" queried Kingsley.

"Probably," admitted David.

"If there was something wrong with me," suggested Kieron, "I'd like to think that I could use the correct word to describe my condition, wouldn't you?"

"It depends," argued David. "What if I were dumb?"

"Good point!" said Kingsley, pouring himself an Earl Grey from his flask.

Kieron seemed a tad miffed. "Okay David. Who's the best painter, Jackson Pollock or Holbein?"

"Vermeer," replied David, countering with "What's the best animal, an Armadillo or a Capybara?"

"A squirrel!" said Kieron.

"Correct answer!" said David. "Now tell me this. If a woman with a lovely pair of breasts is sexy, would she be even sexier if she had three of them?"

"Can we reel this in now?" asked Kieron tetchily. "It's getting a bit silly."

"You started it," countered David. "I thought we were here to discuss my work, not play mind games."

Claude smiled. "My dear boy. It's sharpness of mind that makes a great artist. All the others just paint meaningless pretty pictures. You can go into the studio now and see no end of students with superficial drawing skills, sitting there, knitting."

"You have to knit if you want to make a jumper," argued David. "Besides, you allowed them onto the course, remember?"

Kingsley closed David's portfolio and smiled benignly across the table. "David, you'll do for us. You're talented, hard to intimidate, argumentative and cheeky. In fact, the perfect combination to do well in the art world. Congratulations!"

* * *

Laz stood up and began to pack away his electric piano. He thanked David for the valuable insight into art college life.

"They sound like a bunch of turds. It wasn't like that when they interviewed me at British Leyland. Did they eventually ask you about your work at all, or just talk bollocks?"

David had to admit that his version of events was a little précised, but he reasoned that the work spoke for itself. It was the character of the artist that interested them, and he had to confess that, whilst he found the interview technique a little pretentious and off-putting at the time, nevertheless he could see why they used it. An artist spends his or her entire life arguing their cause and standing up for what they believe in. The lecturers just wanted to see if their applicants were up to it.

With the rehearsal concluded, and the equipment safely returned to Mo's transit van, Nick, Mo, Duncan and Ken retired to the Waggon and Horses to discuss the finer points of the stage show. Laz gave David a lift home so that he could continue to pick up useful interview tips.

"You know, I still don't get the point of it all," said David. "Where's the percentage in it for you?"

Laz thought long and hard, as he dragged deeply on his cigarette. "It's a few things. Do you remember when I bust my arm and had loads of time off from the garage? You were swanning around in Florence as part of your course, and you asked me to drop something off at your foundation college while you were away. Well, I loved it there. Everybody seemed to be doing what they wanted to do, and there was no boss making you clock in and clock out. People were having intellectual discussions over coffees in the canteen, unlike our place, where you just grab a copy of the Sun and take it to the kharsi for ten minutes. The students had dirty hands, but it was paint and modelling clay, not engine oil and Swarfega. What made it worse was me chatting to your mate Katie, and one thing leading to another, and so on. Before long, I was turning up there every day, sitting in the canteen and chatting to her, and it was wonderful, but I knew that it was just while my arm got better. I was bloody jealous of you, you know. I know you've done dirty jobs in your holidays, but that's okay, because you know it's just to earn a few quid, and then you'll be back at college. This was exactly the opposite. I knew I'd have to go back to the blasted filthy car repair garage, and I reckon I'm worth more than that. I've got a brain, for God's sake. I suppose I overstayed my welcome, because the Head of Department told me I wasn't allowed in the place unless I was on the course, and asked me politely to bugger off. I think it just planted a seed in my head, which began to grow when I saw the ad for the correspondence course. I know it's all bogus, but if I can just get in, then maybe I can pick things up and learn a bit, and who knows? I might just surprise you. You said yourself, they don't draw or paint proper pictures up there; they just throw paint around and create 'installations'. Well I can do that, and if I can't, it will have been fun while it lasted, eh Dave?"

David smiled a sad smile at his old friend. He had no idea that Laz's visit to the foundation course had had such a profound effect on him. He hadn't got the heart to mention that, in his opinion, he wouldn't last a day, let alone a month.

"How will you live?" he asked. "You'll have no income from the house clearances, will you?"

"I can still do a bit at weekends," explained Laz, "But if I'm accepted, I'm eligible for a student loan the same as you. It's not a fortune, but I'll get by."

The car pulled up outside David's parent's council house in the quiet little cul-de-sac. He opened the door and thanked his friend for the lift.

"And what if the band gets a recording deal?" he asked, pulling his guitar case from the back seat.

"Oh no contest!" laughed Laz. "The art college can go shag themselves!"

# CHAPTER 6

## Dead Man Snapping

The elegant old lady was dressed in an off-white suit, with a white fluffy hat. She had a powdered white face and thick black mascara, with a string of pearls around her wrinkled and over-perfumed neck, and a white poodle on a white lead trotting weightlessly by her side. Following a successful expedition to the local department store, she was loaded to the gunwales with carrier bags, trying her best to make headway along the shopping precinct to the multi-storey car park at the other end.

Suddenly, a darkly dressed, hooded figure sprinted up behind her and grabbed the smallest of her bags - the type that jewellers frequently use. Rudely jostled to one side, the old lady stood bewildered as she watched the thief hurtle through the precinct, displacing anyone who got in his way.

Unfortunately for him, WPC Hobbins, who had been studying a sausage roll with a view to purchasing same, just outside Gregsons the Bakers, saw the incident take place and, shelving her food cravings temporarily, gave chase.

David was, as usual, waiting for Dylan outside Tweedledum's Coffee Shop, when he became aware of the commotion at the far end of the mall, and realized that a fugitive from justice was heading straight for him at a rate of knots. He also recognized the willowy figure of WPC Hobbins trying to shave valuable seconds off her hundred metres personal best. He figured that he had about four seconds to make up his mind how to play things.

If he stood directly in front of this hooded steam train, it was odds-on that he would come off second best, and end up sprawling across the pavement, whereas, if he rammed the thief from the side as he passed, the low-life would completely lose his balance and go careering into the balustrade that prevented shoppers from falling to the floor below, hopefully breaking his bloody neck in the process. By the time the thief had worked out what had happened to his equilibrium, the WPC would have arrived and banged the cuffs on him.

However, if David mistimed this assault, which was highly possible as the assailant was built very much along the lines of a whippet, the booty would be lost. Thinking on his feet, David decided on a two-pronged attack. Noticing that the bag was in the man's right hand, and therefore ideally placed, he would ram him from the side as he passed, and grab the carrier bag simultaneously. He acted as nonchalantly as he could, all the time keenly observing the rocketing criminal as he approached. Then, with split-second timing, shoulder-charged him with all his might, snatching the bag as he did so with all the panache of an Olympic relay runner taking over the baton. The carrier bag, unfortunately, was made of much flimsier material than the average baton, and the force of the impact saw the bag disintegrate into about twelve pieces as the luckless villain catapulted sideways with an almighty groan, ricocheting off the balustrade like a pinball.

Meanwhile, the liberated contents of the jeweller's bag were arcing across the sky, and on a collision course not only for David but also for the thief, who was now catapulting his way back in David's direction, limbs flailing as he struggled for breath. The two bodies met for the second time at a combined speed of around sixty miles per hour, just as the bag's contents, namely the sloppy and malodorous faeces of Fluffy the poodle, descended with a splat, plastering both criminal and captor with equal thoroughness.

73

The sneak thief and the art student lay spark out on the pavement, winded and gasping for air, as the foul stench of poodle excrement filled the precinct with alarming speed and intensity. WPC Hobbins arrived, breathless and panting, just as she had been in David's dream, and produced the cuffs. She read the miscreant his rights as best she could in-between gasping for air and gingerly applied the equipment, trying her best to avoid the many small dollops of poodle poo that adorned his prostrate body. David, meanwhile, rose shakily to his knees. He had several splatters of the foul substance on his face, with one dangerously close to the edge of his upper lip. It was also in his hair, over his shirt and down his new jeans. A small crowd had gathered to observe the proceedings, and an elderly woman shouted out words of encouragement to the plucky officer.

"Good on yer, love. Throttle the pair of bastards!"

David suddenly experienced an extraordinary feeling of déjà vu, as he pulled himself up from the floor, using the balustrade for support. Dylan had seen the whole incident evolve as he entered the precinct from the other end, and rushed over to help his friend up, but changed his mind having got to within a yard of him. Having always been squeamish in that way, he decided to offer moral support instead.

"Well played, Dave. I bet you'll be in line for a commendation or something. What a hero. I'd have shit myself! Oh! I see you did too!"

"Har pissing har!" snarled David. "Look at me. It's all over me."

WPC Hobbins, meanwhile, had managed to drag her quarry to his feet.

"David. Thank you. I don't think I'd have got him without your help."

"It was nothing."

"Arsehole!" chipped in the disgruntled thief, endorsing the policewoman's comments.

"Shut your ugly face!" retorted the WPC angrily. "David, let me just have a word with the old lady, and then we'll get you cleaned up."

The policewoman cuffed her captive to the balustrade while she went over to speak to the lady. Unfortunately, or perhaps fortunately, the contents of the bag could not be returned to her, but there was still the matter of formal identification of the assailant to sort out, and she needed to make sure the old dear wasn't hurt or in a state of shock. Luckily, she was a tough old boot, built very much on the lines of Barbara Cartland, and she appeared to be more concerned about Fluffy's bowel movements than anything else.

Dylan, meanwhile, made his excuses and left for college, as he had an imminent tutorial with Claude and didn't wish to be late.

After a few minutes, thanks to WPC Hobbins's radio call, backup arrived in the form of Donald and Reg, a comedy partnership second only to Laurel and Hardy, and old acquaintances of David. There was something horribly inevitable about their appearance on the scene. If it were possible to be haunted by coppers, these two were David's personal poltergeists.

He first met them after a band rehearsal, nearly three years previously, when he had missed the last bus and was walking home in torrential rain, carrying a valuable guitar in a flimsy cardboard box which the band's new singer, George, had asked him to try and repair. Donald and Reg had invited him into their nice dry Panda car and asked him if the guitar was his own. Hindsight is a wonderful thing, and had David known what he knew now, he'd have just said yes and that, probably, would have been the end of it. Instead, he chose the honest, if convoluted approach. It wasn't his guitar, nor did he know the name of the man who had lent it to him, as it was the first night they had met. He also didn't manage to explain to them why a very sought-after instrument, a Gretsch 'Country Gent', (as played by Elvis) was in a flimsy cardboard box. Eventually, after an impromptu rendition of Colonel Bogey, the comedy double act seemed satisfied, but baulked at David's suggestion that they should give him a lift home to avoid wrecking the valuable guitar in the rain. As a result of their caring attitude, the instrument took on the appearance of a boomerang with rusty strings, and its market value became comparable with a second-hand pair of dentures.

The second meeting of minds was when David arrived in a battered old mini for the first day of his foundation course. Don and Reg had been warned that a suspected IRA car was parked by the art college, packed with explosives. Mistaking David's dismantled speedometer and a pound of modelling clay on the back seat for an IRA bomb, they duly arranged for the car, which he'd only had for one day, to be blown to bits in a controlled explosion. A few months after that, they were summoned to help David catch a pair of international art forgers at a local aerodrome, but instead sat on a pub car park eating pork scratchings, leaving David and his friend Mo to tackle the armed thugs themselves.

After the initial groans of recognition, Donald was first to speak.

"Kim, don't tell me you know this chap."

"'Fraid so."

"My best advice to you is run. He's like Jonah. I'm warning you. Trouble follows him around. It's uncanny."

"I've already noticed."

"A nice lad, make no mistake, but I guarantee you'll be embroiled in about seventeen different adventures and a murder or two before the week's out, now that he's got his claws into you."

"Excuse me," interrupted David. "I hate to butt in when you're clearly having such a laugh at my expense, but I'm bruised all over and covered in poodle shit. Would anyone mind if I got myself cleaned up? And another thing, WPC Snibbs. I think you'll find it's bloody Abbott and Costello here that are the Jonahs, not me. Whenever there's any trouble, guess who's always in the equation just as much as I am? Apart from when they sit in Panda cars farting while I'm being shot at in aerodromes."

"Boys, boys!" said Snibboh. "Enough bitching. Look lads, could you two escort our shit-snatching friend back to the station while I help get David cleaned up? I'd walk him round if I were you. Your car will stink if you let him in there!"

"It probably does already," added David triumphantly. Not for nothing was Reg christened Pongo by his fellow officers.

Reg countered with a hand gesture which he'd picked up during a previous life as a longbow-man at Agincourt, and was gone.

"Well," grinned WPC Hobbins. "It's a small world, you knowing the boys. Let's get you into Tweedledum's and see if Olga or Helga will agree to hose you down."

They entered the café, which in itself probably contravened some hygiene act or other, and walked up to the counter. Olga came out from her door and appeared to be instantly pole-axed by the solid block of stagnant air, which stopped her in her tracks. It was as if someone had hung a ten week old incontinent kipper under her nose.

"Jesus Christ!" she shrieked, eyes bulging. "Couldn't you hang on?"

"Olga," began the WPC, "can David use your shower please? He's just helped apprehend a shitbag in the precinct."

"A shitbag stealing a shitbag," added David, by way of clarification.

"Come on then, if you must," winced Olga, "but not through the kitchen. They'll close me down. Go down the back and through the door on the right, quickly, before you empty the bloody caff."

David did as he was told. WPC Hobbins said she'd wait for him and grab a coffee and a sausage roll. All the excitement had made her peckish. Ten minutes later, David emerged looking and smelling fresher. He was wearing Olga's fifteen-year-old son's clothes, which gave him the look of a young man who'd had an unexpected growth spurt. Kim bought him a tea, to calm his nerves. Once she had congratulated him once more on his sterling efforts, the conversation turned to Jack Hamphlett.

"Have you made any headway with the case?" asked David, sniffing like a rabbit. He had a good nose, and the smell of poodle waste lingered, in spite of a good scrubbing.

"A little," replied the WPC. "We took away his camera to see if there was anything in it that would give us a clue as to why he jumped. Not that it did of course, but you have to try, don't you? The coroner filed his report too. The injuries appear consistent with a fall, blah blah blah. Deceased died at around three p.m. No traces of drugs, but there was some alcohol in his blood stream. Not a lot. Some of the folks who came forward said he did drink too much, especially after his dad died. A tragic suicide I reckon."

David looked troubled. "Did he leave a note? They're always supposed to leave a note aren't they?"

"Not always, David. It's funny though, because he had the wherewithal to do so if he wished. There was a scrap of paper in his pocket, and a stumpy 2B pencil."

"2B eh? 2B or not 2B, that is the question. Whether 'tis nobler in the mind to suffer the slings and arrows of outrageous fortune, or to take arms against a sea of troubles, and by opposing, end them."

"Very good. What's it mean? Remember, I'm a copper, not a bloomin' college educated boy like you."

"Well," explained David, "by sheer coincidence, it's very pertinent. It's what Hamlet says when he's considering suicide. 'To be' means to exist. He's asking, is it better to exist or not to exist? Is it a better thing to put up with life's crap, as I did half an hour ago, or top yourself and beat it that way?"

"What, you don't think the pencil was a subtle comment? Jack's suicide statement?"

"No, it was just a 2B pencil in his pocket. We all carry 'em. I bet you don't know what B and H stand for on pencils."

"No."

"Don't worry. Not many do. No, I was just interested that he actually had the materials to leave a note, but still didn't bother to. It doesn't seem right. And you say the photos didn't reveal anything?"

David had to be careful. Snibboh wasn't aware that he'd purloined the test strips, nor indeed that they existed.

"No, nothing untoward. Just shots of the town from a high viewpoint."

As they chatted, the man whom David had temporarily christened 'Dry Toast' arrived, looked around the café furtively, and ordered a bacon sandwich. He sat in the next booth to David and the policewoman and waited, looking anxiously at his watch.

"This bloke's worth observing, Snibs," whispered David. "Dyl and I spend hours doing it. His wife's a battle-axe who's forbidden him bacon sandwiches. He's on his own today, and he's ordered one."

Snibboh suspended the interview at precisely one-fifteen p.m. in favour of David's surveillance operation. They sat huddled together in their booth, giggling like school children, and both were aware of a growing intimacy between them - the uniformed officer and the dreamy art student. They say opposites attract. Shortly afterwards, the man's wife, code-name 'The Dragon' arrived, and judging by Dry Toast's reaction, arrived unexpectedly to boot. His whole demeanour was that of a man who had ordered a 'verboten' bacon sandwich on the sly and was in danger of being found out. At the worst possible moment, Helga arrived with the aforementioned foodstuff, laying it before him with a flourish. Dry Toast couldn't have looked more sheepish if he'd covered himself in matted wool and cried 'Baaaaaah!'

"I didn't order that!" he exclaimed, his facial expression an equal mixture of righteous indignation and abject panic.

Helga, to her credit, was a quick-thinking woman who was abreast of the facts vis-à-vis Dry Toast and The Dragon. As a successful café owner, she had to keep a mental list of her customer's wide and varied peccadilloes, habits and quirks. She was on top of her brief, as they say in legal circles. With great panache, she exclaimed: "Oh, what am I thinking of? You ordered the dry toast didn't you? I was thinking you were Eric. He always orders a bacon sandwich. I must be losing my marbles."

The Dragon seemed satisfied with this.

"Look!" continued Helga. "Would you like it? It seems a shame to waste it now it's cooked. I realize you shouldn't, but just once won't kill you."

Dry Toast gave his wife the kind of look normally favoured by eight-week-old puppy dogs when they are trying to convince their owners that they need one more chocolate drop. To everyone's amazement, she relented with a silent, haughty nod.

David turned back to WPC Hobbins.

"It pays to be observant, Snibs, as you well know, being a rozzer. You learn a lot about people that way. I'll wager this drama isn't over yet, methinks!"

The policewoman fixed him a fond look, the way a doting grandmother looks at a thick but loveable grandchild.

"You are a strange lad," she said, touching his hand, and causing every hair on his head to stand on end, like quills on a fretful porcupine. "Every sentence that comes out of your mouth amuses me. I don't think you realize how funny you are, which is even better. Does anyone still say 'methinks' in the twentieth century, apart from you?"

"It's Shakespeare's fault," spluttered David, his cheeks reddening, as they always did on the rare occasions when a girl showed any interest in him. "I did it for O level and A level, and it left an impression on me. I can still quote huge chunks of it. Remind me to show you next time you're suffering from insomnia."

"There you go again," she smiled. "Everything is a joke, usually at your own expense. You shouldn't run yourself down all the time."

"I just get one in before anyone else has a chance to. It's like the footballer who kicks an opponent up in the air for no apparent reason. He's just getting his retaliation in first."

She touched his hand again, causing little electric shocks to fizzle all over his body. If this was just her touching his hand, he thought, what would full-blown sex feel like?

"Besides, you have a lot to be proud of. You did A levels, and now, presumably, an art degree, so you're obviously very bright. You can quote Shakespeare, paint pictures, and I've heard from my spies that you're one of the best artists on your course. I was flipping hopeless at school. Totally unacademic. I couldn't wait to leave and join the police. As to Shakespeare, I can't understand a bloody word of it. It's so intellectual; it just passes straight over my head. In a word, I'm thick."

"Nonsense!" replied David. "You're lovely." His face reddened again. "But you're wrong about it being just for intellectuals.

81

Shakespeare is fantastic stuff. If you were to read one of his stories in modern dialect, and set in the twentieth century, you'd love it. He wrote brilliant plots with believable characters, and gruesome murders. He wrote comedies and romances too, and no one understood the complexities of the human mind like him. His books are all about greed, stupidity, morality, love, you name it. He was a great thriller writer really, just like Raymond Chandler or Agatha Christie. It's just the language that's hard to digest, that's all."

"If you say so."

"I do. Look, do you rozzers ever get days off?"

"Of course."

"Well, why don't I take you to Stratford one day? It's great. I'll take you to Shakespeare's birthplace, Anne Hathaway's cottage and Mary Arden's house. Then we can take a boat down the Avon. I'll row, while you put grapes in my mouth and kiss me every now and again."

WPC Hobbins leaned over to him.

"Like this?" she asked quietly, and gently pressed her plumped-up lips to his. The electric shocks had now moved exclusively to his groin area.

In the next booth, Dry Toast had just finished his bacon sandwich. He said goodbye and walked out of the café, leaving his formidable wife to settle the bill. She paid for two teas and left, leaving the stunned owner staring at the wall in blank disbelief. Meanwhile, David was half expecting his mother to shake him, hand him a cup of tea and tell him he was late for the bus. Now it was the policewoman who looked a little flushed.

"I don't know what came over me then!" she whispered.

"I wish I could say the same," said David, "but it's a substance I'm very familiar with."

82

Sometimes, David suspected that God had forgotten to insert the filter between his brain and his mouth that most other humans had been fitted with as standard. He now resembled a pillar box in a denim jacket. Luckily, WPC Snibboh had a robust sense of humour. Police women and nurses usually have. They rose from their booth and headed for the till, where the constable graciously paid as a reward for David's earlier heroic actions. They left the café and walked through the precinct together.

"I get Wednesday off next week." she said, after a long and slightly embarrassed silence. "If you fancy filling me up with…"

"Culture?" asked David.

"Well, that'll do for starters," she grinned. They swapped phone numbers, and wandered through the little alleyway that led to the Dragonfly Boutique. The chalk line had gone now, as had any signs of the dried blood. Pausing to look in the shop window together, Snibboh noticed a bronze sundial mounted onto a stone plinth, and remarked that she had a similar one in her garden.

Suddenly, David slapped his brow with his hand and turned to the officer.

"There's something wrong with the coroner's report."

Snibboh looked quizzically at her new friend.

"What do you mean?"

David realized that he wasn't supposed to know about the contents of Jack's camera, but he felt that he knew Snibboh well enough to risk a confession, especially as it could help her with the case.

"It was you, showing me that sundial. Something just clicked in my brain. When did the coroner say Jack died?"

"Three o'clock."

"And he couldn't be wrong about that?"

"Not really. Maybe an hour either side, but that's all. They can work out the time of death very accurately nowadays by applying various scientific tests. Why?"

David owned up. "Look, I've done something naughty. I found Mike Sambroke's test strips in the bin, and I was fascinated by this suicide, so I borrowed them and studied them when I got home. Are you mad with me?"

Snibboh became the formal police officer again. "David, that worries me. I was told that I had the negs and the only prints. This fascination with the case could point to you having a vested interest. My superiors could give me a right bollocking for fraternizing with a bloody potential suspect. You've stolen evidence. They'll want to know why you were so interested in something that doesn't really concern you."

David was taken aback by how quickly the WPC reverted to the woman he'd held up at banana-point.

"Come on, Snibsy. Do you really think I'm anything to do with this? I was just wrapped up in it because I stood on the very spot where a chap killed himself. I'm a sensitive soul, and it just got to me. Do I look like a nutter?"

"Yes."

"Thanks. Look, I'm trying to tell you something important here. You can bollock me for nicking off with evidence another time. Remember, I just helped you capture a bag snatcher. Now I'm going to help you solve another crime."

"Go on then."

"I looked at those tests, and I can tell you that Jack took a few shots at around lunchtime or just after, and then he stopped for a considerable length of time."

Snibboh was curious now.

"How did you deduce that, Sherlock?"

"You told me that the pictures told you nothing, but that's because you looked at them with a policewoman's eye, and not an artist's eye. The light on those shots is the kind of light you see around midday or early afternoon. You can tell by where the shadows fall. If you go up to that roof with me now, you'll see what I'm talking about."

"If you think I'm going up on the roof with the chap who stole the test strips, you've got to be joking. I don't want to wake up dead with a Snibboh-shaped chalk line around me, thank you very much."

"Oh come on, really!" sighed David. "The light shows they were shot up until about three o'clock maximum. I'm only guessing of course. You'd really have to compare shadows by going up to the roof, as I said. Then, there's a large pause in the photography. My guess is that Jack wasn't happy with the light. He knew that, come late afternoon, there's a golden glow descends over everything. It's that glorious time just before sunset, when all the brickwork goes orangey coloured, like those pictures of Tuscany you always see in magazines. If you take a look at Jack's later pictures, they've got that quality, and the shadows are all completely different. That indicates a rather long pause in the middle."

Snibboh was enthralled now.

"Look, in a nutshell, these last shots were definitely taken at around six o'clock. Seeing that sundial triggered the thought, as I said. There was something nagging at me and I couldn't quite get it, and now I realize what it was. You said three o'clock was a fairly accurate time of death. You're wrong. It must have been after six. Jeez! Hang on! I can prove it too. If you look at one of the shots under a magnifying glass, you can see a weird woman who always waits for her bus at five to six on Fridays. I know, because I often have to wait there too, and she puts the willies up me. Behind her, there's a van going past, with 'Vincent Gough, Florist' sign-written on it. Why not check it out? Check when he was in town. Those photos revealed a lot more than you think. The coroner is wrong."

"I'm not so sure," replied Snibboh. "He's deadly accurate as a rule. Maybe the weird woman caught an earlier bus."

"Maybe, but unlikely. She is a creature of habit."

"Okay, perhaps the light was just, sort of golden that particular day."

"Impossible. Check the shadows. You can't rearrange shadows. They're creatures of habit too."

Snibboh was perplexed.

"If what you say is correct, we have two choices. Either the coroner is talking out of his arse, or someone else took the 'weird woman photos' after Jack died. In which case, who?"

"How about the person who killed Jack?" suggested David, for once, deadly serious.

# CHAPTER 7

## Vincent Gough's Van

It was a glorious early summer's day. The type of day when a person feels inclined to fling her coat over her shoulder, close her eyes, look heavenwards and, feeling the warmth on her face, utter the words, "I'm glad to be alive!" or some such expression of contentment, as she strolls past the park. We use the term 'she', because the contented human being in question was none other than WPC Hobbins.

It was not just the fine day that has put her in this elated frame of mind either. She had a few reasons to be cheerful. Firstly, or perhaps secondly if the fine summer's day counts as reason number one, she was becoming rather fond of a young art student. True, he was on another planet most of the time, and could only be serious on days that didn't contain the letter 'Y', but he was entertaining, shy with girls (which she found extremely arousing) and scholarly, which she was not. Thirdly, she had made quite a breakthrough with the Jack Hamphlett case, the details of which had seriously impressed her superior officers. She had needed to tell a few little white lies, however, about the time of death query, to protect her new friend from being arrested for stealing police evidence. Purely to shield David, it must be understood, she had claimed that the detective work vis-à-vis the timing of the photography was all her own. So impressed was her commanding officer by her diligence, he had dispatched her forthwith to check out the precise chronology of Vincent Gough's van journeys during the Friday in question. She found the business's address in Yellow Pages, all by herself, without any help from David, and was now proceeding on foot in an easterly direction towards the pleasant and bustling high street of Chapel Ash, where said establishment was situated. This contented young copper had a spring in her step and a smile for every passing school child and shop owner. Had she been physically capable of whistling a jaunty tune, she would have done so.

Fifteen minutes later, feeling a little damp under the armpits, she arrived at the neat little florist's shop, where she was pleased to observe the very van that had cropped up in Jack's photograph, parked right outside the shop and looking very smart indeed in what looked like a brand new livery of bright sunflower yellow. She entered the shop, causing an unseen bell to tinkle pleasantly above her head. The eponymous owner arrived from a backroom, where he had doubtless been snipping and pruning. He greeted the officer jovially.

"Ah, good morning! What a lovely day. And what can we do for the lovely young officer today? A bunch of red roses perhaps? But then again, you surely must have some handsome young fellow buying you those all the time. A bunch of lilies for your mother? We've got some beauties in today, Miss!"

"Nothing to boost your sales I'm afraid!" replied Snibboh. "Just some information, if you don't mind."

"Anything to help."

"Well, I know I'm asking the impossible, but do you keep diaries here? I need to know where your van was on a Friday in April, at a very precise time. Don't worry; you've done nothing illegal, Mr Gough. It's just that the van showed up on a photograph which we need as evidence in a potentially serious crime, and if you could confirm a time it would be really helpful."

"Goodness me!" exclaimed Mr Gough, clasping his podgy hands to his mouth. "How exciting! The trouble is, I deliver so many flowers all over town every day, it'll be a nightmare trying to guess where I was."

Snibboh said that she understood his difficulty and told him the date. Mr Gough looked in his diary for a while and then looked up at the officer with a self-satisfied smile.

"Do you have the photograph on you?" he said. "If I could see it, I'll be able to confirm the exact time."

WPC Hobbins handed it to him.

"Do you know," began the florist, "had it been any other day, I couldn't have helped you. Now, how's this for a coincidence? I was without my van for a week around that time, because it was being re-sprayed yellow. It was green you see, and my wife thought we should brighten up the shop, which was also green, so we repainted it yellow, like a sunflower, and we wanted the van to match, so we booked it into 'The Spray Bay' in Queen Street, which is an accident repair place. I had to hire a van from them while it was being re-sprayed and sign-written, so that's why I needed to see the photo. I picked my van up at ten to six on the Friday. I remember that because Barry, who runs the place, was waiting for me to arrive before he could lock up and go home. I dropped off the hire van with him and I left a few minutes later, so this would have been about six o'clock. As you can see, this van is yellow, so that means I'd taken delivery two minutes before and I was heading home to Chapel Ash. An hour before, it would have been the white hire van, and the week before, the old green version, so this clearly pin-points the exact time, I'm happy to say. Doesn't it look smart on the photo?"

WPC Hobbins had to agree that it did. She was tingling with excitement. David had been right about the Weird Woman's bus stop habits, and Mr Gough had proved it. This now meant that either the coroner was mistaken, which was, of course, possible, or something sinister had happened on the top storey of the car park. She thanked Mr Gough for his help and began walking back towards the town centre, deep in thought.

Laz too was deep in thought, as he pulled up at the petrol station to buy cigarettes. He desperately needed a fag to calm his nerves. In approximately twenty minutes' time he would be sitting before a panel of fine artists being grilled with pretentious unfathomable questions about everything but art, if David's memories of the interview techniques were anything to go by. He should have been grateful, as he didn't have the first clue about art, but somehow this wasn't any great consolation. He wasn't too hot on lateral thinking either, or, for that matter, on interviews in general. His interrogation for the British Leyland job had consisted of more prosaic questions, such as, "You're not a communist are you?" and "How long do you spend in the crapper reading the Sun?" Somehow, he couldn't imagine his Leyland interviewer asking him about making holes in rivers. As long as he could make a hole in a car door with a drill, the job was his. Whether he wanted it or not was another matter.

As he returned from the kiosk with his twenty Benson and Hedges, he glanced nervously at the back seat, where the large red portfolio of work lay in waiting. He took a huge gulp, turned on the ignition and pulled onto the A449, Wolverhampton bound. He picked up his cigarettes and began to impatiently nibble at the strip of plastic that joined the two sections of cellophane wrapped around the box. He was so nervous that he was in danger of gnawing through the cardboard box completely. Technique went out of the window now, as he effed and blinded at the confounded wrapping, which he saw as a completely unnecessary encumbrance, doing its damnedest to hamper the progress of his legally purchased fag to its rightful place in his mouth.

"For f***'s sake!" he screamed, finally tearing the box from the offending plastic with his left hand and tossing it out of the car window, as his right hand steered the vehicle erratically around the large traffic island at Wall Heath. As he exited the island and pointed the car in the direction of Penn, Laz realized that he still had a large piece of cellophane in his mouth. This was strange, as he thought he had just thrown it out of the window.

90

What he had, in fact, thrown away was his brand new packet of cigarettes, which immediately met their makers, (if indeed cigarettes have makers, other than The Imperial Tobacco Group, of course) under the wheels of a council refuse lorry. This did nothing to lighten Laz's mood, and the air turned blue, not from smoke, but from foul language all the way to Wolverhampton.

Screeching into the underground car park behind the college, and realizing that he was far from early for his appointment, he tried to ram the car into a space that it didn't fit, and in another bout of temper, screeched back out again at a higher speed than some old gentlemen can manage on dual carriageways of a Sunday, until the car suddenly stopped with a sickening bang that nearly dislodged the driver's teeth.

Laz threw open the driver's door and stormed out to inspect the damage. Someone had left a two-foot tall concrete bollard in his way, which served absolutely no purpose, and was probably sponsored by The Spray Bay in Queen Street. The back of Laz's car now had this infernal bollard embedded into it, meaning that any money he might make out of David, if he succeeded in hoodwinking Kieron Hastings, was now just the excess amount he'd need to part with to further his insurance claim. Sweating profusely now, like a glassblower's backside, he quickly parked his stricken vehicle into a marginally more comfortable bay only to discover that he now couldn't get the giant portfolio out of the back seat, due to the close proximity of the cars on either side.

A passing student, observing this scene, might have been forgiven for thinking that Laz was either an escaped madman, or else a patient with an extreme case of Tourette's syndrome who had mistakenly arrived at the college car park thinking it was his psychologist's clinic.

Laz jumped into the car, reversed it out just enough to retrieve the portfolio, which he threw onto the ground behind the car, and drove back into the space at a speed Sterling Moss wouldn't have been disappointed with, applying the brake with just as much gusto as he had applied the throttle, a split second earlier. The passing student, had he still been passing, could not have faulted the speed of Laz's driving, but the accuracy was another thing. 'More haste, less speed!' he would probably have remarked to himself, as he wryly observed the driver, trapped in his vehicle, unable now to open the driver's door due to the close proximity of the vehicle to his right. Had the student decided to stick around, on the grounds that he was being royally entertained, free of charge, by a comedy genius second only to Stan Laurel, he would have overheard Laz screaming profanities that would have made a Liverpudlian docker blush, as he reversed over his bulky portfolio in an attempt to re-position his car in order that he could vacate it. A further minute of this student's valuable time would have been rewarded by the vision of Laz looking heavenward, shaking his fists and yelling "F*** off, bastard!" at no one in particular, before gathering up the flattened folder and running, scarlet-faced, towards the car park's exit.

The interviews, mercifully, were running late, and it was a marginally calmer Laz that sat in a corridor on the seventh floor, breathing deeply and staring at the wall, his battered portfolio at his side, with a cartoon tyre track down one side. A few feet away down the corridor, an intense-looking young man with a shaved head and an earring stared at his own portion of wall. Laz didn't like him. The fellow had not spoken to him, or even looked at him during the ten minutes they had sat there, which led him to formulate the opinion that he was an antisocial, stuck-up, pretentious shitbag. Laz was notoriously quick at assessing people, totally wrongly usually, and always saw the world in black and white, (or monochrome, as he would have to start saying if he were to be accepted onto the course)

Nothing was ever 'okay' for Laz. It was either 'shit' or 'brilliant'. People, likewise, fell into two distinct camps, 'bosom buddies' or 'complete arseholes'. Unfortunately for the latter, they were not scrutinized for years before being labelled thus. One comment or facial expression could seal their fate. Laz had even been known to despise someone intensely because they were wearing a shirt that he didn't like the colour of.

Blissfully unaware of all the irrational hatred being focussed on him by the curly-haired character a few feet away, the shaven-headed student continued to fix his gaze on the opposite wall, in case the crazy man he'd seen earlier, smashing up his own car and portfolio in the student car park, tried to engage him in conversation. He'd heard that three-quarters of all art students were barking mad, but this one should really have been locked away in a secure unit somewhere.

A door opened, and a middle-aged gentleman called out "Larry Homer please!"

Laz gathered up his badly bent portfolio and scurried into the interview room, where a panel of three lecturers sat behind a trestle table. Laz was invited to lay his work on the table, where two of the lecturers studied it, while the third, who introduced himself as Kieron Hastings, welcomed him to Wolverhampton.

"Mr Homer, thank you for coming. As you know, we don't usually interview in term time, but we do have one place available on the Fine Art course, which we'd obviously like to fill. Unfortunately, a foreign student had to return home, as her grant didn't materialize. Bad news for her, but maybe good news for you, eh?"

Laz nodded nervously, like a flock-sprayed nodding dog on the parcel shelf of a Ford Anglia.

Kieron looked over to his fellow lecturers, who were making very encouraging noises. Hearing his colleagues waxing lyrical as they leafed through Laz's battered portfolio, he deemed it necessary to take a look for himself. After a brief silence, he resumed his conversation.

"Well Larry, it is obvious from even that brief glimpse at your folder that you are a very talented young man indeed."

"Thank you very much!" replied Laz modestly. He wisely avoided the temptation to add the word "Shucks!"

"Let me ask you," continued Kieron, "How would you make a hole in the river Avon?"

Laz feigned puzzlement, followed by enlightenment.

"Simple! I would throw that chap waiting in the corridor into it."

"And why the lad outside?" asked Kieron.

"Because there's only one place going on this course, and I want it, that's why! The trouble is, when I tell you about my disability, I have a feeling you'll prefer him to me."

"You are disabled?" asked the shrivelled-up little man to Kieron's left.

"Well, sort of," replied Laz. "It's more of a nervous complaint than anything physical."

"We make allowances for all types of problems here," Kieron assured him. "It's an equal opportunity college, of course. What is your precise problem?"

"Well," began Laz nervously. "You see, I think I'm a talented artist, though it sounds conceited to say so...."

"Very talented," agreed the limp, lisping blond-haired gentleman to Kieron's right.

"But I have a psychological problem. I went to a very tough and unforgiving school in the Black Country, where you were bullied if you were artistic like me. Whenever the teacher praised me for drawing a good picture in class, the other boys would beat me up in the playground, or after school, walking home."

"You poor love!" gasped the Limp Lisper.

"To make matters worse, my father was just as bad. If I complained to him about the bullying, he told me it was my own fault for taking up such a sissified hobby, and I deserved what I got. He was an alcoholic and a boxer you see, and he wanted me to follow him into boxing."

"How heartleth!" whispered the L.L. He turned to look out of the window, perhaps to wipe away a teardrop.

"My mother tried to reason with him. She said that every child was different, and should be allowed to follow their own dreams, but he wouldn't have it. I was forced to work in factories when I left school, which I hated. Consequently I could only draw in secret when he was out getting drunk somewhere. I'd draw in the evenings at the kitchen table, and she'd keep an eye out for him returning, so we could hide away the pens and papers. One evening, he caught us at it, and beat me and my mother black and blue."

"You should have left him," suggested Kieron, deeply concerned. "The pair of you."

"It's never that easy," replied Laz dolefully. "You know how it is. Women are funny that way."

"I know, love," added the L.L., his lip quivering.

"Anyway, I muddled through, as best I could, snatching moments with my mother here and there. I often used her as a life model, as you'll see from my portfolio. He finally died this year, which is why I'm here right now."

"A tragic tale, Larry, and I'm sorry you've had such a bad time, but surely that's all behind you now."

"Yes and no," sighed Laz pitifully. "It's left me with what I suppose you'd call a psychological problem. I'm doing my best to sort myself out. I see a shrink once a month, but so far it's not doing me much good. You see, I can't draw or paint anymore when people are watching me. I associate it with my terrible school days. I clam up and begin to sweat profusely. I literally forget how to hold a pencil properly, it's so bad, and I, erm, shake. The only place I can concentrate is at home alone, or with my mother, and that, Mr Hastings, is my confession. If you won't let me carry on working at home, I fear that I will incapable of producing any work worthy of showing. I'm a wreck, aren't I?"

The L.L. spoke up. "Listen, Larry. You are a very brave boy, coming here for an interview, after all you've been through. I may be thpeaking out of turn here, but I for one wouldn't mind you continuing to work at home, with the provitho that you attended hithtory of art lectureth, theminarth, tutorial groupth and tho on."

He looked eagerly around the room at his fellow lecturers, who were slowly beginning to nod in agreement. Kieron eventually spoke.

"I agree. It's a bit unusual, but if you're happier in that environment, and you're happy to travel in when we ask you to show work or whatever, I can't see the problem. It means we can't just sidle up to you as you paint and suggest an improvement here and there, technique-wise, but to be honest, not many of us do that anyway. It would be downright wrong of us to deny you a place, after you've worked in secret for years and suffered at the hands of philistines in the bargain."

Laz gave them his best 'humble and overcome with emotion' look, the one he had been saving for when he won his first Oscar. Some would say he'd already won it. He thanked them for their time, gathered up his work and walked towards the door.

"One last thing," he added. "Is there another way out of this interview room, other than this door?"

"Yes" said Kieron, puzzled. "You can go through that door there, which will take you through Studio One and into the lift area. Why?"

"Well, I shouldn't mention this really," said Laz nervously biting his lip. "That lad out there, I know him, you see. I couldn't believe it when I saw him sitting there, in an art college of all places. I'm pleased that he's obviously changed his ways, but I

96

broke out into a cold sweat when I saw him. I'm sure he was one of the boys who bullied me at school."

* * *

Raymond Homer was sitting in the front room with the cat on his lap, tickling its ear, when the familiar figure of the postman flashed past the bay window, followed seconds later by Raymond's favourite sound; that of a heavy pile of letters sliding through the letterbox onto his Minton tiled floor. He eased his way out of his favourite armchair with a groan, unceremoniously displacing his cat, and scurried out to see what had arrived with all the naïve enthusiasm of a ten-year-old waiting for his Beano.

It was there! He picked up the pile of post, sifting out the horrible brown envelopes and leaving them the hall table for his wife to deal with. That left just two items of interest. His Matchstick Modeller's Monthly Magazine, and a white enveloped letter. He had been patiently creating a model of a Victorian Grandfather clock, following the step by step instructions each month, and he was itching to continue. He removed the ten free matchsticks which were glued to the front of the magazine in a sealed plastic bag, and hurried back into the front room to plan his next session in the garden shed, where his works of art were patiently constructed. Pausing at the door, he called up the stairs.

"Larry! There's a letter for you. It looks important!"

Laz flew down the stairs, landing on every sixth step and snatched the letter from his father's hand.

"Ta, dad. Put the kettle on."

He pulled him close and planted a sloppy wet kiss on Raymond's brow.

"Get off!" laughed his father. "He's never right, Vera. If he's right, I know a hospital full of 'em just up the road!"

Laz sat down at the breakfast bar in the kitchen and tore the envelope apart. It read:

*Dear Larry,*

*Thank you for attending our interview on Monday. We have great pleasure in confirming that a place has been allocated for you on the Fine Art Bachelor of Arts (Honours) degree course, with immediate effect.*

*We discussed your needs in more depth after you left, and we all agree that you can work at home, as long as you are prepared to visit the college for lectures, criticisms and so on. Could you initially report to the seventh floor next Monday at ten o'clock to fill in the necessary forms and take your first brief?*

*Incidentally, we interviewed the student waiting in the corridor immediately after you had gone, and you will be relieved to know that he was not accepted onto the course, as his work was not of the required standard.*

*However, it is quite heartening to be able to report that he seems to have matured since his school days, and now seems quite a decent young fellow.*

*In a world where there is so much violence, cruelty and deceit, it is encouraging to see that a leopard is capable, after all, of changing its spots!*

*Let us now hope that you can put your bad educational experiences firmly behind you, and go on to fulfil your huge potential.*

*Yours Sincerely, Kieron Hastings. Head of Department.*

What is often referred to as 'the gamut of emotions' ran through Laz's head as he placed the letter in his back pocket. He would dearly have loved to sit there for a few more minutes, reading and re-reading that letter until it began to sink in, but he had promised to pick Sammy Chinn up from his house so that they could visit an old lady in Dudley. She wanted them to organize a house clearance, and work had to come first. After all, wasn't it work that had given him his big break at the art college? Where would

98

he have been now, had he and Sammy not cleared a house in Stourbridge a few weeks earlier, and discovered an attic full of treasure?

It was a typical call, from a lady who was trying to remove the clutter from her life, and make a few pounds in the process, before she moved to a small one-bedroomed bungalow. Her husband had died two years previously and both her sons had left home to pursue their artistic careers. She was justifiably proud of them, and chatted with Laz and Sammy about their various achievements.

Roland had moved to London to manage a successful theatre in the West End, whilst Jeremy was a top professional scenery artist in Hollywood. She was a little upset that he had moved so far from home, but he was a good boy who phoned his lonely mother each week to tell her about the exciting projects he was working on. It wasn't so bad with Roland, because, for some reason, in spite of his good looks, he'd never found the right woman, and often popped home to stay with her when he could, even bringing his best mate occasionally. Jeremy however, was a family man with two kids, and getting home was becoming more and more difficult, what with the work and their hectic social lives and so on.

She'd been trying to clean out the loft for absolutely ages, and couldn't bear to dispose of their old things, but Roland didn't wish to keep the various costumes he'd created on his Fashion Design degree course, and Jeremy had insisted that he would never need his old college work again, so with their blessing, she reluctantly agreed to have a clear out, after carefully selecting a few special items to remember them by. She felt just as awful about disposing of her Henry's old suits, ties, shoes, golf clubs, gramophone records and P.G. Wodehouse first editions, but one could only harbour so much, and it was nice to think that someone else would get pleasure from them.

Laz and Sammy were sympathetic, as they sat and sipped tea with her in the elegant drawing room, but they had to be business-minded too. They hoped she'd understand that certain items, such as the complete set of signed Wodehouse first edition hardbacks with perfect dust wrappers may have had sentimental value, but would fetch next to nothing in a sale. The grandfather clocks too would be hard to sell, but Sammy kindly offered the lady fifty pounds per clock, which was apparently more than generous, according to Laz.

Sammy confessed that he was no art expert, and could offer no sensible opinions on the three bulging portfolios of college work. He could only identify two famous pictures, namely Constable's The Haywain and Leonardo da Vinci's Mona Lisa, neither of which was present in the pile of student work before him, so he gracefully declined to commit himself. Laz, who regarded himself as a superior intellect when it came to the arts, flicked through the mountain of work until he settled on a rather beautiful terra cotta portrait, which he propped up against the drawing room wall in order that he could perform a simple test of its worth. He strode purposefully from one side of the room to the other, much to the bemusement of both Sammy and the old lady, staring at the drawing from various angles as he did so. Finally he returned to his seat and pompously deemed the work to be of quality, as its eyes appeared to follow him around the room. He offered her ten quid for the lot.

Having brought the work home and gone through it more thoroughly, he discovered that the first folder contained foundation course work from Birmingham College of Art, circa nineteen-sixty-nine, and the other two were full of fine art degree course work, circa nineteen-seventy to seventy-two. It belonged to one Jeremy Westfield who had achieved a first class honours degree before concentrating on scenery painting, which had taken him to the giddy heights of Hollywood.

It was the foundation folder that had impressed Kieron Hastings and his colleagues so much, just as Laz hoped the other two folders would, once his degree course began. The bogus correspondence course Laz had spoken to David about, with its qualification that was purportedly equivalent to the foundation certificate, simply didn't exist. It was a figment of Laz's fertile imagination, and no one was more surprised when his gullible friend took it hook, line and sinker.

\* \* \*

Laz jumped into his car and drove to Sammy's house, with his acceptance letter safely stored in his pocket. He may have pulled the wool over David's eyes in one respect, but he hadn't been lying when he waxed lyrical about the time he had spent visiting the foundation course. Compared to the soul-destroying, grim conveyor belt job he was used to, and the deadheads he had to co-exist with, the art college and its inhabitants were from another, brighter, more carefree universe. That was where he longed to be. The only drawback, as far as he could see, was that he couldn't draw a straight line, with or without the aid of a rule. That said, if David were to be believed, no one else on the seventh floor could either, so he'd be in good company.

The deal he had struck with Kieron Hastings was perfect. He could lounge around the college whenever he fancied, after he'd delivered his project work, and chat up Katie Black in the refectory. He would naturally participate in the various art college parties, which often ended up back at the halls of residence, putting the average Roman orgy to shame, and he would reluctantly endure the critiques, seminars, lectures and slide shows, just to keep his masters sweet. The rest of the time he would continue to do house clearances with Sammy, secure in the knowledge that, if the money didn't flood in from robbing old ladies, there was always his student loan to fall back on. Life was looking rosy, but there was one small cloud on the horizon.

The foundation folder had done its job admirably, and gained him a place on the degree course. He felt sure the degree level folders would likewise serve him well, but there was a little irritating niggle in the back of his mind, caused by his lack of understanding of how these colleges operated. Did the tutors merely allow the students to express themselves willy-nilly, and paint whatever they wished, as the mood took them, or was there some kind of structure? David, for example, had often told Laz about his various projects, such as the Tiffany glass one he was currently working on. Had he just bowled into old Claude's office one day and said, "Look Claude, old chap. I fancy doing a bit on stained glass. How about it?" or had Claude pinned up some communal notice in reception telling them what was on the agenda that week? If the latter route was par for the course, there could well be trouble ahead. Kieron might inform them, for the sake of argument, that they must draw pictures of old bottles and fruit, and where would that leave Laz? He would have to riffle through the two huge folders in the hope of finding the aforementioned items in two-dimensional form, only to discover that Jeremy had never developed a taste for them as still-life subject matter, and had concentrated entirely on sketching flowers in vases. The following week Kieron might ask for the students to draw their mothers asleep in a chair, only to find that Jeremy had nothing of that nature in his repertoire, resulting in Laz having to reluctantly hand in a painting of two puppies in a basket. The whole scenario was one that could easily give him sleepless nights, but Laz was made of sterner stuff. After all, had he not blagged his way onto a fine art degree course? The hardest task was already done. Surely, a man of his intellect could quickly sort out a little problem such as this. He resolved to not worry about it until it happened, instead giving some thought to how he and Sammy could persuade the old gentleman they were about to visit that his three Victorian marble fireplaces were virtually worthless.

# CHAPTER 8

## Friends Reunited

Jim Weston was a large man with large sideburns and a white nylon shirt, through which his incredibly hairy body was clearly visible, whether he was viewed from the front or the back. He was virtually bald on top, but his black, greased-back hair began to curl a little when it got past his ears, and a sharp-eyed social historian would have noted the ancient remnants of a D.A., which dated him fairly accurately as being from the Teddy Boy era. Jim was in charge of silk screen printing, which every student was encouraged to dabble in during their three years at the college. He was an affable character from Stoke on Trent who enjoyed helping the students, providing they came equipped with breasts and a skirt. This form of natural selection permeated throughout the printing disciplines, and was perfected by Dom Bentley, the etching lecturer, or lecherer as most of the female students preferred to call him. One could virtually guarantee that the girl sharing a Guinness in the refectory bar with him on a Sunday night would coincidentally be the same one getting her project printed ahead of schedule first thing on Monday morning.

Jim Weston was the kind of person who didn't seem happy unless he had lots to occupy his mind. Running a busy print room would be enough for most people. The salary was good and the holidays long, but Jim didn't like to idle away his time once the college closed down. He also ran a commercial silk screen printing company in Stoke, and a small holiday cottages business.

The print room was quiet, for a change, with not a pretty student in sight. David had booked a screen for the morning to print a Tiffany glass design for his degree project. The only other student in the room was a fine artist called Laurence Fuchs, who was printing a picture of the current pope with most of his entrails hanging out.

David walked over to observe.

"Nice!" he volunteered.

Laurence said nothing, and continued to ink up the screen. He was a tall, thin, bony-faced young man with a neatly trimmed black beard and wiry black hair. His eyes were soulless and dark, and his complexion an unhealthy yellowish white. David had been wrong on a few occasions, but he could generally work out if he was going to like someone or not fairly quickly. He couldn't imagine Laurence being a bosom buddy. He seemed like the kind of man who had been allocated just three thousand words to last him for his whole lifetime, and he didn't want to waste them.

David gave up and returned to his own screen.

Jim sidled over and said hello. He'd have preferred David to have had breasts, but it was a slow morning, and if there were no pretty girls to chat up, the next best thing was a funny and friendly student to talk to. Given the competition, which admittedly was not much, David was the easy winner.

"Howdy Dave!" he grinned, gripping him by the back of the neck and nearly shattering his spine. "How's it hangin'? Hey, you'll never guess what? I just went for a piss, and that bastard Claude has put a sign up on the bog door saying we have to book the cubicle lavvies now! The cheeky bastard. He can go and bollocks."

David smiled for two reasons. He loved the way Jim pronounced 'book', with around five 'O's, Stoke on Trent style. He was also pleased that someone had at last fallen for his childish little prank.

"The place is going down the pan," agreed David. "You can't even shit in peace anymore! I can't wait to break up for Whitsun. I'm knackered with all this degree show stuff. Everyone is on edge."

"Are you going away anywhere?" asked Jim.

"Can't afford to," said David. "Have you seen the cost of hotels lately?"

Jim smiled the smile of a refrigerator salesman who had just met a very gullible Eskimo. "Scandalous! Have you ever thought of hiring a cottage instead?"

"They're even dearer, aren't they, Jim?" asked David.

"Depends who you know. I've got a cracking little cottage in Dittisham, near Dartmouth, which I could let you have for next to nothing, if you're interested. You could take that pretty young policewoman with you."

David blushed. "How do you know about her?"

"I was in Tweedledum's getting a sausage roll, and I spotted you canoodling in the end booth."

"I'll have you know I wasn't canoodling," insisted David. "I don't even own a canoe, as a matter of fact. I was helping the police with their enquiries. I've discovered something of great importance to the Jack Hamphlett case, which has led to a major breakthrough, as it happens."

"Such as?" smiled Jim.

"It's confidential. I'm not allowed to talk about it, but suffice it to say, the net is drawing in."

"What?" Jim washed his ink-stained hands in the sink. This was good stuff. "He committed suicide, didn't he? Who's this net going to draw in on then?"

"I can't say," stated David firmly. "Not even to you, Jimbo. Incidentally, did you ever teach Jack? He was a nice chap by all accounts."

"Says who?" snarled Laurence, pausing from his printmaking.

David stared at him, taken aback by this sudden venomous outburst. Laurence strode over to where David and Jim were chatting.

"I don't see why I should pretend to like the little shit, just because he jumped off a car park and broke his bloody neck. I'll let the sycophants do that. There was more to Hamphlett than met the eye. He was no bloody saint. If your policewoman friend wants to do something *really* worthwhile, ask her to investigate the paintings that have gone missing. I've had one of mine stolen from the seventh floor exhibition space."

"Careful," advised David, "You'll use up your word allocation for April."

Laurence glared at him. "I knew Hamphlett all too well, unlike you. He went out with my sister and treated her like dirt, but that was nothing compared to something else I could tell you about."

"So tell us," urged Jim.

"It's confidential. I'm not allowed to talk about it," sneered Laurence, mimicking David's Black Country accent. "He jumped off the car park, and I, for one, cheered. Okay?"

Debate concluded, Laurence returned to his silk screen press and began throwing things around.

"Anyway," continued David, somewhat shaken, "I've got to go and have a word with Claude Beardsley in a few minutes. There's something I need to discuss with him, and I know it won't go down too well. I shouldn't be long, and then I'll get cracking."

Laurence suddenly stormed out of the print room, leaving his screen covered in ink and in danger of drying out. Another messy job for Jim to take care of.

"He was delightful," said David.

"A charmer," agreed Jim. "Laurence Fuchs!"

"I'm sure he does, but who'd volunteer to do it with him?" asked David, shuddering theatrically.

"He's a nasty piece of work who paints nasty pieces of work," said Jim. "Have you seen them? He's a gifted painter, but he will insist on painting folks just after a demented surgeon's been at 'em. I mean, it stands to reason, he can't be right in the head, can he? I wouldn't mind if he restricted his horrific imagination to his art, but he isn't a nice chap to know either. I've heard this tale....."

"Go on."

"Shall I put the kettle on?"

"Yes please!"

"He used to share a flat until very recently with a nice chap called Tim, a ceramics student from the fifth floor, who had a cat called Molly. Pretty little thing. Molly, I mean, not Tim. The flat was Tim's but he sub-let to Laurence, who apparently hated this cat, right? So one day last week, Tim was out. When he got home, he asked Laurence where his cat was. Laurence said he hadn't got a clue, but Katie in graphics reckons he killed it and buried it somewhere over West Park. They're all talking about it at The Castle."

"They begin with animals, these psychopaths," frowned David. "It's well known. They cut their teeth on animals, but after a while they're not satisfied with chopping up a gerbil, and they need to kill humans. I saw a documentary on it."

Jim had seen the documentary too.

107

"My aunt's cousin's friend's little child was weird, you know," said Jim, flicking his used teabag in the scrap paper bin. "He began by pulling the wings off butterflies and nobody took any notice. Before long he was shoving straws up frogs' arses and blowing them up like balloons, and then he graduated to filling his rabbit up with water at the sink."

"Jeez!"

"One night he was with his parents at the Conservative club in Stoke, reading his war magazines, when his mother casually mentioned that there was a German gentleman sitting in the corner - a friend of one of the members who'd popped to see him while he was in England on his holidays. The next thing you know, this kid, who was about eleven by then, ran over to this bloke and smashed a beer bottle into his face, shouting, 'Die! Nazi pig dog', or some such thing, and the stewards had to drag him off."

"Nice welcome to England," winced David. "Look, I must go and see old Claude. I've got a tutorial with him on Wednesday at eleven, and I want to skive off for the day so I can take the policewoman to Stratford. He won't be best pleased."

Jim winked horribly. He made a fist with his right hand and pulled it towards his chest, grabbing his upper arm's muscle with his left hand at the same time. The inexplicable lecher's gesture to symbolize sexual intercourse.

"I knew you were shagging her, you dirty bugger."

"I'll have you know," insisted David, "that I am taking her there for a bit of culture. We intend to visit the historic houses, followed possibly by a bit of canoodling up the Avon."

"And does your Suzanne know about this?" asked Jim, but David, who was feeling guilty enough without this probing printmaker prodding his protruding proboscis in where it wasn't wanted, declined to comment further and scurried off in search of Claude, promising to return forthwith.

Finding Claude was proving more difficult than David had imagined. He wasn't in his office on the third floor, nor was he sauntering around the studios putting the fear of God into his students. David wandered down to the reception office on the ground floor and stood impatiently behind a new Chinese student who was endeavouring to make herself understood to Betty, the college secretary. The girl appeared to be saying, "Possiboo now book toyret?" which made very little sense. Eventually, she gave up trying and staggered off into town, with a gait that suggested she'd got something unpleasant secreted in her trousers.

David smiled at Betty through the glass partition, and asked if she knew the whereabouts of his Head of Department.

"He's gone home for the afternoon because he had a bit of stuff he had to do," she replied. "If it's really important, you can catch him there. I'm sure he wouldn't mind, as long as you don't hold him up. It's two minutes from here, past Tarmac's offices and the football ground, turn right and it's on the left. Number six. It's a white terraced house with a red door."

David didn't really want to turn up at Claude's place unannounced, but if he didn't, there'd be trouble when he didn't show up for the tutorial the next day. He decided to risk it. It was a beautiful day, and he fancied a walk in the sunshine. It would give him time to ponder, and there was much to ponder upon. First on the agenda was Laurence. He was a nasty piece of work, for starters, but almost certainly nothing to do with Jack's demise. Either that or he was really dim. David had seen lots of whodunits on TV, and the golden rule was, the killer was never the bloke who was the obvious baddie. It was usually the one nobody suspected, like, for example, Dylan, but this wasn't a film. It was real life.

Laurence had been quite open about his dislike of Jack, though less open about *why* he disliked him. He had hinted that Jack had mistreated his sister, Leonora Willowbrook, but the amount of venom he released upon hearing Jack's name mentioned was completely disproportionate to that of a disgruntled brother who wasn't keen on his sister's choice of soul mate. There were stories about Jack drunkenly arguing with Leonora at The Castle, but that was merely par for the course with these art college romances and nothing to get so vitriolic about, unless of course Laurence knew that Jack was secretly beating the living daylights out of her. Somehow, from what David had gleaned from various sources, this seemed unlikely. Laurence had hinted about something far worse than his sister's relationship problems, but clammed up when quizzed about it. Whatever was eating him, it was intense, if his storming out of the print room was anything to go by.

Then there was his sister's surname. Why was she a Willowbrook when her brother was a Fuchs? Had she been married, or, intriguingly, was she still married? David had only ever seen her once, floating along the corridor in a purple crushed velvet dress, with two thin plaits at each temple, tied with ribbon at the back of her head, which made her look like a woman in a Renaissance painting. She was pale and beautiful with a distracted, haunted face, but that was probably because David had seen her not long after Jack had died, and despite their problems, he was very much the love of her life.

Another beautiful face popped into David's mind as he strolled past the huge façade of the football club. It was that of his girlfriend, Suzanne. Circumstances had conspired to separate them in recent weeks, and he was feeling guilty, not least because he had arranged to see a pretty young policewoman the following day. How could this new, mutual attraction be so wrong, he wondered, when half of the world was killing the other half? All he was guilty of was liking someone, after all. Was this such a terrible crime? He loved his Suzanne, but did that mean that he was forbidden from ever liking another female? If he and Snibboh made love in the long grass by the river in Stratford, surely this was just two people getting on and giving each other pleasure, and certainly not an insult to Suzanne, providing, of course, she never got to hear about it.

He had just about convinced himself when Suzanne's face popped into his head again, causing havoc.

The trouble with women, he felt sure, was that they were so serious. They always complained that relationships weren't 'going anywhere', whilst the average male didn't feel the need for them to travel at all. What was wrong with standing still, if it felt nice? Why did romances need a beginning, middle and end? Besides, the female of the species spoke in riddles, and one had to be an expert code-breaker to be able to read between the lines. 'Going anywhere' really meant getting married, buying a house and having babies.

David had been doing a lot of thinking about this particular topic of late, and he was convinced that his theory was correct. For a start, it wasn't entirely women's fault. He realized, in fairness to the fairer sex, they were genetically conditioned to push for these relationships that 'went somewhere' by God, who needed to keep the old planet kicking along, with all the inmates reproducing and so on. After all, He'd invested a lot of His time getting His planets business off the ground, and He didn't want to see them go bankrupt after a measly few million years. The problem really early on was that men, with a few exceptions, didn't really want to have sex with the women, as most females back then were extremely hairy and some had beards. He quite quickly realized this fundamental mistake, and a lot of cosmetic changes were made. This, however, was apparently not enough.

God then re-programmed the females to paint stuff all over their faces and wear skimpy tops, so that the males would want to have sex with them. David had long been fascinated by this weird ritual, which involved the females spending an inordinate amount of time covering up their existing faces with ones they'd painted on top, paying particular attention to their mouths. This was the bit they wanted men to kiss, so they drew attention to them by colouring them bright red or garish pink. The plan, though primitive, worked a treat, and quite soon women were having babies left, right and centre, which was God's hidden agenda. The

111

excitable and overly eager male was merely the means to that end, as Desmond Morris has been trying to explain to everyone for years.

From then on, once God had redesigned the females and given them make-up, nice smooth skin and skimpy tops, men became second class citizens, faring only slightly better than the male Praying Mantis and certain species of spider, which as most people know, are devoured by the female shortly after intercourse. There's gratitude for you. The females shut up shop, sexually speaking, having achieved their goal, which is not really marriage at all, but children, and the men feel unwanted, except by Gloria in the typing pool, who is still unattached and painting her lips bright red. The man is then vilified because of the resulting affair and hands over half of his worldly goods to the wife, when all he really wanted in the first place was the odd cuddle after Junior was born. David was completely convinced that around ninety percent of divorces could be avoided if only women would remember that their men feel unloved and dispensable once the child arrives.

Thoroughly depressed, he turned his thoughts to the band's final rehearsal which was scheduled for the following Saturday, but he had only got half way into humming the opening number when he spotted Claude's small terraced house. Daydreaming was suspended for the time being. He opened the front gate and rang the doorbell.

After a gap of a minute or so, he repeated the exercise, but still no one answered the door. To the left of the property was a narrow passage that led to another gate, which in turn led to the small back garden. David walked down the passageway and called out 'Is anyone home?' But the house was empty. Then he heard a harrowing cry coming from the direction of an old potting shed at the bottom of the garden. He hadn't figured Claude for a serial killer, but he was clearly engaged in sawing the limbs off an old lady inside the shed, judging by the unearthly racket emanating from within.

David nervously made his way towards the shed door, trying to decipher what the limbless old lady was trying to say, but it was impossible. As he approached, the volume of noise led David to believe that not one, but several old ladies were suffering mutilation. Whoever was being dismembered also seemed to be scratching at the door with their remaining, unsevered hand, trying in vain to attract a passing bobby.

Swallowing deeply, David opened the door, stepping sharply to one side as he did so, just in case. The noise ceased instantly. He popped his head cautiously around the door to be met by a pair of beautiful orange eyes, staring up at him from the darkness. They belonged to a small smoky grey cat that looked frightened out of its mind. David bent down to stroke it, and to his surprise, the cat came to him immediately and wrapped itself around his legs. He gently held onto its collar and looked for the identity disk. The cat's name was Molly, the very animal that Laurence had allegedly buried over West Park. The hapless creature had got itself locked in a potting shed, and was almost certainly starving. David needed to find some sort of box to contain the cat so that he could take it back to college and find Tim, whoever he was.

There was a decent sized length of string wrapped around a nail on the back of Claude's door, so David unravelled it and made a makeshift lead to prevent Molly from disappearing once more. She wasn't overly keen on this new development, but one sometimes had to take a firm line with cats for their own good. He walked into the shed and looked around for suitable cat box material, settling on a crate that had previously been home to several bottles of vintage port, judging by the typography on the side. These college lecturers obviously earned good salaries.

The problem was; a creature as agile as Molly would have no difficulty in leaping out of this open-topped box. What was needed was a lid. David's prayers were answered by God, who is renowned for moving in mysterious ways, His wonders to perform. On this occasion, He had decided to leave a large rusty sieve on top of the old oak plan chest where David could find it without hours of rummaging. He called the frightened little cat to him in the time-honoured tradition, by twiddling his fingers together as if rolling a bogey and mouthing the words 'Choo choo choo choo'. Quite why cats fall for this patently ridiculous charade is not clear, but Molly did so, and was gently lifted into the box for her troubles, an action that saw her body language change from domestic pet to ferocious predator in the batting of an eyelid. To slam the rusty sieve into position and thus avoid multiple lacerations was, with David, the work of an instant.

The string, which had served admirably as a lead, was now employed to secure the sieve; a not entirely scratch-free operation that left David leaking blood from several incisions. Trying desperately to staunch the flow of his vital fluids in order to keep his essential eight pints inside of him where they belonged, he began searching the various shelves for a piece of clean cloth, after a cursory rummage through his jeans' pockets produced only a crumpled 'Epitaph' business card which Jim had printed for them at a heavily discounted rate. He pulled open the top drawer of the oak plan chest and found not cloth, but a pile of drawings. These must, David thought, be Claude's personal work. He opened the second drawer, which revealed more of the same. The remaining four drawers were also crammed with paintings, etchings and prints, all of a very professional standard. Claude was obviously a talented artist, as was only right and proper for a Head of Department at a well-respected college. Two things puzzled David, however. Firstly, the work seemed incredibly varied in terms of style, which was unusual. Claude, it appeared, was nothing if not versatile. Secondly, why did he keep such good quality artwork in an old chest in the garden? Was his house so full of pictures that these had been relegated to his shed? If so, and these were the pictures he deemed worthy only of his shed, what did the ones in his house look like? They must have been very special indeed.

Then David spotted a rather beautiful pencil drawing. It was a still life of two bell peppers in an old basket, with the light from a window streaming onto them. The picture was signed Dylan Weldon. Another picture, on canvas this time, featuring a reclining nude on a chaise longue with her throat cut from ear to ear, was by Laurence Fuchs. David quickly riffled through some of the other pictures. Signed by many different people, none bore the name Claude Beardsley. These had to be the stolen pictures that Laurence had spoken about in the print room; the ones Kieron Hastings had mentioned as they caught the lift to the lecture theatre to see Snibboh.

David was confused. Why on earth would his Head of Department want to steal his own students' paintings? It made no sense. He had experienced similar feelings to the ones now surfacing when his car was stolen from a car park, just after he'd passed his test. He'd returned to the spot where he'd left the car and it wasn't there. His first reaction was to think that he hadn't come in the car in the first place, and that he must have arrived by bus. No, he distinctly remembered driving to Dudley that evening. Had he perhaps parked somewhere else? He was scatterbrained, after all - it was common knowledge amongst his friends. The car was probably just round the corner. Maybe he was looking for the wrong car. Had he sold it and purchased another, or just forgotten what colour it was?

The possibility that someone had actually stolen the damned thing was around eighth on his list of scenarios, just after the one where it was all a dream and he was about to wake up with his mother handing him a cup of tea. He tried desperately to come up with a believable reason why Claude would hoard all this work in a shed. Maybe someone else had stolen them and hidden them in his shed. Stranger things had happened, but not much stranger. The truth was staring him in the face. Claude, for reasons as yet unfathomed, was a thief.

David grabbed Molly's box, shut the shed door and made a speedy exit down the passage way. There was still the vexed question of his one-to-one tutorial with Claude the following day to sort out, but now wasn't the time to be worrying about that.

Luckily, there was not a soul in sight, least of all Claude, who was currently a mile away at Gertie's house, giving her a one-to-one tutorial of a different nature, which involved demonstrating his extensive range of artistic techniques and giving her a pointer or two.

Breathless after running all the way back to the college with a heavy box, and streaked with blood from Molly's frenzied attack, David arrived puffing and panting at reception and asked Betty if she knew of a student called Tim in ceramics. A few minutes later, a very grateful Tim Finlay and Molly were reunited, and all was sweetness and light. Having done his boy scout's good deed for the day, David slipped away quietly from the reunion celebrations to clean up his wounds in the third floor lavatories, leaving Tim and his colleagues to ask each other, "Say, who *was* that masked man?" or words to that effect. David then made a visit to the payphone and dialled Mo's number. He urgently needed to borrow the band's transit van.

# CHAPTER 9

## Historic Warwick and Alas Poor Yorick

Claude Beardsley sat in his office seething. He picked up his coffee mug and threw it at the far wall, breaking it into fifty pieces. The polite knock on his office door heralded the arrival of Katie Black, his eleven-thirty tutorial, and he wasn't in the mood to discuss her work right now. There were darker, more sinister things occupying his mind. He walked over to the door and opened it a few inches, holding his head with the other hand.

"Ah, Katie, love," he groaned. "Can you be a dear and come back tomorrow, and inform the others that I've cancelled tutorials for today. I've got a migraine and I can't see a bloody thing. It's all flashing lights and blurred vision, so I wouldn't be able to criticize your work."

Katie sympathized, as she also occasionally suffered from 'classical' migraine. She turned to go.

"Just one thing, love," added Claude wearily. "Is David Day about this morning?"

Katie said that she hadn't seen him, but he had told her the previous evening that he was taking the day off.

"Did he say why?" asked Claude. "He was my eleven o'clock tutorial; not that I was in a fit state to have seen him."

"Not really," replied Katie. "But he mentioned something about going somewhere with a policewoman. I know he said he wanted to 'probe' her, because I remember replying 'Ooer, missus!'"

"Why would you say that?" asked Claude, who didn't do jokes.

"Because it sounds like something from a Carry On film; you know, 'probe her'?"

"Did he say what he was probing her about, by any chance?"

"No. He seemed a bit secretive. I must say, it's unlike him to miss his tutorial. He's a real swot!" replied Katie.

Claude made his excuses and returned to his desk. He took a small piece of card from his leather jacket and studied it. It read:


### EPITAPH
Progressive Rock Band.

Telephone Brierley Bank 62566.


He dialled the number and waited a while. Eventually, a female voice answered.

"Hello, Ruby Day speaking."

Claude apologized, explaining that he'd dialled the wrong number.

He picked up his ashtray and threw it at the far wall. He was not having a good day, and when that happened, items of crockery suffered. On Tuesday, in sharp contrast, he had enjoyed a very pleasant afternoon at Gertie's house. After a leisurely love-making session which lasted most of the afternoon, she had cooked him his favourite coq au vin, and they had seen off two bottles of red wine. He eventually got home at half past nine, a little the worse for wear, but sufficiently alert to notice that his

118

shed door wasn't shut properly. Fearing that some petty thief had stolen his bicycle or lawn mower, he looked inside, discovering, to his absolute horror, that his entire art collection was missing, and that the intruder had left him a calling card into the bargain. Imagine then, his state of mind when several other jigsaw pieces began to fit together.

Laurence Fuchs had telephoned him later that very evening to tell him that a student called David Day had been mouthing off in the print room about how he and a policewoman were collaborating over the Jack Hamplett case. David doesn't show up for his tutorial, and then the phone number on the band's card belongs to a woman named Day. Claude paced the room, like Napoleon probably did just before he declared war on Russia, throwing desktop items this way and that. Then he returned to his chair and dialled a number. He filled in the irritating time waiting for the person at the other end to pick up by slinging a saucer at the filing cabinet. To his chagrin, it remained intact.

"Is that Rosie?" asked Claude gruffly. The woman at the other end confirmed that it was.

"Is Gilda there?" asked Claude, nervously straightening paper clips as he spoke.

Gilda came to the phone. She had a gruffer voice than Claude's.

"We were shagging. It had better be important."

"It is," Claude assured her. "This is your pen pal. I need you to do something for me, girls."

\* \* \*

Blissfully unaware of the massive impact he was having on Claude Beardsley, David was feeling pretty pleased with himself as he tootled through the pretty country lanes in his Mini, with a pretty policewoman by his side, looking gorgeous in a floral summer dress, with her shiny hair cascading around her shoulders. He had dropped his dad off at the factory in order that he could borrow his own car back for the day, and had promised faithfully to pick him up at five-thirty that evening for his lift home. This time constraint meant that he would have to cram things in a little, but at least it gave him an excuse to get back if time was weighing heavy and they ran out of stuff to talk about.

First port of call was Anne Hathaway's Cottage, but a few miles short of his destination, David was a little dismayed to find the road dug up with barriers all over the place and diversion signs.

"Oh bugger!" he moaned. "We can't go the way I know now. We'll just have to go Anne Hathaway!" suddenly bursting into a self-satisfied fit of laughter at his dubious pun.

Snibboh stared at him blankly.

"It sounds a bit like another way, you see. Anne Hathaway." explained David.

Snibboh stared at him blankly.

"So," she said eventually. "Run this past me again, David. You broke into a man's shed last night and stole a load of pictures from it, aided and abetted by your friend Mohammed? Not content to rob any old bloke, you choose Claude Beardsley, a man I shared a platform with during the appeal for information on Jack Hamphlett's suicide - your head of department - and then you tell a police officer all about it, expecting me to congratulate you on a job well done. What did you do it for, Rag Week?"

"I can explain," replied David, "If you'll hear me out, my old Snibboh. Just ask yourself where you'd have been without my help in re. the photographs. I haven't just turned into a kleptomaniac overnight."

"And you wore gloves, did you?"

"Er, no."

"So when the forensic boys turn up to fingerprint the place and find that yours are plastered all over the place, along with some

Asian that's built like a brick shit-house, you'll be happy to continue learning how to paint from behind bars?"

David was not overly worried. "My dear Snibs. Let me finish. There has been a spate of art thefts from our college over a few years now, usually from the most gifted students, with one notable exception - me, but I'm sure it was only a matter of time. My act of kindness in rescuing that cat led me to discover the loot in Beardsley's shed. Now, I don't know about you, but I can't think of one rational explanation for how they came to be there, other than that Claude nicked off with them over a period of time. He's hardly going to call the pigs in - no offence - when it was he who was the real thief, and I the Robin Hood figure, is he now?"

Snibboh pondered.

"But why would he steal artwork from his own students? It doesn't make sense."

David turned to her, wagging his finger, causing his Mini to veer across the country lane and put the fear of God into a woman walking her Labrador.

"That's what I thought originally, but then it dawned on me. Think about it, Snibbs. Thirty students per year graduate from our department alone at college, and out of that number, one, maybe two do well in the big wide weird and wacky world of art, if you'll forgive the alliteration."

"I would if I knew what it was."

"Anyway, imagine that David Hockney had trained at Wolverhampton, for instance. How much would a few of his early works be worth?"

"Who's David Hockney?" asked Snibboh.

David sucked his tooth but continued undaunted.

"What price an early painting by Peter Blake, now that his originals fetch mega-bucks?"

121

Peter Blake too was a closed book too, as far as Snibboh was concerned.

"So these names," she ventured, "Are all big earning art superstars, I take it?"

"Exactly, and anyone with a decent eye for talent, as Claude has to have in his profession, could borrow a piece here and a piece there over a period of time. After all, he's the last one that we'd suspect. All he has to do is sit on them and wait to see which of the pile becomes famous. Then he's rich. Did you know that he has three properties? I bet he didn't get those on his lecturer's salary."

David pulled to a halt on the car park near to Anne Hathaway's cottage, and they walked across the gravel in the blinding sunshine, towards the house.

"So what now?" asked Snibboh. "Presuming I leave my police responsibilities along with my uniform, back in my Wolverhampton flat, just for today, and promise not to arrest you, even though you just confessed a serious crime to me."

"Ah!" said David. "I have a cunning plan. I need to have a word with Jim Weston, our silk-screen printing lecturer, and Dylan's uncle Martin. I will reveal all when the time is right, but for now, let's forget Jack Hamphlett, Claude and the rest for an hour or two and get some culture, after which I intend to canoodle you on the Avon."

Snibboh smiled a smile so sensual that David felt all of his blood rush to his groin, leaving him light-headed. He paid the entrance fee and they disappeared inside. The guide who was usually on hand to show visitors around had called in sick at the eleventh hour, but David wasn't unduly concerned, as he'd visited the old place several times before and knew the patter off by heart. In fact, he was secretly quite pleased, as he could now take on that role and impress Snibboh with his knowledge.

He showed her the old bedroom and explained that Elizabethan beds had canopies, which had to occasionally be tightened up to prevent nasty insects from falling on the unwitting sleeper, giving rise to the expression 'Sleep tight, don't let the bedbugs bite.'

This tale of creepy crawlies prompted his lovely companion to slip her arm under his and shudder at the thought of it, which was very satisfying. The arm stayed in position as he charged around the house pointing out the origins of other oft-used expressions such as 'Threshold' - the raised doorstep that prevented the floor covering of straw, or thresh, from spilling over into another room. He showed her the large chimney breast, where meals were cooked in large black pots, and explained how the soot was removed by throwing a hen down the chimney pot, attached to a piece of string. Snibboh, by now well and truly fascinated, asked if this practice had given rise to the less widely used expression, 'Last one at the dinner table gets the sooty chicken's arsehole.'

Next stop was Mary Arden's house, mother of the Bard, where David showed her the baby walker, which consisted of a central pole with a metal harness attached, thus allowing a child to toddle around in circles without fear of it colliding with the open fire or the boiling pans on the range.

"I'm getting the hang of this now!" piped up Snibboh excitedly. This device gave rise to the expression, 'Going round and round in circles like a sooty chicken!"

David gave her a hug, holding on to her beautiful bare arms. He could feel her soft skin beneath the thin cotton dress, and for the umpteenth time that day he was cognizant of little involuntary twitches from within his Y Fronts. He drove off in search of Stratford town centre, hoping and praying that his excitement wasn't too obvious through his tight loon pants. As they drove, Snibboh fondled his hair with her right hand, and glanced down at the extra gear stick that seemed to have formed within his trousers.

"Shall I change to fourth for you, now that we're doing fifty, or do you prefer it stuck in second?" she asked, nodding at his short, racing model.

David flushed red and informed her that she'd have to pull it up and across if she needed to find reverse. Too much culture in one day can be off-putting, and something unexpected had arisen, which resulted in Shakespeare's birthplace being put on hold in favour of a trip to the river, where they planned to commandeer a boat and meander down the Avon. David, ever conscientious, filled her in about what she had missed.

"It's similar to the other two places really, but I don't think it's as good. There's a nice feature about Will's will though. Apparently, he left his second best bed to his wife. There's gratitude for you!"

The constant light petting that Snibboh was subjecting him to while he bored her rigid with Shakespearian facts was having an enormous effect on the gear stick, which now resembled a fleshy crook lock in search of a steering wheel. David drove into the rough old boat yard car park while he could still steer his vehicle and skidded the Mini to a halt amid clouds of white dust. Snibboh leant over and gave him a slow, lingering kiss, while seeming to try to find reverse at the same time.

"Erm, the boat man is watching," groaned David. "Shall we hire one so that we can have some privacy?"

"Good idea," agreed Snibboh, licking the inside of his ear.

"You go," whispered David. "I can't walk in this state."

David removed his denim jacket in order to cover up his embarrassment, while WPC Hobbins commandeered a vessel. After a two minute talk from the boatman on safety and how to work the outboard motor, they were allowed to cast off. Snibboh sat alongside David, stroking his inner thigh, as the boat careered all over the river. After several near collisions with pleasure cruisers, it was deemed a good idea to pull over beside a farmer's field, before anything more serious happened. They flattened an area of long grass where, unseen by passing boats, they lay down to continue their canoodling. Shakespeare was all very fine and dandy, but this was, for both of them, the climax of their day out, and when the canoodling eventually ceased, they both lay still, staring at the cloudless sky.

"David?" whispered Snibboh.

"Yeah?" whispered a near comatose David.

"Have you ever thought about how birds build nests?"

"No."

"How do they keep the very first twig in place, till they come back with more to start intertwining them?"

"Good question. They probably gob on the first one, and it acts as a sort of bird glue."

"David?" The Stratford trip had made Snibboh hunger for knowledge.

"What?"

"What's your girlfriend's name?"

"How do you know I've got one?" asked David sheepishly.

"I asked your mate, Dylan."

"Suzanne. What's your boyfriend's name?"

"How do you know I've got one?" asked Snibboh.

"I don't, but I bet you have!"

"I haven't," replied Snibboh, somewhat nervously. "I have a husband."

David shot up from his second-best bed. "What?"

"I'm married," repeated Snibboh. "And suddenly I'm feeling shitty."

"So am I," agreed David. "As soon as I saw you, I fancied you like mad, but I knew it was wrong to. Suzanne's never done anything to hurt me, and if she found out, she'd be distraught."

"Steve would be too. He'd probably kill you."

"Oh cheers!" said David. "He'd kill me, not you?"

"Both of us," said Snibboh. "He's in the police too. We coppers marry each other because no one else will have us."

"I've just had you," said David, gallantly.

"I didn't think I'd feel as guilty as this though," she sighed. "What we just did was lovely, and anything that feels so nice should be made legal, I think."

David agreed. "I was only thinking about that yesterday. The trouble is, it causes so much unhappiness too, for those that it affects. Look at Jack Hamphlett for instance. He was so upset by his father's death and Claude's affair with his mother that he killed himself; that's if he did kill himself of course. If my Suzanne found out about us, she'd go mental, and I don't want to think about your Steve removing my entrails with a rusty pen knife, thank you very much."

Snibboh looked at him long and hard.

"Do you think it's best if we remain good mates, but stop the sexual stuff then?"

"Probably. I'm good at that. Most girls end up just being my mates. There was one called Katie on foundation. A quick fling and then relegated to best mate. It'll be Suzanne next, probably. I don't think I'm fascinating enough to keep them interested, to be honest."

"I think you are," said Snibboh. "I've learnt loads of stuff about Shakespeare today. I don't think he's a boring old twat anymore."

"Thank you," said David. "And I've learnt that policewomen can be kind, funny and very sexy. Snibboh?"

"Yes?"

"Can we do it one more time and *then* be just mates?"

"Okay, but our boat's due back in five minutes, so hurry up!"

David leaned over her and kissed her.

"Five minutes is more than enough for a chap like me."

* * *

The boatman thanked them for their custom and tied up the boat. It was getting late, and David had to get back to give Len a lift home. Snibboh also needed to get back to the station, as she had asked Reg and Donald to interview the Mander Centre's caretaker in the hope that he had seen something on the car park roof on the Friday of Jack's death. David started up the Mini and headed for home. Snibboh rummaged around in her shoulder bag and produced a Pentax camera.

"Before I forget," she said. "Here's Jack's camera, but I can't think what use it'll be to you."

"It's just a hundred to one shot, I admit," replied David, "but I've had an idea. I'll ring you tomorrow about it.

They drove home in virtual silence, each pondering the events of the day. They held hands in between gear changes, and looked poignantly at each other, star struck lovers who both realized that what they were doing was wrong, even though it felt so right. David dropped her off at the police station, kissed her for what was probably the last time, and sped home to pick up his dad, his mind in turmoil.

Len was waiting outside the gates when David arrived, and greeted him with a moan about his awful timekeeping. As the car pulled up outside the small council house ten minutes later, he complained to David that someone had taken his parking space, and then realized that the white van in question belonged to

127

Graves Brothers, whom Ruby had called to mend the ailing gas fire.

"About time as well!" mumbled Len, as they walked up the steps to the back door.

Inside, the living room was in a state. Horace Graves, the elder of the two, was drinking tea and chatting to Ruby, whilst his younger brother, Douglas, was prostrate on the floor with his head in the chimney breast and his plumber's cleavage on show to all who wanted to admire it. There were copper pipes and wrenches all over the carpet, and the stricken gas fire in bits, propped up against the settee.

"Evening folks!" said Horace cheerfully. "Sorry about all this lot, but we won't be long now, will we, Dougie?"

Dougie didn't answer. He seemed preoccupied. After a few moments, he backed out of the fireplace, covered in soot, like a man who'd forgotten to throw a hen down his chimney. He was holding a tiny, white skull.

"Look here," he said. It looks like a rat's been back here, a long time ago, wouldn't you say Horace?"

David asked Dougie if he could see it. He sat on the edge of the settee, holding it gently in his hand.

"Poor little Jennings!" he said at last. A tear formed at the corner of his eye as he studied the delicate little bleached skull, running his finger against its minute teeth. "I knew this little creature, Dougie. This was Jennings, my hamster. He was the loveliest, gentlest, tamest thing. He used to run up and down my back and into my pockets. He was so funny. One day we thought he'd died, but he was only hibernating. I laid him down in a little bed by the gas fire, and when he woke up, he disappeared underneath it. We never saw him again. When I was a child, I used to cry myself to sleep each night worrying about whether he'd be okay for food and water. I made myself believe that he'd found his way out somehow and he was living in some field with a lady hamster. Now I know what happened to him."

Dougie, Horace, Len and Ruby looked on as David's eyes welled up and he suddenly began to weep.

Horace offered to wash the cups up in the kitchen, while Dougie shuffled from foot to foot nervously. David mumbled embarrassed apologies and disappeared upstairs to his bedroom. A few seconds later, his mother popped her head around the door and asked him if he was feeling all right.

"I'm sorry," said David. "I don't know what came over me then. It was like I was eleven years old all over again. I can't explain it. It's as if someone squeezed some kind of emotional trigger in my head, and I felt exactly as I did all those years ago. If you don't mind, I'm going to have a lie down. It's been a funny day. I can't very well face that lot downstairs now, can I? They'll think I'm a big bloody baby!"

Ruby left him to his complex emotions and retreated downstairs to make Dougie and Horace yet another cup of tea. David carefully placed Jennings's skull on his shelf, and vowed to build a respectful display case for it as soon as he was able. Either that or he would give it a decent Christian burial, to make up for the hasty pedal bin treatment favoured by Len all those years ago, when the poor creature went into hibernation. Around half an hour later, David had drifted into a fitful sleep, when he was rudely awakened by his bedroom telephone extension.

He picked up the receiver and said hello. It was Laz.

"Hello chap. Just thought I'd tell you some good news and some bad news."

"Go on. Good news first. I need some."

"I can give you a lift into college tomorrow, that's if you're still lending Len your Mini."

"I am. Thanks. What's the bad news then?"

"You owe me forty quid, old pal, once you've deducted the gorilla bus pass money I owe you. I am officially a fine art degree student."

"What?" shouted David. "You're having me on."

"I'm not. I prefer it in fivers by the way. I'll pick you up at eight thirty, promptish. Bye!"

David had no time to ponder this bombshell, as the phone immediately began to ring again. This time it was Snibboh.

"David, I just wanted to thank you for a great day. I will always think you are lovely, even if we can't, you know, do it anymore, but that's not the only reason I rang. I've spoken to Donald and Reg. They've interviewed the caretaker who looks after the Mander Centre. Guess what? He was up on the top level of the car park on the Friday Jack died. He reckons it was virtually deserted by half-five, but he did see one vehicle up there, parked near the end wall, and he saw a man in a bobble hat taking pictures. He returned around six-fifteen and there was no one there by then, so he locked up and went home. Even better, he recognized the vehicle. He's seen it before."

"Fantastic! What was it?"

There was a slight pause on the other end of the line.

"David, it was Vincent Gough's van."

# CHAPTER 10

## Mystic M

WPC Hobbins strolled once more in the sunshine down to Chapel Ash, with a lot on her pretty mind.

It was a wrench having to go back on the beat after her wonderful day out in Stratford, and it was an even bigger wrench having to consign her new beau to the 'just friends' filing cabinet, when she really wanted to phone him up right away and arrange another fling. This WPC, however, had a strong moral streak, which was, albeit belatedly, shouting loudly at her to do the right thing, if streaks can indeed shout at people.

Her Steve was a dull man, but honest and caring too, in his own way, and the sense of guilt which now engulfed her was overbearing. It was very easy, and not a little tempting to say, 'just one more won't hurt', like a fat lady eyeing up a large box of chocolates, but one more begets one more, which in turn begets a few more, and before you know it you are divorced or obese, depending on which example you've been following. Claude Beardsley had the same problem, but luckily the main obstacle in the way of his happiness had chewed on a dodgy sandwich and died in a rowing boat.

WPC Hobbins fancied David something awful, but she wasn't going to dip Steve's chocolate digestives in arsenic for the promise of the odd trip to Warwickshire and a quick romp in the long grass. She was a romantic, but it was tempered with practicality and a sense of fair play. Unfortunately, the second and third qualities only managed to kick in after the first had allowed her a quick fling, which meant that her filing cabinet was rather too full of discarded brief encounters.

Another cloud on WPC Hobbins's horizon was Vincent Gough's van. How could it possibly have been on a car park roof at nearly six o'clock, when it was being re-sprayed or else driving home to Chapel Ash at the same time? Her final worry was Claude Beardsley. She knew that, as a police officer, she should step in and question the man about the art thefts, but David had begged her to let him sort it out his way, and he had a way of wrapping her around his little finger. Look how he'd stolen the test strips and sweet-talked her into keeping quiet. The boy was a menace who would one day land her in it, just as Donald and Reg had intimated. He only had to look at her with that stupid, dopey face and ask her something, and she was putty in his hands. Now here she was again, running an errand for him. Next door to Vincent Gough's Flower Shop was The Regency Gallery, a small picture framers and art gallery, which was, coincidentally, owned by Dylan's uncle Martin. Dylan often sold his paintings through the gallery to subsidize his meagre student loan, and had recommended David to his uncle as another talented artist worthy of exhibiting. The shop, though small downstairs, had a long narrow gallery upstairs which was ideal for exhibitions and private views, and had often hosted art college events.

David, on hearing that his pet police officer was heading that way, had persuaded her to pop in and have a word with Martin about staging a special event the following week, once she'd spoken to Mr Gough. She walked into the flower shop first, setting off the loud bell to alert the owner. Vincent was in the back fiddling with his wife's clematis, which looked like it had seen better days. He breezed into the shop looking flustered.

"Well, if it isn't the prettiest bobby in town. Good morning! What can we do for you?"

"Hello again," said the WPC. "I'm sorry to pester you, but something rather intriguing has happened. You know you said that your van was at the body shop till almost six? Well, I have an eyewitness who recognized it, and said it was on the roof of the multi-storey at the same time. Any theories?"

Mr Gough seemed completely stumped by this bombshell. He wilted so badly that the constable thought she might have to fetch the watering can to revive him.

"But it can't have been!" he insisted. "You saw it in the photograph."

"And there's only one van, I take it?"

"Yes," replied the florid florist, his brow corrugated by thought. "But I did have another van, before this new one. I sold it with a private ad in the Express and Star."

"Ah!" said Snibboh. "Can you remember who you sold it to, by any chance?"

"I can. I can!" replied the honest gentleman, wiping the perspiration from his pebbled glasses. He was innocent, and knew he was, but that didn't stop him getting damp around the armpits when the police began turning the screw. It had been the same at school. The headmaster addressed the assembly, wanting to know, not unreasonably, who was responsible for putting a cricket ball through the science block window, and inviting them to visit his study for a session with the bamboo stick. Young Gough of 3C may have been as pure as the driven snow, but when confronted thus he felt as guilty as a fox in a hen house, and was often within a toucher of sticking up his hand and admitting to a crime he hadn't committed. This same feeling engulfed him now, at the age of sixty-two. It was, therefore, a blessed relief to have remembered the old van's new owner.

"I remember him because he looked like a cartoon version of a mad professor. You know, bald head, bow tie, eccentric tufts of hair at the sides, like a clown with no make-up on. I asked him what he did, and he told me he worked at the Polytechnic. I naturally enquired as to what kind of work he did, and he said he was something to do with the sciences. A boffin! You'll have to forgive me though, because I can't quite remember if it was Chemistry, Biology or Physics. My money is on Physics."

"Thank you," smiled the WPC "That's most helpful. Tell me, did the van still have its sign writing on the side?"

"Yes, it did, and I was a bit worried about that at the time, not knowing if I was going to receive parking tickets, or find that it was used in a robbery or seen in the red light district, but he assured me that he was going to remove it forthwith, and to be honest, it saved me a job."

WPC Hobbins thanked Mr Gough once more for his cooperation, and left him to his floral displays.

\* \* \*

Migraine sufferers seldom pretend they are having an attack as an excuse for getting out of situations they would rather not be in. They are a superstitious lot, who think that such deceit could lead to God punishing them with the real McCoy, in much the same way that He punished the boy who cried 'Wolf'.

Claude Beardsley was a migraine sufferer who had just cause to feel this way. He was having the mother of all migraines and had taken a day off work. The incidence of such attacks had greatly increased over the past month or so, and most doctors were of the opinion that stress was a factor. In Claude's case, this was certainly right.

David Day was rather relieved to discover that his boss was absent. He had been dreading a chance meeting in the corridor, even though he believed that Claude had no reason to suspect that he was the 'Shed Art' thief. For all David knew, Claude might not have even realized that his ill-gotten gains were missing, but, like Vincent Gough, one stare from that tough-looking Oliver Reed face would be enough to have him owning up to all sorts of things, some of which he probably hadn't done.

Thankfully, also absent that morning was Laurence Fuchs, whom Jim Weston had seen earlier that morning on the way to hospital for a dental operation.

"I hope they pull them all out without any anaesthetic," growled David, as he made Jim a cup of coffee, in the hope of buttering him up for a favour.

"So, Mr Day," grinned the lecturer. "What can I do you for today? Come to put a deposit on my cosy Devonshire cottage have we, or are you after a foreigner perhaps?"

"Both, as a matter of fact, my rotund teddy bear of a man," replied David, ducking to avoid a deft left hook. "I've been on the phone to my girlfriend this morning, and we both agree that we need to spend more time together, so I'll take the cottage for Whitsun, at an incredibly generous knockdown student price."

"Oh, you're taking the official bird, not the rozzer?"

"I'll thank you to keep a civil tongue up my arse. The rozzer and I are not an item, as I believe the fashionable new expression is. We are merely friends."

"She wouldn't let you shag her then?"

"Au contraire, mon ami. Now let us elevate our conversation from the dirt track you frequent to the black tarmac highway that I'm used to, if that's not too mighty a leap for you. I need some invitations done for next week. I'm having a soirée at the Regency Gallery in Chapel Ash. An exhibition, a few peanuts, a glass of cheap and undrinkable Spanish wine; the usual college do."

"I didn't realize you had enough work to show, you lazy bastard."

135

"I am full of surprises. I contain multitudes. Now how much, you Stoke on Trent robdog?"

"Twenty quid."

"Sod off."

"Tenner?"

"I'll invite your wife and tell her about Jodie Stone."

"Fiver?"

"Done. Here you are, the fiver and the details. Can I have 'em tomorrow?"

"Sod off."

"Jodie Stone."

"Okay. Blackmail is an ugly word, Mister Day."

"Not as ugly as you are, you big fat ugly bastard."

"Fair enough. Call round at eleven and pick 'em up."

David slapped him jovially on the back and left the print room, en route for Mrs M's place on the fifth floor, leaving Jim Weston to ruminate on how the teacher-student relationship had changed since he went to school in the late forties.

Mrs M was her usual cheerful self, and sporting a new henna-coloured wig, which David complimented her on as they sat on the huge mound of foam rubber drinking tea. He handed her the Pentax, omitting to mention who it had belonged to, and asked her what she thought of the camera, as he was considering buying it.

"You do ask me some strange things, our David," she said as she examined it. "You should know by now that I haven't the foggiest idea about photography."

"I realize that, M. I just thought you could give it the psychic once-over and tell me if it's a happy, contented camera or one that'll give me out of focus crappy pictures out of spite."

Mrs M, however, wasn't listening any more. She seemed to be in a dream. David clicked his fingers theatrically to wake her, but she remained silent for what seemed like an age to her unnerved young friend, before finally intoning, in a voice that The Weird Woman would have been proud of; "If thou hold'st me dear, revenge my most foul and unnatural murder."

David shook Mrs M by the shoulders, trying to bring her round.

"Murder? Did you say murder?"

"Murder most foul, as in the best it is, but this most foul, strange and unnatural."

"Mrs M, wake up. Why are you quoting from Shakespeare? Are you in an amateur dramatics society? Come on now, stop having me on, this is frightening."

"Jack and Jill went up the hill, to fetch a pail of water. Jack fell down, and broke his crown, but did he jump or was he pushed? Humpty Dumpty sat on a wall. Humpty Dumpty had a great fall. All the King's whores, and all the King's men, couldn't put Humpty together again."

"Mrs M, that's enough now, this is creepy!"

"None of woman born shall harm him. Only when the woods move unto the castle will he be o'erthrown. Damned villain. Cursed, smiling, damned villain!"

"Come on Mrs M, enough's enough, and besides, you're getting your Hamlets mixed up with your Macbeths now, if you don't mind my saying so. I'm quite an expert on Shakespeare you know. Now snap out of it please, you're scaring me!"

David ran over to the sink and filled a beaker with water. He had already stolen pictures from his Head of Department's shed.

He had called his silk screen lecturer a fat ugly bastard. Now he was about to throw half a pint of cold water over his textiles tutor. He gulped, and released the liquid, which hit her square on, sending her huge black-framed spectacles tumbling onto the foam rubber mound. For a few seconds, she didn't react at all, but gradually she rejoined the real world.

"Why am I so wet, David? What's wrong? One minute I'm looking over your camera and the next I'm soaked. It's not one of those squirty ones from a joke shop is it?"

"Er, yes, and you fell for it! Sorry M, I didn't realize it was so powerful."

"Can I see it?"

"No, it's empty now. I'll have to fill it up again first."

"I went dizzy for a second. It must be the force of the water in my face. Do you know, I'm sure I blacked out, just for a split second. It's most peculiar."

"Probably just the shock. I'm ever so sorry. I got it from Kettle's joke shop in Brierley Bank. I shouldn't have played a trick on you. Here, use this tea towel. Look, I have to go, I'll pop back later."

David left the textiles room only slightly less bewildered than Mrs M must have been, and wishing he'd been straight with her. Her deranged ramblings were seemingly random quotes from Shakespeare and nursery rhymes, all jumbled together. They didn't make an awful lot of sense, but from past experience, it paid not to underestimate the lady. His hunch had certainly paid off, for the camera had affected her in the most dramatic way; so dramatic, in fact, that she seemed to have absolutely no memory of what she'd just uttered. He needed to see Snibboh right away to pass on what he'd seen.

To this end, he rang the police station in search of her. The desk sergeant said that she was in Chapel Ash, but promised to let her know that David was going to be in Tweedledum's at one o'clock with Dylan and Laz, if she could make it. They had arranged to have lunch there so that Laz could give them a match report on how college life was going, and maybe pick up a few tips on how to conduct himself and impress his tutors.

Life, as usual, was getting a little too hectic, and David was beginning to suspect that it was he, after all, who was the catalyst for most of the weird incidents that plagued him. As far as he knew, his father, Len, went to work each day, made a few precision tools and came home at teatime. His mother, Ruby, walked up Brierley Bank High Street, did some shopping, came home and cooked the dinner. Neither of them was troubled by Russian spies, abducted by Aliens or transported back in time to the Neolithic period. If they were, they were keeping very quiet about it. If their lives could be so ordered, why couldn't his?

No, he was the catalyst, and that was it. He couldn't do anything about it, so it was best he just learnt to live with it, at the same time hoping that none of the strange things that happened to him on a daily basis would put him in a box six feet under. The problem wasn't just the strange happenings; it was the fact that there were several all happening at once. One at a time was just about manageable, but when sorrows came David's way, they came not in single spies but in battalions, as Bill the Quill himself once put it.

He examined the facts, and made a mental list, because he found that this helped to clear his head.


1. He had assaulted a WPC in a shopping centre and then had a whirlwind affair with her, which had lasted one day. Now they were just friends.

2. Jack fell down and broke his crown. Thankfully Jill didn't come tumbling after, which, at least, was something. However, it was still early days.

139

3. Claude, far from being a mentor and inspirational leader, appeared to be no more than a common thief and adulterer.

4. Laz, a lad he had known for years; who had no artistic talent whatsoever, was now a fine art degree student.

5. Laurence, though not a cat murderer, was fond of painting people's entrails, and as such, almost certainly barking mad. At least, in Wolverhampton he wouldn't stand out.

6. Gertie, mother of Jack, widow of Kingsley and mistress of Claude was, as yet, a closed book.

7. Mrs M was getting spookier by the minute, and speaking in tongues. What, if anything, did it all mean?

8. Vincent Gough had a van that could travel through time and space, like the Tardis.

As if all this wasn't enough for his brain to cope with, there was the small matter of the degree show. Compared to some in his group he was ahead of the game in terms of finished work, but he couldn't be complacent. He wanted a good degree, at least a two-one, or even a first. He tried to buoy himself up by comparing his lot with Gordon Bradford, the third year's no-hoper. For two terms now he'd been doing a drawing of Gary Glitter, which still wasn't finished. When questioned by Claude as to why he had only three tubes of paint and a dog-eared brush, Gordon had huffily replied that he *did* have a new set, but he was saving them for a special occasion. The lad was using oxygen that more deserving causes would have been glad of, and the kindest thing would be to have him put to sleep. There was virtually no difference between that and his current state anyway. Then there was Judy. The stress of the impending end of year show had robbed her of all reason, and rendered her incapable of performing the simplest task.

"Measure twenty centimetres and strike a line."

"Which ones are centimetres? Can you help me, David? What does strike a line mean? Oh shit! Look, I've started crying again now. Can you do it for me? Please! Help me, look, I'm shaking."

No, compared to some, he was on course. There was no need to panic.

He arrived at Tweedledum's earlier than the others and took a seat in the far booth. Dry Toast had just arrived and was looking dapper. Wearing a black suit with a tie, he appeared to have just returned from a job interview. The Dragon was nowhere to be seen, so he ordered the full English breakfast and an extra portion of fried bread.

Helga, once bitten, twice shy, remarked pointedly that if his wife arrived unexpectedly he would still have to pay up this time, and reminded him that the previous bacon sandwich was still chalked up on the slate. Dry Toast waved an imperial hand and assured her that this was not a problem. His wife would definitely not be showing up, as she was dead. He had just returned from her funeral and was getting outside of a huge breakfast by way of cheering himself up in his hour of need. It was, he reasoned, a kind of tribute to her - what she would have wanted. He seemed remarkably cheerful, David thought, for one who had just said goodbye to his wife. When Helga enquired as to the cause of her demise, Dry Toast informed her that she had suffered a heart attack caused by high cholesterol. Still, it was an ill wind that blew no one a bit of good, so he resolved to keep his chin up and struggle on.

Helga's conversation was rudely interrupted at this juncture by a man of about thirty, who suddenly rose from his table, where he had been nursing a cold cup of tea for over an hour, and began wailing in a grief stricken way as he approached the counter.

"What on earth is the matter with you?" she enquired, but in a brusque, rather than sympathetic way.

"I am in love," he volunteered, whereupon the inconsolable sobbing moved up a gear to border on the hysterical.

"In love with whom, for goodness sake?"

"Kate Bush."

Helga was losing her patience now.

"Right," she barked. "Stop that right now, and I mean right now."

"Sorry Helga."

"I should think so. You'll lose me all my customers."

"Au contraire," David mused. For him, that was the attraction of the place.

Dylan and Laz arrived together, just as Helga was showing the man the door. They spotted their friend, ordered a coffee each and sat in the booth.

"Dave, you have to help me!" pleaded Laz, before he'd even sat down. "I'm out of my depth. We've just had this lecture, right, and I only understood every sixty-ninth word. You people speak another language. Welsh is easier. You owe me forty quid, by the way."

David held his brow, as if trying to stop it bursting and spewing ten thousand wriggling thoughts all over the Formica table.

"Laz, I don't know how or why you did this, other than to experience the joys of the college social life. They'll find you out, mate."

"I'll have you know that Kieron said my portfolio was exceptional, and that I was a rare talent. It's just that I don't speak the lingo like the others do. Listen to this. He wants us to read this book by next week. It's about Post Modernism, whatever that is.

*'Following a prescription of Albrecht Welmar, Habermas considers that the remedy for this splintering of culture and its separation from life can only come from 'changing the status of aesthetic experience when it is no longer primarily expressed in judgments of taste', but when it is 'used to explore a living historical situation', that is, when 'it is put in relation with problems of existence'. For this experience then 'becomes part of a language game which is no longer that of aesthetic criticism.'"*

David looked at Dylan, who looked back at him.

"I'd need to study it a bit," he admitted.

"Come on lads," implored Laz. "It's bollocks. It doesn't mean anything."

"If I were you," suggested Dylan, "I would write the following words down, and just use them every now and again. Do you have a pencil? Chiaroscuro. Impasto. Pictorial Shorthand. Juxtaposition. I particularly like that one, Laz. Are you taking note? You seem to be staring out of the window."

Laz was too busy observing something truly artistic that had just entered the café. Snibboh had arrived, looking extremely easy on the eye. She took the remaining seat and said hello. David introduced her to Laz, who, to his credit, stopped just short of actually drooling.

"David," she said. "A new development. I need to speak with you privately, if you two will excuse us."

Laz and Dylan reluctantly shuffled off to the counter to refill their cups.

"I've seen Vincent Gough. It appears that it was his *old* van that the caretaker spotted on the roof. He sold the van to a man he referred to as a boffin type from the Polytechnic, so I called in and visited the Physics department. I saw a very nice secretary there, a very informed lady, and I asked her if she knew a bald-headed mad scientist. She said they all were, near enough, so that was no help. Then I asked her if she was familiar with their vehicles, and I described the old green van. She reckoned that it was owned by - wait for it - a lecturer named Wilfred Fuchs, who had been killed in a hit and run accident in the town centre. He had two children, one Laurence Fuchs and a daughter called Leonora Willowbrook, who was married to an accountant in Sutton Coldfield or Solihull, or somewhere like that. Life as an accountant's wife had bored her stiff, so she had returned to college to discover herself, whatever that means. I think that I need to have a word to our Laurence, don't you?"

"Absolutely. He may not have killed that cat, but I bet he took it for a long walk and tried to lose it. He's a charmer, I tell you. Watch him though. He may want to paint your intestines. I just hope he uses his imagination, and doesn't insist on working from life."

"Have faith, David," said Snibboh coolly. "I can handle myself. Remember?"

"It's etched on my mind, Snibbs. I still have the scars. Now! I have information for you too, my little Piranha fish. I took the camera to show Mrs M, and the results were even more dramatic than I expected. She touched the thing for a while and fell into some form of trance. Then she began to spout all this mumbo jumbo which I recognized as extracts from nursery rhymes and Shakespeare plays. It all came so fast that it completely freaked me out, so I can't remember it all. She mentioned Jack, and went on about 'Murder most foul and unnatural', which is from Hamlet. Then she rambled on about Humpty Dumpty, and all the King's men, but I'm sure she said 'All the King's whores' instead of 'horses', which was a bit weird. Then she started saying stuff that I vaguely recall from Macbeth about 'none born of woman' and the bit where the forest advances on the castle, just before the King is overthrown. You know, the stuff I told you about on the way to Stratford."

"I can't remember," admitted Snibboh. "I was too busy playing with the gear stick. By the way, I went to see your mate's uncle Martin like you told me to, and it's all arranged for next week. I explained who'd foot the bill, and told him about organizing the food and so on. You just need to deliver the stuff by the weekend."

"But soft!" whispered David. "The travellers return. I'll phone you later about that."

Laz and Dylan came bearing gifts, namely a sausage roll and a tea for the officer.

"Dyl and I have been talking," said Laz, rolling a cigarette. "He reckons I should stop fretting about college work and let my hair down a bit. We're going to the third year canal boat trip tonight and we're going to get pissed."

"Bloody hell!" moaned David. "I'd completely forgotten the trip. I don't want to miss that. I need a bit of mindless relaxation myself!"

David's social life was indeed gathering pace. Within the space of a week there was a boat trip, his band's gig at The Crypt, the private view in Chapel Ash and his holiday in Devon. At least the cottage would allow him a restful, trouble-free week before the frantic build up to the degree shows began.

They finished their coffees and made for the exit. Helga took their money, and continued trying to defrost a large cod steak which she intended to have for tea, prompting David to burst into an impromptu soliloquy, for Snibboh's benefit.

"Oh, that this too too solid fish would melt, thaw and resolve unto a dew, or that the everlasting had not fixed his canon against microwaves."

Laz gave him a withering look. "Is it compulsory for all you bloody artists to talk bollocks?"

* * *

Back at the art college, Jim Weston was begrudgingly trimming a large sheet of white card with the names of all the graphic design staff and students silk-screen printed onto it. Above each name was a gap, which was reserved for a small black and white mug-shot, so that the inmates could easily identify each other. Jim hated having to do jobs which were covered by his weekly salary, much preferring to be occupied with 'foreigners', which made him a few quid on the side.

Having dealt with his chore of the day, he now turned his attention to more lucrative projects. He picked up and carefully inspected one of the hundred or so small aluminium plates that were drying out on every available surface in his office, and laughed out loud at his self-penned caption.

I AM A FULLY INSURED,

DOUBLE-GLAZED ATHEIST.

PISS OFF.

All he needed to do now was to drill the two screw holes and shrink-wrap the plates and screws onto the packaging cards.

'Tired of being pestered by door-to-door salesmen? Fit this discreet sign above your doorbell or knocker, and they'll never pester you again!'

Manufactured by Weston Silk Screen of Stoke on Trent.

Jim's inventiveness didn't end there. He had persuaded a couple of students to go around the town's housing estates at what he'd estimated was the time when most people sat down to their evening meal, and knock on their front doors, offering to sell them his door bell plates. If the bottom ever fell out of the silk-screen printing market, Jim could easily have retrained as a psychologist.

Satisfied, he allowed his handiwork to carry on drying in peace and turned his attention to a far less lucrative freelance job, namely, David's private view invitations.

He picked up the flimsy piece of letrasetted artwork and checked it for spelling mistakes.

Wolverhampton Society of Artists

PRIVATE VIEW

The Regency Gallery

Chapel Ash

May 20th. 6.30pm till Benny Hill.

Wine and Buffet.

He took the artwork and began the process of converting it to clear film, so that the image could then be transferred to the silk screen. He was interrupted by Mike Sambrokes, who had emerged, blinking and disorientated from his bat cave and made his way to the third floor to collect Jim's name board. Mike could then glue down the mug-shots he had taken and printed, and laminate the board in clear plastic to protect it from the inevitable graffiti. Jim pointed to the large sheet of card, which was in the drying racks, made his excuses and disappeared into his office, so that he could get on with trying to earn an honest living.

Handling the board carefully, trying his best not to dent the edges, Ken caught the next lift back to the photographic department. He had already trimmed the forty, two-inch photographs of the staff and students and backed them with double-sided tape. All he had to do now was identify each student and place the picture squarely above his or her name, making sure they all lined up neatly. Claude was very particular about this, and had kicked up a fuss the previous year when they were a little higgledy-piggledy. Once the pictures were in position, he would lay a large sheet of self-adhesive plastic over them and laminate the sheet on his press.

An hour and a half later, he had just three students left to do - namely, Dylan Weldon, David Day and Katie Black. He peeled off the backing tape on David's picture, and stuck it in the space immediately above Dylan's name, and then stuck Dylan's picture where David's should have been. Finally, he positioned Katie's picture, and the job was done.

Ken was always getting Dylan and David mixed up, probably because they were friends that were often seen together. They both had long hair and wore Levi's denim jackets, both were talented artists and both came from the same town. It was an easy mistake to make, but one that was to have dire consequences for one of them.

# CHAPTER 11

## A Cosy Chat with Laurence

WPC Hobbins was in the seventh floor tutorial room; the one where Laz had pulled the wool over Kieron Hastings's eyes only a few weeks before. On the other side of the desk sat Laurence Fuchs, with a look of contempt on his face for the uniformed officer of the law opposite; a person he regarded as mentally negligible and an irritating interruption to completing his latest painting. A slimy smile flashed across his face, as he suddenly realized that she had some worth after all. Once he had finished his 'Dead Popes' series, he would immortalize her on canvas.

'Policewoman's Entrails' had a nice ring to it. The crimson red of her bowels would juxtapose quite beautifully with her black uniform. His pulse quickened at the thought.

"Laurence," she began, thankfully unaware of what was going on in his cesspit mind, "I hope you don't mind my asking you a few questions. There's nothing at all to worry about. I just wondered if you could tell us a little bit about your father."

"Of course. He's dead. How's that?"

"I know. I'm sorry. How did he die?"

"Ha!"

"I'm sorry?"

"He died like a hedgehog, with his entrails spilled all over the road."

"Oh dear, I am sorry. That explains a few things."

"Such as?"

"Well, er, your style of painting perhaps?"

"Ah, right. I presume you mean that I don't paint abstracts like the others. I've always painted in a realist, traditional style."

"Is it traditional to paint people with their insides on the outside then?"

"What did you want to know about my father? I need to get back to my canvas before the paint dries."

"How he died."

"He was hit by a drunken driver. A hit and run."

"How did you get on with your father?"

"Bloody hell! That's the kind of question you ask a murderer! Jesus Christ, you stupid woman. I didn't kill him."

"No one said you did, Laurence. I was just asking."

"Yeah, right! Look, he was a tedious, irritating old eccentric scientist. He used to bore the living shit out of my sister and me, lecturing us on the perils of art college life, telling her to beware of Jack Hamphlett, whom he regarded as a 'loose cannon.' He got that bit right at least. Father told her to ignore Jack's promises of undying love, and get herself back to her boring accountant husband where she belonged. He used to lecture me on a daily basis about leaving the college to become a solicitor, or a doctor, or anything that he could understand. He regarded artists as worthless, undisciplined 'wastrels', to use his exact terminology. Father used to bore his students rigid too. He always had his head in the clouds, pondering some unfathomable physics problem. He was probably doing just that as he crossed the ring road that night, instead of looking around at the traffic. Strangely enough, I miss him now. We didn't get on, but I didn't want him to end up flattened by a drunk."

"Why didn't you like Jack?"

"How long have you got? Okay, I'll tell you. He had a family tragedy, fair enough. His dad died, and that was awful – so did mine - and then he finds out that his mother's been shagging Claude, just to add insult to injury. He turned to drink and began treating my sister badly. Standing her up, arguing with her in public and so on."

"Hardly something to hate him for, nor to justify unguarded comments in a print room about being glad he was dead."

"Ah, so that's what all this is about? Has your little friend David been telling tales then?"

WPC Hobbins felt her face redden.

"No, not really, there is something else, which I'll get to shortly. There's more than you're telling me. What caused you to hate Jack so much?"

"Well, if you'd really like to know, I'll tell you. I think he killed my father."

"Do you have proof that he was the driver? That's a serious accusation."

"Not now that he's dead."

"So what makes you think it was him? We appealed for witnesses and none came forward."

"There was one. A colleague of mine."

"And why didn't you or your colleague tell the police?"

"Two reasons. Firstly, he only told me about it after Hamphlett jumped off the car park roof and went splat! Mm! Now that's an idea! Maybe I could commemorate him with an oil painting."

"Charming!"

"Secondly, my colleague was somewhere he shouldn't have been, and I didn't wish to drag him into the resulting quagmire. There was no point. I'd got the result I wanted by then anyway. Justice done! It seemed a waste of time telling you about what a friend of mine thought he saw. What could you do? Arrest a dead man?"

"You could be charged with withholding information; you know that, don't you?"

"So arrest me."

"That's not my decision, Laurence. What precisely did your colleague tell you, by the way? It may still be important."

"He said that he was with a 'lady of the night', when he saw what looked like Jack's car veering all over the road, travelling in the direction of the student halls of residence, like the driver was pissed up. He said my father walked into the ring road looking 'vague', and the driver hit him at breakneck speed. He then got out, saw the damage and drove off."

"And he was sure it was Jack?"

"That's what he said."

"I'm very sorry. It must have been a nightmare for you and your sister."

"It was."

"One last thing, and I'll let you get back to your picture. Did your dad own an old florist's van?"

Laurence stared at her.

"Yes. How did you know that? He sold it some time ago. Why do you want to know?"

"Oh, it's nothing of any consequence. Do you know who he sold it to?"

"A student I think."

"No name?"

"No, sorry."

"Thanks for your help; I'll let you get back."

WPC Hobbins saw him out and sat on the edge of her desk chewing the life out of an HB pencil, deep in thought.

Eventually she took a coin from her pocket and tossed it to see who she'd visit first. The Spray Bay won, so Leonora Willowbrook would have to wait.

* * *

Laz felt like a frightened little boy wearing a hissing rubber ring in the twelve-foot end of the public swimming baths - totally and utterly out of his depth. He had just handed in his project work, which was met with blank looks by Kieron Hastings and his colleague, till now known only by the rather cruel pseudonym of 'The Limp Lisper'.

Michael Wiggins, to give him his real name, was puzzled. How, he wondered, could such a talented and good-looking boy be so clueless? They had quite clearly asked for monochrome sketches, and he had produced work in full colour. They had entitled the project 'Chiaroscuro', yet there was no evidence of extreme light and shade in his composition. Despite that, the work he had handed in was of an exceptional quality. It appeared that not only was he incapable of working within the college walls, but he was also incapable of doing what was asked of him. When questioned as to his motives, the young man's response had been laughable.

Michael called his friend Quentin over to take a look. Quentin was not an art college lecturer. He had taken the day off from The Birmingham Conservatoire, where he taught violin and guitar, and was hoping to take his lover out to lunch at Luciano's, a

153

small, discreet Italian restaurant in Tettenhall. Though not a practising artist anymore, Quentin had once been a foundation student in Birmingham many years ago, and Michael valued his opinion.

"This boy's a paradox, Quentin," said Kieron. "Lovely work, but he seems to be in a world of his own. You ask him to do one thing and he goes home and does another. I reckon he's autistic or something."

Quentin flipped through the drawings silently as the other two continued to discuss Laz's shortcomings and brilliance in equal measure.

"Bloody hell!" he said suddenly, causing them to halt their debate.

"What ith it, love?" asked Michael.

"This work. As soon as I saw it, it was like déjà vu. You see here, down the bottom right hand corner, where he's rather crudely signed it 'Laz'? If you look carefully, you can just about make out another, rubbed out signature beneath."

"Oh yeth!" agreed Michael, intrigued.

"Gentlemen," announced Quentin rather grandly, and making the most of his big moment, "this is the work of Jeremy Westfield, who I was at college with briefly in Birmingham."

Kieron stared at him in blank disbelief.

"Are you sure? It was a long time ago, after all."

Quentin was adamant.

"Anyone else but him maybe, but he was the best student at the college. Do you have a magnifying glass handy? I'll bet you twenty quid I'm right. Look here, on these other pieces, the same rubbed out signature."

Kieron was rummaging around now in his drawers, until, triumphantly, he pulled out a glass and held it to the picture. It was faint, but the remnants of the J and the W were quite legible. An immediate search for their rogue student revealed that, in typical enigmatic style, he had returned home. Tony Hemmings, who sat next to Laz on the rare occasions that he graced the college with his presence, told the red-faced tutors that Laz had gone home to get changed, as he was gate-crashing the Graphics narrow-boat trip that evening. Further probing revealed that he would be at The Crypt the following night, which prompted Kieron to comment on what a busy social life the lad seemed to enjoy for one who was so reticent to put pen to paper in public. It was agreed there and then that the three hard-working lecturers needed a night out, and where better than at The Crypt on a Saturday evening. There was usually a decent band on, the beer was cheap, and most importantly of all, a student they wanted a quiet word with would be going there.

* * *

WPC Hobbins - Snibboh to her friends - needed to rush if she was to get through her workload before she clocked off. She, like Laz, needed to rush home and get changed into her best frock (not that Laz was intending to wear a frock, of course). Ray, one of the partners at The Spray Bay, had been most accommodating, and had promised to examine Jack Hamphlett's car, currently parked at Gertie's house, first thing Monday morning. That just left Leonora, who was taking a little time off college to get over the death of her boyfriend.

Snibboh rapped the brass knocker, fashioned in the shape of a dolphin and situated in the middle of a large purple door. A minute later, the willowy figure of Leonora Willowbrook appeared. She was wearing a dressing gown and holding a large scented candle that she'd purchased from the Dragonfly Boutique, a shop that regarded her as the difference between profit and loss.

The young policewoman asked if she could come in for a few minutes.

Leonora made them both a cup of something she referred to as fruit tea, but which tasted to Snibboh like drinking a stale air freshener.

"Firstly, I'm sorry about your father and Jack." she said, easing her way in. "It must have been unbearable, two bereavements in quick succession like that."

Leonora said that it was, and that she had been unable to concentrate on her work, which had led to her doctor prescribing anti-depressants. These helped, she added, but made her feel dozy all the time. Snibboh wondered to herself how a young woman who collected statuettes of fairies sitting on toadstools could get much dozier without becoming comatose. She glanced up at the ceiling of the flat, which was painted deep blue, and twinkled with a thousand painted stars.

"Nice ceiling," she observed.

"Yes, I always think that the stars are God's daisy chain."

"Do you?"

"Yes!"

"Anyway, I just wanted to ask you a few quick questions. Were you with Jack, the night that your father was killed?

"Yes," replied Leonora. We'd gone to the Castle for a drink, but he was in a strange mood. He wasn't a bad person, contrary to what my brother keeps telling everyone. Laurence didn't know Jack like I did. He was thoughtful and kind, but he was troubled too, and his mood darkened when his dad died. It changed him. He began to drink and argue about silly things. But you know, I forgave him because it wasn't really me he wanted to hurt. He was in turmoil, and angry about his beloved dad, that's all.

That evening he'd had too much, and he stormed out of the bar after calling me 'an empty headed vacuous hippy'. Can you believe that?"

"Yes. No, I mean I can believe it now that you've told me about his state of mind. Carry on."

"I started to cry and went home at around ten, so I don't know what happened to him after that. I didn't see him the next day either, but he turned up that evening with a bandage on his head and a black eye. When I asked him what had happened, he just said that he didn't want to talk about it."

"Oh really?"

"Yes. Can I ask you why you're asking about this? Did he do something wrong?"

"I'm not sure. Do you ever discuss this with your brother?"

"No, we're not close. He can't stand coming here because of Cleopatra and Nefertiti."

"Why, are they here?"

"My cats. He doesn't like cats."

"I gathered that. So he's never shared his theories about Jack with you then?"

"Only that he didn't like him one bit. Why?"

"Oh nothing. Did anyone see where Jack went when he stormed out of the Castle?"

"You could ask his friend Glenn behind the bar. He dashed after him but came back a few seconds later. Other than that, I wouldn't think so. Look, I'm very sorry, but I have to get ready now. I'm going to a boat trip tonight. Is that all?"

Snibboh smiled.

"Yes thanks. I may see you later."

Time was really tight now, but she had one more place she needed to visit. Five minutes later, the breathless WPC staggered into the bar, walked up to the counter and asked the barman if he knew Glenn.

"I know him better than anyone," he replied, "and he's a really nice chap too. Who wants him?"

"I do."

"Pleased to meet you. I'm Glenn, what'll it be?"

Snibboh was tempted but she was still just about on duty. She decided to go for the pork scratchings.

"Glenn," she spluttered, spraying crispy pig skin all over his freshly wiped counter, "can you remember what happened to Jack Hamphlett on the night he had a row with Leonora in the bar?"

"Which night? It was a regular occurrence after his dad died."

"Oh right! How about the night *her* dad died?"

"I remember it well! He stormed out in a huff, and I followed him into the street to reason with him, as usual, but I thought either he'd become a dab hand at the one-minute mile or he'd caught a bus, because he'd disappeared. I carried on serving till closing time and put my coat on to go home. I decided to use the loo one more time before I walked back to my flat, so I went upstairs; the art students call it 'La Trek to Loos' because it's such a way. You have to go up a flight of steep stairs and turn right for the gents. Right opposite is another door, which is usually locked, because it goes nowhere. It's an old loading door for barrels and so on. It used to be a home brewery up there in Victorian times, and there was a kind of winch above the door for lowering stuff down. Now it's a sheer drop into the old back yard. There's a corrugated plastic roof affair underneath, which the gaffer had put in to stop him from getting soaked in the winter."

"Is this going anywhere, Glenn?" asked Snibboh, nervously studying her watch.

"Oh yeah, sorry. Well, I'm up having a pee, when I hear this quiet moan, and I noticed the door was open on the other side. I looked through it and there was Jack in a heap, two flights down. He'd gone straight through the corrugated roof and he was lying on the yard, with a nasty bump on the head and scratched to bits. He'd obviously decided to go for a pee too, before calling it a night. Everybody but me had gone home, so I shot downstairs and picked him up. He seemed a bit delirious. I didn't know if it was just the drink or the bang on the head, so to be sure I took him to the hospital to be checked over. They decided to keep him in because they said it might be concussion, and they didn't want him dozing off in his flat and dying on them. He was let out the following day, and I arranged to fetch him; he was dead embarrassed, and asked me not to tell anyone, especially Leonora. He said that storming off dramatically didn't work quite as well when you fell through a mid-air doorway and cracked your head open. It's like making a theatrical exit and walking into the broom closet. You have to re-enter the room where they're all laughing at you and have another go! Anyway, here's the spooky thing. As we drove home from the hospital, he was reliving his nasty experience, and he said that he was terrified of heights, and falling that distance had scared him to death. He said that he couldn't think of a worse way to die, and had it not been for the gaffer's corrugated roof breaking his fall it would have been curtains. Strange eh, considering that not long after, he decided to end his life the same way."

Snibboh grabbed Glenn's hand as he swished his dishcloth about on the hammered brass surface of the bar, removing bits of scratching here and there.

"Thanks Glenn. I'm late, but you made my trip well worth the effort."

The barman watched as she skipped out of the pub.

"The woman fancies me. It's so obvious," he mused. "After all, she's only human!"

159

# CHAPTER 12

## Three Men in a Boat (and a girl called Snibboh)

Two seventy-foot narrow boats were moored side by side at the Stewponey Wharf, near Kinver, South Staffordshire. They were decorated in the traditional colours of bright red, yellow and green, with tubs of colourful flowers along their roofs.

An idyllic setting welcomed the students as they tumbled out of the coach that the college had laid on for their annual canal-side treat. The early evening golden sunlight twinkled on the water, ducks guffawed at each other's jokes, and an electric blue kingfisher darted from tree to tree in search of minnows. Contented anglers ate their sandwiches with maggot-stained hands and shoved their empty Sunblest wrappers into the hedgerows, hoping that no one would notice. Cyclists tootled by, waving to the passing boat owners and occasionally crunching over the angler's giant roach-poles, which lay arrogantly blocking the towpath.

Not that the students noticed any of this. Their chief concern was getting to one of the two floating bars before the others and drinking as much lager as they could stomach before eleven o'clock. Sadly, both education and the wonders of the English countryside are wasted on the young.

David had arrived on foot, as his parents lived nearby. He greeted Dylan and his fellow merrymakers and climbed aboard in search of refreshment. The plan, such as it was, was to meander

160

gently down the canal, once all the students had arrived, and anchor at the Vine public house in Kinver, which held large stocks of alcohol, just in case the booze on board ran out. After a couple of hours, they would chug back again at the regulation five miles per hour, stagger onto the waiting coach, and irritate the surly bucket of congealed lard who was driving the vehicle by singing obscene rugby songs. Then they would crawl home to their dismal bed-sits to witness their bedrooms spinning round, before crouching over their toilet pans and praying for an early death to put them out of their misery.

The party was mainly made up of graphic design students, with or without their partners, but a few dedicated revellers from other Polytechnic departments had snapped up the unwanted tickets and joined in. David was surprised to see Laz making his way from the car park, accompanied by a striking young girl in a pretty floral dress, with hair like a shampoo advertisement. As they drew nearer, he was able to identify this vision of beauty as none other than his crime-fighting colleague, Snibboh. He mused wryly to himself that the girl seemed to possess a mind similar in construction to that of a goldfish, with a three second moral memory. Had they not both made a pact to be faithful to their official partners in a field just outside Stratford, only days before? Now here she was on the arm of his best mate, a fellow who made Casanova look like Mahatma Ghandi. It must surely be just a matter of a few hours before she embarked on the passionate but brief fling, followed immediately by the overwhelming guilt, and the inevitable relegation of poor Laz to the pedal bin labelled 'Just Good Friends'. At least there'd be lots of people he knew in there to talk to.

What made it worse was that Suzanne couldn't attend, as she'd promised to baby-sit for her sister. Now David had to endure an evening of watching his mate snogging a gorgeous policewoman whom he could easily have been snogging himself. It wasn't a promising start. Luckily, his other friend, Dylan, hadn't brought his girlfriend Kathleen with him either, so at least he had someone to talk to.

Noticeable by his absence was Claude Beardsley, who had purchased a ticket but cried off at the last minute, blaming yet another migraine. David was also pleased to see that Laurence Fuchs had given it a miss, presumably so that he could spend the night in some morgue or other, painting a still-life. His sister Leonora, however, was amongst those present, floating about on the towpath, singing a Celtic lullaby and gathering wild flowers which she intended to weave into a garland for her hair.

David stood transfixed as he watched the Pre-Raphaelite nymph bend to pick a daisy. He shuddered as he imagined her approaching an unfortunate lover from behind at the breakfast table, clasping her hands over his face and whispering, "Guess who?" He was just on the verge of thinking the unthinkable about Jack being spared a fate even worse than death, when his attention was drawn to a whooshing noise and a blur of day-glo colour to his immediate right.

A determined cyclist dressed in fluorescent Lycra skin-tight shorts catapulted by, narrowly missing him and causing angry art students to dart this way and that to avoid being flattened. Just as he came level with Leonora, a Mallard duck emerged from the canal and decided to dice with death by crossing the towpath in search of its mate, who was having a nap in the hedgerow. The cyclist, who had clearly not been expecting Mallards to get under his wheels, and had not formulated any contingency plans for avoidance of same, careered towards the canal in a last ditch attempt to miss the creature and was met by the shapely, velvet-clad backside of a young woman. He desperately swung the handlebars to the right to get himself back on track, his legs now off the pedals and flailing around like the sails on a windmill.

There was an awful predictability about what happened next.

Blissfully unaware, Leonora plucked her daisy, just as a size eleven cycling shoe caught her square on her elegant bottom,

162

doing an estimated twenty-three miles per hour. Time seemed to stand still for a few seconds, before an almighty splash sent ducks scurrying for cover. The cyclist, knowing full well what he'd done, and equally aware that he was no match for sixty angry art students who would no doubt be baying for his blood, held his balance by the skin of his teeth, miraculously righted himself and literally could not be seen for dust.

Leonora had unwittingly performed a rather stunning triple somersault with toe-loop which would have impressed any passing Swedish judges, and now lay flat out in the water, buoyed up by the air in her billowing clothes, with wild flowers strewn all around her. The unkind observer would no doubt have commented that she was now well and truly wet, in both senses of the word. At first, in a state of shock, she continued to sing her plaintive melody as the water slowly engulfed her and dragged her under. Then she snapped out of it and began to scream.

"Help me! Help me! I can't swim."

David would have loved to spring to her aid, but he couldn't swim either.

Suddenly, a girl in a floral dress ran past him and leapt into the water. She grabbed Leonora with ruthless efficiency and dragged her to the canal bank, where David and several others were waiting to haul her out. Once she was safely ashore, Snibboh emerged in her clinging, bra-less summer dress, looking like a Bond girl striding out of the ocean. Both women stood breathless and shivering on the towpath.

The canal boat owner, obviously well prepared for such occupational hazards, quickly joined them with large warm towels, old pairs of jeans and sweaters, and the two were promptly taken on board to dry off in front of the log-burning stove. This unavoidable delay in the proceedings allowed Dylan the time to stroll along the tow path, Guinness in hand, communing with nature and enjoying the sunshine, while David and Laz fussed around Snibboh, ostensibly to make sure she was

163

okay but secretly hoping to catch a glimpse of her naked, or at least see her pert breasts and alert nipples through her thin wet dress.

Dylan was as gregarious as the next man when it suited him, but also liked his own company, and was quite content to explore while the two girls were dried off and given new clothes. He'd seen a very old, traditional narrow boat further up the canal, which he wanted to inspect. As he walked towards the vessel, he became aware of a very pretty young lady standing amongst a clump of bushes, around twenty yards ahead of him. At first, he thought that she was waving to someone behind him, which caused him to glance around to see who it was, but there was no-one in sight. It was indeed himself she appeared to be waving at, but her face was not familiar. He carried on walking towards her, hoping that he would recognize her when he was closer. He was, after all, very short-sighted, and could not recognize his own mother if she was more than ten feet away.

Then, a remarkable thing happened. The young lady lifted her dress, to reveal that she had left her under garments at home for the evening, and presumably wanted to get a bit of fresh air to her most intimate parts. Dylan, being the perfect gentleman, faltered at this point, not sure whether he should continue to walk in her direction or turn away. He needn't have worried; the lady beckoned again, and began to rub herself down below, in the most provocative way.

Neither one to look a gift horse in the mouth, nor one who was particularly backwards at coming forwards, he quickened his step, eager to see exactly who this was, and why she was prostrating herself in this way. Poor Dylan had obviously neglected his study of classical literature, which warns quite plainly about the perils of sirens on rocks and suchlike. He was within feet of the lady now, and she was, as he had suspected, a total stranger to him, but nevertheless a cracker in the looks department. She had changed her tack now, and had given up the previous routine in favour of rubbing her fulsome breasts.

"Er, do we know each other?" asked Dylan somewhat awkwardly. It wasn't the best line he'd ever used, but the circumstances, in fairness, were a little unusual.

Suddenly, he experienced a feeling that roughly equated to the Dudley to Wolverhampton 58 bus hitting him in the small of the back. Some unseen but powerful force had rammed him from behind, sending him sailing into the canal with a magnificent 'Bladoosh!' which appeared to displace most of the surrounding water. As he flailed around, trying to get his bearings and locate his Guinness, he became vaguely aware of two ladies climbing a stile before legging it across a field at a rate of knots. After that he lost interest in their careers and decided that there were more pressing things to concern himself about.

Dylan's accident had not escaped the notice of the long-suffering boatman, who had already resigned himself to the prospect of a long, hard night. He sent David and Laz, whom he suspected of ogling the two wet women, along the towpath bearing towels. This time at least, the victim was a good swimmer, but his escape from the murky waters was not without incident. Dylan's cowboy boots, which had filled up with canal water, were having a similar effect to that of the concrete blocks affixed to the feet of gangster's victims. It had taken every ounce of his energy to drag himself from the muddy and malodorous waters. He lay flat out on the grass, a spent force, vowing to lay off the booze, as it was giving him hallucinations.

Fifteen minutes later, the canal boats finally got underway, with no really serious consequences for the three victims, other than sartorial. David grasped the opportunity to try to embarrass Snibboh and her date for the evening by endeavouring to look lovelorn, hurt and miserable. He and the WPC reserved an old beer barrel-style table whilst Laz and Dylan drew the short straws and had to go to the bar for the first round of drinks. Snibboh seized the opportunity to snatch a private word with her hurt ex-lover.

"Sorry about this, Dave. I know it's embarrassing, but what could I do? He asked me out."

"You could have said no. Weren't you supposed to be feeling guilty about your husband?"

"Well, I was, but not as guilty as you seemed to be about your girlfriend. I could have coped, but I sensed you were in a moral dilemma."

"Well, I was, but if I'd known you weren't so concerned it might have made me less concerned, if you know what I mean. Anyway, we're still mates and superhero crime fighters. Any news?"

"Yes, quite a bit. I managed two Fuchs in one afternoon!"

"Wish I had the energy. It's pronounced Fooks, by the way. How was old Laurence?"

"Horrible, but maybe he has a lot to be horrible about, what with his dad being killed."

"There's an epidemic going round. I hope mine's okay."

"He suspects Jack of being his dad's hit and run driver. That's why he was so off-hand with you in the print room."

"What?"

"Yep! He reckons that a colleague of his saw it happen, but didn't report it to us because it would have compromised him, as he was with a prostitute at the time. This witness clearly saw Jack's vehicle hit Mr Fuchs. He says he saw Jack drive off, once he'd seen what he'd done. No wonder Laurence is bitter and twisted. Then I went to see that drip over there. Jesus!"

"So now what?"

"I'm going to see Jack's car tomorrow to check for damage. I'll keep you posted. Also, I've got your friends Donald and Reg out trying to locate Vincent Gough's old van, so Lord help us! Do look a mess?"

"No, I *like* chunky knit orange pullovers. Are your boobs flopping around in there unhampered by a brassiere?"

"Yes."

"Can we be platonic starting from next week, perhaps?"

"Behave."

Laz and Dylan arrived with the drinks and squeezed round the barrel.

"God almighty, there's a lot of wet folks here tonight," quipped David. He sniggered at Dylan. He was wearing a lime green chunky knit sweater and his glasses were steaming up.

"Very funny," sneered his friend. "I still can't understand what happened. One minute she's trying to seduce me, the next I'm in the canal. Women! I'll never understand 'em. What did I do to deserve that?"

"Well, joking aside," said David, "If anyone's thinking of playing the fool later, can I remind you that I can't swim. If that had been me, it would have been curtains."

He shuddered at the very thought, and chewed on a contemplative peanut. After a few silent moments he decided to steer the conversation in other directions.

"How's college, Laz?" he enquired.

Now it was Laz's turn to shudder.

"I don't want to talk about it, alright?"

He had obviously taken drummer Nick's correspondence course on how to avoid awkward situations, and the topic of conversation became up for grabs one more time. This time it was Dylan who spoke.

167

"Did you sort anything out with Uncle Martin?"

David smiled his best enigmatic smile. "Yes, thanks. It's all arranged for next week."

* * *

Meanwhile, in a telephone kiosk in a country lane near Kinver, two languages students from Germany were relaying the night's events to their employer.

Rosie Kranz and Gilda Stern were from a small town not far from Frankfurt called Idar Oberstein, which is famous for jewellery - or Schmuck as the Germans would have it. Rosie was a tall, pretty girl with typically German blonde hair and a sprinkling of freckles across her nose, which drove the German boys wild. Unfortunately for them, boys didn't do it for Rosie; at least, real boys didn't. The love of her life was a short, stocky, cropped-haired boyish woman called Gilda who favoured sweatshirts, jeans and Dr. Marten's boots. Gilda was built roughly along the lines of an ox, but slightly uglier. It was she who had provided the muscle to propel Dylan into the drink.

When the two had first arrived in Wolverhampton, money was tight, and they needed a regular income to afford the little flat that they co-habited. Rosie had worked at The Castle as a barmaid for a period, but had been sacked for fiddling the tills. Gilda had worked briefly on a building site, but was let go after she fought with a plumber and broke his nose. It was a Godsend then, when an etching lecturer called Dom Bentley approached them one night in The Crypt and propositioned them about a little film-making venture he was about to embark on. He paid them good money to do what they did for free each night in the privacy of their flat. The only snag was, they had to do it in front of him and a movie camera.

Dom was a raffish, good-looking man of about forty, who had a way with the girls. Most weeks he got away with at least three, some just providing good company, while others gave him considerably more. Occasionally, one would come along that showed promise, and she would be offered a part in one of his films. Rosie and Gilda were his first ever same-sex couple, which gave him a chance to exploit new areas and appeal to a different type of consumer, thereby maximizing profits.

Copies of their film, 'Beating about the Bush' were soon circulating around the Polytechnic, in spite of the fact that Dom had promised them faithfully that they were for export to the USA only. It was, therefore, only a matter of time before one Claude Beardsley got to see it. By sheer coincidence, his house was two doors away from theirs, and he instantly recognized the actresses, in spite of the fact that their heads were often buried in acres of someone else's flesh.

A quick check with his opposite number in the languages department had revealed that these two came from very influential families back in Germany. Rosie's father was a local member of parliament, while Gilda's parents were big in the church. If the news of their daughters being seen in a pornographic movie ever got back to them, it would cause a massive scandal. Both sets of parents were blissfully unaware that their daughters were even co-habiting, let alone starring in titillating movies.

Claude, using a false identity of course, was kind enough to ring them one afternoon, just to put their minds at rest that their sordid secret was safe with him, providing, of course, they helped him out when help was needed. Just when the girls must have thought that things had blown over and they wouldn't hear from Claude again, the call came that they were dreading. He was reeling in his favour. All they had to do was shove a man into the canal, and they'd be let off the hook. He omitted to mention that the man could not swim, just in case they became reluctant. It was a simple task. They were to pick out their victim from a large chart on the third floor which had black and white photographs of all the students laminated onto it. Having identified him, they should then drive down to the canal wharf and use their feminine charms to lure him well away from the crowd.

* * *

Rosie replaced the receiver and smiled to her friend.

"Well, zat was so easy! I couldn't believe it when he began to walk away from his friends in our direction! Now, maybe, zis man vill leave us alone, ja?"

Gilda smiled back at her, but something told her that life was never that simple.

## CHAPTER 13

### Shocking News for Duncan

WPC Hobbins showed Spray Bay Ray around Jack's car, which was parked at Gertie Hamphlett's house. Gertie was making them both a cup of coffee and wondering to herself why on earth the policewoman needed to see her son's car.

It only took Ray a few seconds to reach his conclusion. "This car hasn't had any work carried out on it at all. I can guarantee it, Miss."

"I didn't for one minute think it had," confessed the officer. She turned to Gertie, who had just arrived with the coffees and a packet of digestives, because Snibboh had complained of a rumbling stomach.

"Mrs Hamphlett, did Jack ever use another vehicle, like yours, for instance?"

She pointed to the other car on the drive.

"Oh, that's not mine," she replied. "I can't drive. That belongs to Claude."

She went back into the house to answer the phone. Snibboh walked up to the car and looked it over.

"So you're telling me, Ray, with your expert eye, you could spot if a car had had bodywork done?"

Ray examined the front section of Claude's car. "Yes, as a matter of fact, I think I could. Take this one, for example. This has had a dent or two knocked out of the bonnet, for a start, but it's so well done, you need to be experienced to spot it. I'd say it was done by a top firm, that's for sure."

"How do you know that it's such a good job? Explain it to me," she said. "How can you be sure Jack's hasn't had a facelift but this one has?"

"I know, my dear, because we did it!" laughed Ray. "I remember having it in."

WPC Hobbins walked into the house to return the coffee cups, and found Gertie sitting on her settee, head in hand. A closer inspection revealed that she had been crying. She quickly dried her eyes and smiled at the officer.

"Sorry, dear. It's all been a bit much this last month."

The policewoman sat beside her and stroked her hand.

"I know," she said quietly. What she omitted to mention was the possibility of more to come. She said that she'd let herself out, and thanked Gertie for her help.

\* \* \*

It was Saturday, but Jim Weston was hard at work. He often came in at weekends so that he could avail himself of the college's facilities and catch up a little, without the students getting under his feet. Saturday morning was handy for doing a few commercial jobs, without having to fork out for expensive materials.

However, on this particular morning he had spotted Claude's car in the car park, meaning that he was on the prowl somewhere in the building. To make matters worse, there was a student in the print room who'd popped by to finish off a degree show print, and all these unwanted intrusions were cramping his style. The fifty 'House for Sale' signs he'd promised for Jolliffe and Co, the estate agents would have to wait until Claude had buggered off home and the lad was sorted out.

"Morning Edwin!" he called, trying his best to sound cheerful. "If you need me I'm in my office. How's that girlfriend of yours, by the way? Shagged her yet?"

Edwin Binks was not, by any stretch of the imagination, the playboy type. He was a shy, spotty-faced little Herbert who had just landed himself his first girlfriend, and was not a fast mover. This crass language, especially from a lecturer, offended his sensibilities. He had made the mistake of opening up to Jim the previous week, during a long spell at the printing press on a slow day, about his new love and his lack of courage to move things on from the holding hands and pecking stage, to what Jim referred to as 'The Full Monty'. Every time he felt the urge to delve a little deeper, his nerve went; he was beginning to sense that his girl was feeling a little frustrated by his lack of progress.

"It's not as easy as that, Jim," he complained. "I've got nowhere to take her. My mom and dad never go out, so we can't go to our house."

"Let me give you some advice," winked Jim, ex-Teddy boy and man of the world.

"Wait till *her* folks go out on a Saturday night. Pop round with a bunch of flowers and a bottle of Liebfraumilch. Sit on the settee with the lights off, with just the glow of the artificial coals on the gas fire to give the place a romantic atmosphere. Then do a bit of snogging, like you usually do, and slide your hand onto her boobs and give them a bit of a rub. If she starts panting and moaning, you're in, pal. Repeat the exercise down below. Remember the etiquette of sex. Tits first, and if there's no complaints, fanny next. If she pushes you away, try again. If she still pushes you away, give up, turn the lights back on and sulk. She won't though, I guarantee it. I reckon she's dying for it, and disappointed with you for being too half-soaked to have a go."

"I suppose you're right."

"I *am* right. You mark my words. I know women. Try it tonight. If she pushes you off, I'll give you a tenner. How's that?"

"Okay, I'll try it tonight. What if she doesn't?"

"You owe me a fiver. Deal?"

"Okay. Thanks for the advice, Jim."

"Pleasure! Now piss off so I can get on with my jobs."

Edwin pissed off. They say, however, that there is no peace for the wicked, and this was borne out by the arrival of Claude Beardsley.

"Ah, Jim, nice to see someone at work on a weekend, even if it seldom benefits the college. I need a few sheets of white cartridge paper, and then I'm off. How's the holiday cottage business going? Still renting those two damp, dingy shit-holes in Devon?"

"Yes thanks. Can I interest you in one for the summer?"

Claude laughed out loud. "You *are* joking. After the last time? I'm surprised you get anyone to rent them. Besides, I've just bought myself a place down there, to add to my considerable property portfolio. It's called The Old Rectory. Do you know it?"

Jim was miffed. He was familiar with the house, a superior detached place in a prime spot, with a view of the river from the rear garden.

"Very nice, but then, I'm not in your tax bracket, am I? Anyway, I'll have you know, both cottages are taken for Whitsun. David Day's had one and the other's almost certainly booked. They've promised to get back to me today, so bollocks!"

Claude's ears pricked up. "David Day you say. Have you, erm, seen him today, by any chance?"

"Not yet, but he phoned me an hour ago. He's popping in with the money."

Claude's face clouded over. It looked as if a thunderstorm was imminent.

"I see. Could you let me have the address, do you think? I'll need to send letters out to all the students about the degree shows during the Whitsun holidays, so I may as well send his to your holiday place."

"Sure." said Jim. "It's Honeysuckle Cottage, Old Harbour Road, Dittisham, Devon. As he was first to book, I gave him first choice."

"What choice was that then?" asked Claude sarcastically. "Damp or Depressing?"

"Don't you go mentioning that to him," warned Jim. "You can have a word with him though, if you need to mention the degree show letter. He'll be here in ten minutes, or if not, his band's playing at The Crypt tonight, if you're going. He's enlisted the usual college rent-a-crowd."

"I think not," replied Claude icily, and with that, he was gone.

Just as Jim turned his attention once more to his foreigners, David arrived, bearing cash. He picked up the keys for Honeysuckle Cottage and made his excuses, explaining that the band were shortly going to be over at The Crypt setting up the equipment and sound checking, and he needed to fly.

"Aren't you forgetting something?" called Jim, as David headed for the door. He waved a wad of Private View invitations.

"Oh excellent!" said David. "Here's your money, and keep an invite. Try and come. It's going to be a night with a difference!"

* * *

At The Crypt, Mo was manhandling huge speaker cabinets from the back of his van and lugging them into the venue, while the rest of the band busied themselves by watching him struggle. Mo's girlfriend, Desdemona Wilcox, sat in the front of the van, applying her bright red lip gloss with the aid of the rear view mirror.

There was a lot of equipment, but slowly, the stage was taking shape. In the middle, Nick began to assemble his double drum kit, whilst to his left, Laz was setting up three keyboards and three guitars, one electric and two acoustics, a six and twelve string. Ken was looking at the stage and drinking his selfish, sugar and milk-free tea, in the firm belief that the equipment would somehow assemble itself. David unpacked his Gibson Les Paul, placed it on the stand, and then wandered around, viewing it from several angles so that he could judge which one was the most flattering to the glossy maple wood finish.

"I don't need any help, lads," called Mo, his T shirt soaked with the sweat of honest toil. "I'll carry all these by myself!"

"Thanks!" replied Duncan, who was popping out to get a bag of crisps and a bottle of cider.

"Who's got the opening tape?" asked David, panicking as usual.

"Me," replied Mo calmly as he set up the mixing desk at the back of the hall.

"Who's got the stage clothes?" asked Laz.

"Me," replied Mo calmly as he unpacked the microphones.

"Where's our other roadie gone?" asked Nick. "I thought you'd recruited some bloke to help you, Mo."

"He's got the flu," replied Mo. "Dave's arranged for a mate of his to help out, just for tonight, haven't you Dave?"

"Yeah! Dylan's coming later. He said he'd stick around and load up the van, which is good."

Dylan walked into the hall, bang on cue.

"The man himself!" smiled David. "Come over and I'll introduce you to everyone."

Dylan strode over and shook David by the hand. "Good afternoon Dylan!" he said.

David could make nothing of this. His old friend must have been in the sun too long, or perhaps the canal water had addled his brain. Either that or the Guinness.

"What, if anything, are you talking about?" asked David, perplexed.

"You are Dylan Weldon. I am David Day. It's official."

"Now you take me into deep and uncharted waters. Are you sure you're not on a bender? I told you that Guinness was habit forming."

"Nonsense. I've had one every day for ten years, and never found it habit forming. No, I refer to the official notice board on the third floor, showing pictures of all the students with their names printed below. Haven't you seen it yet? They've got our two names mixed up."

David reeled. "Surely I've come off worse there. Obviously, you would be proud to be mistaken for me, a handsome rock star, whereas I would rather not be mistaken for you, a bespectacled alcoholic canal dweller."

"Ha ha! Amusing! I've had a word with Mike Sambrokes. He's promised to put it right when he has a second, which, knowing him, will be in around two years. I can't stand the thought of being you for that long."

"Ditto, ratbag. Anyway, Mo, this is Dyl, who's promised to help you today in return for Guinness vouchers. Let him know what you need doing, and I'll start tuning the guitars."

By five o'clock, everything was set up and working, and the band had run through a few songs so that Mo could mix the sound from the back of the hall. There were three hours to kill before the club opened, so everyone dispersed to grab some food and relax a little before the real nerves set in. David was especially prone to

177

pre-gig nerves, and typically used the lavatory at least sixteen times before walking onto the stage, somehow producing results each time. He also became very quiet, which tended to worry Laz, who eased the pressure by smoking what seemed like twenty roll-ups a minute. Nick, who talked too much at the best of times, talked even more - most of it complete gibberish - whilst Ken, given the choice, would head for the bar and end up comatose. Last, and in David's eyes least, Duncan tended to become even more pompous and insufferable, and would often talk to himself, like a mad man. At the back of the hall, Mo, usually unflappable, was having a row with Desdemona, whom he suspected of infidelity with a friend of his from the gym.

Everyone had agreed to split up and meet back at The Crypt at eight. They were scheduled to play at nine-thirty, so this gave them plenty of time to unwind. David and Dylan headed for Tweedledum's for an omelette and a pot of tea, whilst Laz took a delegation to the Castle pub, a move that was permitted by the ever-nervous David on the understanding that no one, least of all Ken, was allowed more than two pints. Mo, who had brought sandwiches, agreed to guard the equipment until their return.

Refreshed by their unexpected but nevertheless enjoyable vegetable pasties, David and Dylan arrived at exactly eight o'clock, just as the doors were being opened by Billy the Convict, the club's bouncer and odd-job man. Billy was not the dinner-suited, bow-tied type of doorman; his attire of choice being the sweat-stained vest and jeans, which revealed a body so well-muscled that short-sighted folk had often confused him with an animated Leather Chesterfield settee. His shaved head and large earring gave him the look of an eighteenth century pirate - the sort that would slit a man's throat for a piece-of-eight or a doubloon, or sometimes just because he fancied it. For all his menace, The Crypt had a reputation for being a safe place to go to, due in no small part to the fact that, if Billy hit a troublemaker, the troublemaker stayed hit for a long time, and ceased to make trouble for the assembled multitude from thereon in.

Recognizing David and Dylan from the afternoon's sound check, Billy let them in with a smile. Even with the man's cheery approval, they stepped gingerly past him, as if they expected him to turn ugly at any minute. This trepidation was unwarranted, however. Billy, beneath the fearsome image, was a teddy bear; if people were nice to him, he was nice to them. He grabbed David's shoulder as he slipped past, causing the poor lad's heart to cease beating for around eight seconds.

"What kind of music do you play, lads?" he asked.

"Oh, a bit complex and orchestral. Genesis, Yes, Van der Graaf, you know the kind of thing."

"Poncy shit!"

"Er, yes, that about sums it up."

"Catch yer later, lads. The punters are arriving."

The first little gaggle of students were making their way up the front steps, and a steady trickle were vacating The Castle and the halls of residence, in search of cheap beer and live entertainment. Kieron Hastings and a few colleagues from the Fine Art department were next to arrive, followed by a rather pretty freckle-faced German girl who was holding hands with what looked like a Russian shot-put specialist.

Inside, the house lights had been turned off and the disco had begun. As more and more students filed in and headed for the bar area, Mo was busy making minor adjustments to the singer's microphone sound, which he felt was a little tinny. Dylan stood on stage repeating the musician's moronic mantra, 'One Two, One Two', while Mo experimented from the mixing desk until, after a few minutes, he gave Dylan the thumbs up.

This mundane pre-gig ritual was watched with great interest by the two German girls at the bar, and after some conspiratorial whispering, Rosie - for it was she - wandered over to Mo, whose girlfriend Desdemona had stormed off in a huff an hour earlier.

She revealed to him how fascinated she had always been with sound engineers, citing them as the great unsung heroes of the rock world; the ones who made bands sound better than they really were. Mo responded to this unexpected flattery as any self-respecting man would have done, and offered to buy the nice young lady a beer at the bar, glancing nervously around as he did so, just in case the fiery Desdemona had decided to come back. Gilda, meanwhile, having vacated the bar area, had managed to slip onto the stage unnoticed, and was currently rummaging around, roadie-style, with a huge bunch of keys attached to her jeans and showing, in time-honoured tradition, a revolting amount of bottom cleavage as she did so.

Laz and The Castle Crew had also arrived and were mingling with friends and hangers on, glancing nervously at the stage every now and again, in much the same way that a condemned prisoner glances out of his cell to the gallows that have been set up in the courtyard. The crowd had grown considerably now, and was swelled even more by the arrival of George, the band's ex-vocalist and Beatles fanatic, who'd magnanimously come to wish his old friends well in their new venture. He was accompanied by a carload of lads from the factory where he worked, testing light bulbs.

David, in an attempt to take his mind off things, was busying himself handing out his private view invites to selected audience members, in between trips to the toilet. It was now nine-fifteen, and the stage was in darkness except for the green and red stand-by lights that twinkled on the control panels of the amplifiers. This was the magical time for bands and audiences alike. The excitement and sense of anticipation were palpable. David decided to visit the toilet for the last time, just to be sure. The room was empty, except for the long-haired, denim-clad young man standing against the urinal, emptying his bladder while sighing ecstatically and issuing forth the occasional machine gun burst of trapped wind. Dylan was recycling his Guinness in order that he could take on some more.

David crept up behind him, squeezed his buttocks and whispered, "Hello big boy!" whereupon the young gentleman turned around sharply and punched David in the eye with much gusto. Staggering backwards in a state of shock, David was taken aback to discover that someone who looked so much like Dylan from the back could look so little like Dylan from the front. The heavily-tattooed character raised his fist as if to finish the job, and enquired, not unreasonably, "What's your game, pal?"

David, still reeling from the blow, with an eye that was beginning to close as he spoke, answered the question as politely as he could, under the circumstances.

"I'm sorry. I thought you were my friend." He made a dash for the nearest cubicle toilet, locking it after him and sitting still and terrified within.

Back in the hall, it was time for the show to commence. Laz asked Dylan to round up the band and tell Mo to put on the opening tape. It was a five-minute piece of Debussy, the desired effect of which was to create a classy atmosphere designed to invite people to sit up and take notice. Within a minute, everyone except David was assembled backstage, but there was a problem. Mo didn't know where he'd put the tape. The disc jockey, who twice already had announced that the band were on stage and ready, did so once more. The audience were now full of expectation and all facing the stage, eagerly awaiting the start of the show, but nothing was stirring. To compound the problem, the disc jockey had stopped playing records in anticipation of the opening tape beginning, and the room was now in a state of stupefied silence.

David, in the meantime, was on the floor of the cubicle toilet, wallowing in around half a pint of stale urine and trying to peer under the door to see if his assailant had disappeared. Eventually, satisfied that the coast was clear, he darted into the silent hall and handed the cassette tape, which he had placed for safe keeping in his denim jacket, to Mo, just as Billy the Convict strode purposefully across the stage and bawled,

"Will somebody put the f***ing tape on, or there'll be blood and snot all over the place!" whereupon, with perfect timing, the strains of Debussy began to filter through the room.

David nervously struggled into his white stage clothes with seconds to spare, as Duncan paced up and down, with ever wilder gestures and facial tics. The Debussy piece had started quietly, but was now gathering apace and becoming more and more majestic by the second. Hairs were standing up on necks all over the hall, as the five ghostly band members walked on stage to cheers and wolf whistles from the crowd. The guitarists stooped to turn on their amps and adjust effects pedals, and then stood, still and haughty, heads bowed, instruments slung around their necks, ready.

The Debussy was reaching its triumphant, ethereal peak now, as Laz began to play along with the soundtrack on the huge white Mellotron, which perfectly impersonated the strings of an orchestra. Dry ice pumped and gushed around the band's legs, billowed over the fold-back speakers and into the front rows of the audience. There was a blinding flash, and the multi-coloured stage lights were on, revealing the band in all their glory, strutting arrogantly, heads tossed back in ecstasy as the magnificent power chords surged around the room. Then, the handsome figure of Duncan Lake emerged from the right hand side of the stage. He walked cockily and slowly across the stage; a trick he had perfected in rehearsals, which ensured that he reached the microphone at the precise moment when he needed to sing, adding greatly to the drama. He arrived centre stage, into the bright white light and grabbed the microphone.

His eyes, which were manic at the best of times, suddenly disappeared into the back of his head, and he appeared to be doing a strange tribal dance. Instead of the opening line to the first song, which should have been 'In the maelstrom of my memory' he began wailing like a voodoo witch doctor, and as he did so, he sank to his knees.

This act was having diverse effects on the audience. Some whooped and hollered their approval, whilst others gazed in blank disbelief. Duncan, who by now didn't care either way, fell flat on his face. It was at this point that Mo realized something was seriously wrong. He leapt from his stool at the mixing desk and pushed his way through the crowd towards the stage. The band, meanwhile, played on, looking at each other in horror as their opening song became an instrumental. It was only when Mo ripped the microphone lead out of the amplifier with a blood-curdling scream that the penny dropped.

Duncan had suffered a massive electric shock.

David and the rest of the band quickly turned off their amplifiers and rushed over to Duncan, who was by now unconscious. The audience, which previously had interpreted his bizarre behaviour as some form of radical theatrical presentation, were now looking on with concern, hands nervously clasped to their mouths. Suddenly, the stricken singer opened his eyes and began to weep uncontrollably, followed shortly afterwards by most of the band. They had not expected him to rally round so quickly, and it was a blessed relief for both parties.

Billy the Convict had phoned for an ambulance, which thankfully had arrived in world record time, due to the fact that it was literally passing the front door of the club at that moment. The two paramedics carted poor Duncan away on a stretcher with promises that he would be okay, as long as he didn't do anything strenuous such as sit up. Laz had offered to ride with him to the hospital, but they insisted that it was best if he wasn't over-excited, as he had just had his brains boiled, his left arm was dislocated and his microphone hand looked like a pork scratching.

Inside the club, the disco had resumed, and the disc jockey was in conference with the band. He suggested, rather naively, that the show could go on in some form or other, perhaps instrumentally, as they had a captive audience and it was a shame to waste the opportunity after they had spent hours setting up and sound checking. Laz was about to explain to him in words of one syllable that his idea was ridiculous, and that he deserved to be buggered with a rag and bone man's brass trumpet, when an old friend appeared from the milling throng of the audience and tapped him on the shoulder. It was their old singer, George. He put a proposition to them that he thought might rescue the evening.

"I understand completely if you're all too shaken up to go on, but all these folks have paid to see you, and there's nothing any of us can do for Duncan just now. Why don't you get up there and play our old set, and *I'll* sing. Let's send them home happy, eh?"

Laz, dazed by recent events, could only gawp uncomprehendingly, but David intervened.

"Why not, Laz? George is right. None of us can help Duncan at the moment. The ambulance man said he'd probably be okay, and Mo's gone off to phone his mom and dad, who'll go to see him. It's what Dunc would have wanted - the show to go on. Stiff upper lip and all that jazz."

Couching it in this heroic way seemed to strike a chord. Laz walked back onto the stage and turned his amp on. One by one, the others followed. The only musician who seemed reluctant was George.

"Come on then!" called David. "It was your idea."

"I know, but I'm not using that bloody mike!" shouted George, not unreasonably under the circumstances.

"Don't worry," shouted Mo, who had just returned from the call box. I'll go take a look at the problem now. Just get that DJ to announce that you're still going on, and ask him to play two more records. I reckon I'll be done by then."

It was a worried looking Mo who walked across the stage minutes later, demanding a quick scrum down with the lads before they got underway.

"Listen," he began, his voice full of drama. "Someone had sabotaged the mike. The wires have been tampered with. I know full well that they weren't like that this morning. I checked them, like I always do. We'll get to the bottom of this later. It's all mended now, so off you go."

"You talk through it first then," suggested George.

"Ladies and gentlemen," said Mo. "Duncan is at the hospital now, and they assure me that he's okay. We didn't want you to go home with no music, so the lads have bravely decided to carry on. They're unable to play their set without him of course, but thanks to George here, they're going to treat you to some of the best music ever written. Let's pretend we're at the Cavern, which, let's face it, was a bit like The Crypt. Before this band became Epitaph, they were known by another name. Let's hear it for The Stubbles!"

David's powerful crash chords introduced 'She's a Woman', and the band was in full flight. The audience response was instant and gratifying. Everyone was up on their feet and dancing. As the song ended, Laz immediately broke into 'I'm Down' causing the eager crowd to move up a gear into near hysteria. From then on, the classics followed relentlessly with barely a second between songs. George looked across at David and was met by a grin that was considerably bigger than the legal limit. Sweat poured from all of them as they pumped out hit after hit, each met with rapturous applause, until, three encores later, they took the stage for one last song, and what a song. 'Hey Jude' had couples holding each other close in that lovey-dovey way that heralds the end of a good night, and opens up the initial negotiations for the sexual activity that inevitably follows.

The band were all singing away now, "Nar-nar-nar, nanana-nar, nanana-nar, hey Jude." Hands were held aloft and bodies swayed

185

to one of the greatest anthems ever written. George shouted above the noise of the mantra, "This one's for Duncan!"

By now, there was not a soul in the hall who wasn't joining in. Victory had been snatched from the jaws of defeat. This had been a night to remember, in more ways than one. It was a shame that Duncan couldn't have been there. He'd have enjoyed it.

Laz jumped from the stage, exhilarated but in desperate need of a toilet. He didn't have David's cautious nature, and as a consequence, had walked on stage two hours previous without emptying his bladder. Now that the euphoria was subsiding just a little and reason was being restored to its throne, he became acutely aware of what seemed like ten gallons of lager swilling around inside him. He made his way through the throng of friends, well-wishers and back-slappers to the lavatories where David had so recently collected a black eye, and seeing the trough section fully occupied by clubbers, opted for the sanctity of the cubicle.

He sat down and began to empty himself, cross-eyed and sighing with sheer ecstasy as the pain subsided. Just at this moment, Kieron Hastings, who had seen his fraudulent student heading for the urinals and was desirous of a private word, walked into the crowded lavatory looking this way and that, and deduced that the object of his attentions was not amongst those present. Realizing that there was no way that he could have missed Laz in transit, he presumed, correctly, that he must have been in situ within Cubicle One, and duly slipped into Cubicle Two.

After discreetly waiting until the orgasmic sounds of the desperate urinater were concluded, he politely tapped at the partition wall, coughed the way Reginald Jeeves always did when desirous of a word with the young master, and spoke.

"Ahem, is that Laz?" he began.

"Who needs to know?" asked Laz cagily. This fame business had its pluses and minuses. Now the fans were hassling him on the toilet.

"Kieron Hastings. Could I have a word?"

Kieron couldn't see Laz's face as those words left his lips, but it was a picture. People who have just been electrocuted often favour a similar expression.

"Erm. Yes."

"Shouldn't you really be saying something along the lines of, 'Forgive me Father, for I have sinned', these cubicles being somewhat similar to the confessional?"

"I, er….."

"'I er' was precisely my next line, Larry. I er, know what you've been up to."

"What do you mean?"

"You *know* what I mean. Your brilliant portfolio of work. The inability to draw in front of people due to a cruel and overbearing father. I spoke to him today, Larry. He was just doing a jigsaw at the time, while he waited for his matchstick model to dry."

"Oh shit!"

"Exactly. I was extremely angry about it, as you can well imagine, but I didn't come in here to have a row. I have a proposition to put to you."

A voice from outside spoke.

"Sorry to interrupt when you're trying to proposition that young man, but could I get in there? I'm desperate for a crap!"

Kieron answered.

"I presume that I am hearing the voice of a Fine Art student named Tony Hemmings. This is your Head of Department

187

speaking. One more comment and you will get nothing higher than a third. Is that understood?"

"Yes."

"Thank you. Now Larry, as I was saying before that student almost ruined his career, I have a proposition. I'm a fairly intuitive person, and I have a feeling that you badly wanted to be part of college life, so you cheated to get in. Am I correct?"

"Yes."

"Your parents are lovely aren't they?"

"Yes."

"And you've never drawn a picture in your life."

"No. I suppose I'd seen David's lifestyle and I was envious. I wanted to be like him, instead of getting my bloody fingernails broken and filthy in a car repair garage every day. I felt like I was worth more than that. I'm very sorry."

"You *are* worth more than that. You are a gifted musician. I really enjoyed tonight."

An unseen hand banged the toilet door. Kieron barked in its direction.

"Can't you see I am holding a tutorial? Now piss off before I downgrade your exam marks. Now, Larry, listen to me carefully. I watched you tonight and you are a good musician. That is of course, unless you were miming and Eric Clapton was behind the curtain and you were up to your old tricks again. Have you ever considered going to Music College?"

"No."

"Why not?"

"I don't know. I thought you had to be grade eight or whatever."

"It depends who you know. Would you be willing to study hard and do your grades if someone fixed it for you to go to the Conservatoire in Birmingham?"

"Are you kidding me?"

"I don't have a sense of humour. I'm a fine art lecturer."

"So do you have contacts there?"

"Yes. Do you remember the man who sat in on your interview? Blond hair, lisp?"

"Yes."

"It's his, erm, partner. They were here tonight, and liked what they saw, but any more subterfuge and you're dead. Understood?"

There was an impatient bang on the cubicle door.

"Will you pair vacate the bloody toilets so those who need them desperately can get in?"

Kieron, though small, was not a man noted for his patience.

"Knock on that door again," he bawled, "and I will rip your f***ing head off at the roots and dip sticks of buttered toast into your neck."

The Dean, who was also not noted for his intuition and patience, nevertheless sensed that he would be better off waiting until he got home, and like Elvis, promptly left the building. Had he not been preoccupied with thoughts of his potentially imminent bowel movement, he would have observed two shady looking women also heading for the exit. Germany's own lesbian version of Beauty and the Beast departed, fearing that there would be more unpleasant work to be done in the near future. Had they been cartoon lesbians, they would almost certainly have been mouthing the words, "Curses, foiled again!"

Three miles down the road at Newtown Hospital, Duncan's parents had just arrived to pick up their char-grilled son, who had been thoroughly examined and allowed home, with the proviso that he went straight to bed with a hot milk drink. The shock, for all its bad points, had also had a cathartic effect on him. In a moment of extreme clarity, as he lay motionless and smouldering, having his blood pressure checked by a tired junior doctor from Sri Lanka, he vowed to turn his back on the Rock and Roll lifestyle and take up his father's offer of a place in the family accountancy firm.

# CHAPTER 14

## The Private View

It was the final day of term before the Whitsun holiday. Snibboh was at the far booth of Tweedledum's with David, eating a mushroom omelette and chips that she hadn't ordered. David was tucking into a Cornish pastie, which was excellent, if lacking the vital ingredients of spaghetti and toast which was what he had actually paid for.

The subject under discussion was 'Claude Beardsley. Mere rogue or much worse?'

They were agreed that he had certainly stolen work belonging to the students and ex-students of the college, presumably for monetary gain at some future date, and as such was not fit to continue running a department. That in itself was bad enough, but Snibboh suspected him of more.

"That car was definitely repaired by The Spray Bay. They took it in the day after Laurence and Leonora's father died, to repair a dent at the front. We need to interview the man, pronto."

David agreed. "Anyone who could rip off his own students is callous by nature. Who knows where he draws the line? I bet you any money that he whacked into Laurence's dad by accident, probably because the doddery old fool walked in front of him whilst daydreaming about the disintegration of matter or some such nonsense. Instead of doing the decent thing, Claude buggered off."

The pieces were falling into place.

"So," pondered Snibboh. "Let's suppose that he was the so-called colleague who told Laurence that he'd identified Jack as the hit and run driver, only he conveniently didn't bother to mention it until Jack had even more conveniently jumped off the car park roof. It's perfect! He creates an alibi for himself and at the same time fires Laurence up with hatred for Jack, who's unable to defend himself against the allegation."

David seemed troubled. "But it probably doesn't end there, Snibs. Did Jack jump or was he pushed? You know what Mrs M said. She might ramble on, but often she's bang on the money, once you've deciphered her riddles. What about the van? Any news on that?"

"Not yet. Don and Reg are on the case, but it's disappeared off the planet. Laurence reckoned a student bought it off his dad, but we can't find any evidence of that. It hasn't been taxed or insured since Mr Fuchs had it, so whoever was in it that day was driving it illegally and he or she doesn't show up on any records. Unfortunately, Mrs Fuchs is no help, as she suffers from Alzheimer's, and doesn't even recognize Leonora, let alone know where an old van went."

They walked over to the counter to pay Olga, who was having a conversation with the man who had earlier declared his undying love for Kate Bush. He seemed much calmer, and was explaining in detail the outcome of his last trip to the doctor.

"I'm so happy," he exclaimed, "now that they've got me sorted out. It turns out that I wasn't a manic depressive after all. I'm a schizophrenic!"

David congratulated him as he handed Olga his money. "Well done! You must be thrilled."

192

They strolled together through the shopping precinct, pausing at The Dragonfly Boutique to go their separate ways.

"I'll see you tonight," said David. "I'm excited and dreading it in the same breath. I'm pretty sure all the invites have been handed to the relevant parties now, so we just sit back and watch the fireworks."

Snibboh gazed up at the car park roof and shuddered.

"What a horrible way to die. After what that barman told me, I can't believe he threw himself off there. What Laurence said about Jack being the hit and run driver made me think initially that he'd committed suicide out of self-loathing, to atone for killing an innocent man. Maybe he hated what he'd done so much that he deliberately wanted his own death to be awful; a self-inflicted punishment if you like, but the barman assured me that Jack was incapacitated and couldn't have knocked Mr Fuchs down that night. Then I see Claude's car with its freshly repaired dent and it starts to tell a tale, don't you think?"

David nodded in agreement. "Unless…the barman was lying to protect Jack, and he did indeed flatten Mr Fuchs, but not with his own car."

"Meaning?"

"Well, what if Jack was the student who bought his father-in-law's old van? The caretaker said he saw Vincent Gough's old van on the roof near to six, which is when I reckoned the final snaps had been taken. What if that van is damaged at the front and hidden somewhere?"

"But if that's the case, David, who removed the van? Jack wasn't in a position to, was he? He was lying where you're standing now, in fifty bits."

David edged away from the spot.

"The caretaker saw a man taking photographs at nearly six o'clock with a bobble hat on, just like Jack," she continued. "He

193

only saw one person, and that must have been Jack. What I don't get is why the coroner insisted he'd died at three or thereabouts, and not six."

"Jack didn't have his bobble hat with him," interjected David excitedly. "I've just remembered. Mrs M had it. He called around to collect it just before he set off for the roof, but forgot to take it."

"Perhaps he had a spare."

"Possibly, but why make a special trip to collect a hat when you have a spare one? Maybe the person up on the roof was pretending to be Jack, with a hat and camera, but what on earth is the point of that?"

A light bulb came on in Snibboh's head. "There *could* be a reason. What if Jack was already dead, and in the van, where the caretaker couldn't see him?"

"And the man in the bobble hat was his killer?"

"Correct!"

"So why would the killer be standing around taking photographs? Surely he'd want to bugger off sharpish."

"He couldn't go before he'd thrown Jack over the car park, could he?"

"So hang on a minute," frowned David. "Go slowly. You're saying that Jack was killed."

"At three, like the coroner said he was."

"But the killer wanted to make it look like suicide, obviously."

"Correct."

"So why not sling him over at three so that the post mortem results tallied? He'd just have to whack his head with an iron bar and turf him over the side. By the time he'd hit the deck, one more head injury would be difficult to detect."

Snibboh fixed David with her best Sherlock Holmes expression.

"Because, my dear Watson, that car park can get very busy at that time of day. Let's suppose that someone arrived on the roof, drove over to where Jack was photographing away in a world of his own, whacked seven shades of crap out of him with an iron bar, dragged him into the back of the van and thought, 'Great! Now I'll sling him down there so he can look at the Tiffany lamps.' Then he finds his progress hampered by carloads of shoppers coming and going, so he dons the bobble hat, grabs the camera and amuses himself with a few shots of the town till the coast is clear, which unfortunately for him isn't till six o'clock."

"Brilliant!" said David, impressed. "I'll buy that, but why did he need to start taking photos? Why not sit in the van with Jack for company? A bit grisly I'll admit, but nevertheless…."

Snibboh was champing at the bit now. "Because he was a photographer or an artist. He couldn't resist it. It was something to do that looked natural to passers by, and those photos were good, according to you."

"Yes," agreed David. "They were better taken than Jack's, in fact."

"So we look for a photographer then?" asked Snibboh.

"Not really. All of us are more or less competent with a camera, I'm afraid. It's part of our course, being able to use one. But I must admit those photos are well taken. Look, I have to go. I'll see you later."

And with that they parted company, Snibboh returning to the station and David to The Castle, where he'd promised to play Dylan at pool for half an hour before the afternoon's life drawing session began. This was, for a Snooker player, the equivalent of a gourmet chef being reduced to cooking hotdogs, but Glass Eye's Snooker Club was closed for a week due to refurbishment, and any game with a chalked-up cue was better than no game with a chalked-up cue, in Dylan's opinion.

David slinked into the poolroom at half past one, in time to see Dylan making mincemeat of a gentleman in a natty little bowtie, as his rotund and jolly wife looked on with glee at her husband's miserable performance.

"You'd think he'd let me win in my own pub, wouldn't you?" asked the man as David approached and removed his jacket, placing two coins on the cushion to secure the next game. This comment had rather confused David, as he knew the pub's landlord well. Either this man's face was the result of pioneering cosmetic surgery, or else he was lying about his position. The answer was far more prosaic. Henry and Alice had moved on, and were now proud owners of the Frog and Whistle in Bridgnorth. This, as Dylan explained whilst simultaneously going off three cushions to sink the black, was Bernie and Doris Wood, the new landlord and his wife.

"Pleased to meet you, mate," said a deflated Bernie, packing away his two-piece cue and returning to his rightful place behind the bar. "You can play him. I've had enough; he's made a donkey of me!"

David looked disdainfully at the little table and assembled his cue. He affected an ignorance of the rules, protesting in a loud voice that he normally only played Snooker. Ten minutes later, Dylan was just about to pocket the black ball, whilst David still had five reds on the table. The new landlord offered words of sympathy and a complimentary half of lager, which he stressed was an introductory offer and not repeatable.

"I was merely waiting till he'd removed most of his balls from the table, in order that I had a bit more space," insisted David. "I admit I mistimed my comeback, but tomorrow will be another day."

He begrudgingly handed over a pound to the victor and the two friends headed for the door.

When they arrived at the life room, they were greeted by The Limp Lisper, who informed them that the session was cancelled due to the fact that their model had slipped up on a piece of orange peel in the refectory and skidded into the snacks dispenser. She had consequently been sent home with her nose in a sling. As it was the afternoon of the last day before Whitsun, the L.L. magnanimously decided to send the students away to do whatever they wished, but strongly advising a spot of work on their final exhibition projects. Taking these wise words on board, David and Dylan agreed that they would go to the cinema.

The Regal was showing a black and white French film with English subtitles about a manic depressive circus clown in a run-down village who befriends a goat, which, due to his straitened financial circumstances, he later has to eat. The critics had all rated it highly, but somehow the premise of the film wasn't setting either of them alight, so they wandered across town to the Gaumont, which was showing, for the umpteenth week, The Exorcist. Dylan was all for seeing it, as he was fascinated by the publicity that surrounded the film, and wanted to judge for himself if it was worth all the fuss. David, on the other hand, didn't care for scary films, because he had a very vivid imagination, and he feared that he'd be seeing horrible young girls with rotating heads and projectile vomiting every time he opened his wardrobe doors.

The film had caused outrage in some sections of the community, and cinemas had seen mass protests by Christian pressure groups. If the press stories were to be believed, these picture houses were having to tend to collapsed and fainting cinema-goers by the barrow load, and a large percentage had been in padded cells or at the very least, therapy, ever since. None of this filled David with any confidence as his friend manhandled him past the ticket booth and towards the sweet shop.

"Don't worry," said Dylan. "Things like that don't bother me. I'll be there to hold your hand in the dark, if it all gets too much."

This latest development seemed to trouble David even more. He bought himself a packet of wine gums to lighten the mood, while Dylan chose a Kit Kat. The cinema trip had originally been mooted in order to distract David from thinking about the Private View, which had been worrying him for much of the week. He had absolutely no idea how Claude would react, and the only consolation was that the man couldn't possible know who'd organized the event. The film would undoubtedly be successful in taking his mind off things, but he was now more concerned about how long it would be before he could have his mind back, and the state it would be in once it was returned.

They shuffled into the darkened room and sat down half-way back and near the middle, where the picture quality was at its best. Had David had his way, he would have chosen seats in the Regal and suffered the French depressed clown chewing on his deceased goat. He wasn't keen on depressing films, but in his book they beat being scared shitless hands down.

The usual string of awful advertisements came to an end with the one about tubs of ice cream and Kia-Ora drinks being available from the lady down by the screen. David decided that he would invest in a large tub of popcorn, as his wine gums were disappointingly hard and tasteless. He wandered down the aisle and reached the front of the queue just in time to be served, as the room had gone dark in readiness for the main feature. He fumbled for the right money, and after much confusion, caused mainly by him emptying around a hundred-weight of small change from his pockets all over the carpet, he staggered back towards his seat, with the hairs on the back of his neck rising in anticipation of what was about to come. The debacle with the refreshments lady had made him late, and behind him, Mike Oldfield's haunting music from Tubular Bells was well under way. It suddenly reached an unexpected crescendo as the blood red film title hit the screen, causing David to jump about seven feet into the air and scream, throwing the entire contents of his popcorn tub down the necks of the people sitting either side of the gangway in the first six rows. He hurriedly apologized and scurried back to his seat.

Though not especially prone to homosexual tendencies, especially since his encounter with the Amorous Asian, nevertheless, a hug from Dylan would have been most comforting at this stage. The film was hardly sweetness and light from the off, but by the halfway stage both of them were in a state of near terror. Surprisingly, there were no scenes that actually made them jump, in true horror film tradition, but what they were witnessing was far worse. This nightmarish demon child, who spoke in tongues and spewed out profanities with a voice that came straight from hell, was upstairs, tied to her cesspit of a bed. The director clearly knew that here was something so awful that resorting to corny 'make them jump' techniques would only serve to cheapen his vision. What he'd created was pure evil, and each time the petrified priest entered that bedroom the audience would have their hearts in their mouths in anticipation, waiting for the sudden fright, which never happened.

David was doing his best to keep up with the action, which he was following through the narrow slit between the second and third fingers of his right hand, whilst Dylan seemed to be fascinated by what was going on at the back of the room every time something unspeakably grotesque took place, such as the vile black tongue that appeared to be crawling out of the poor unfortunate girl's throat like a giant leech. It was at that moment that David was aware of a tap on his back. He ignored it the first time, thinking that the person behind had touched him accidentally, but when it came tap-tapping again, he turned around to confront the tapper.

He met The Weird Woman's gaze head on, their noses around three inches apart.

No words can ever adequately describe his feelings at that juncture, so 'Abject terror' will have to suffice.

Those in rows one to six who thought they had heard the scream of a terrified young man the first time had to seriously think again. What had gone before was but a warm up, no more than a bit of lightweight throat-clearing to prepare for the main event. What they heard this time around was a fully-fledged, blood-curdling wail, as practised by Banshees, or torture victims just after the rack has been tightened just that bit more. The sudden and unexpected noise in Dylan's right ear caused him to leap like a salmon from his seat and poke the old gentleman next to him in the eye, causing him, in turn, to yelp like a dog and throw his boiling hot coffee down the neck of a fat middle-aged lady in front of him. Meanwhile, oblivious to the terror she had caused, The Weird Woman proffered a leather wallet and stared silently at David. With shaking hand, he thanked her and returned it to the back pocket of his jeans.

Half an hour later, the two friends emerged, clammy and shaken, into the sunlight.

"Not as bad as I was led to believe," said Dylan, less than convincingly.

"It scared the shite out of me!" confessed David, somewhat more honestly. They virtually jogged back to Dylan's flat, nervously glancing behind them every now and again. The plan to take David's mind off the private view had certainly worked. He hadn't thought about it once for two hours.

* * *

WPC Snibboh was making her way down to Chapel Ash. She did a lot of walking, which explained her svelte shape, but also her undying appetite. Spotting the little corner shop by the art college, she darted in to refuel.

The owner, Mrs Timmins came out of a little back room and welcomed the officer, who asked for a packet of crisps, a packet of peanuts and a Mars bar, just to tide her over till the buffet at David's private view.

200

"Would you like ready salted or the ones that smell like somebody's broken wind?" asked Mrs Timmins, giggling at her witticism.

"Well," pondered Snibboh, "Being as you put it that way, I think I'm being swayed towards the ready salted. I must say, I haven't had any nuts for ages, but I just fancied some today. I'm the officer who's been investigating the death of Jack Hamphlett, you know, the lad who fell to his death from the Mander Centre, and whose dad died of a peanut allergy. It put me off a bit, to be honest."

Mrs Timmins looked flushed and upset, as if someone had raked over some forgotten and painful memory and rekindled it.

"Oh, I wish you hadn't mentioned that," she said sadly. "We are the shop that sold poor Mr Hamphlett the tainted sandwich. I had a lad working for me who prepared his sandwich, and I forgot to warn him about the allergy. It turns out that he thinks he had nuts himself and might have forgotten to wash his hands. I've had sleepless nights ever since."

"You can't blame yourself," said Snibboh sympathetically. "It was an accident. No one's to blame. That's why they're called accidents, if you know what I mean. Do you know David Day, by the way?"

"Oh yes. He's a lovely lad. Some of the college lot are a bit stand offish, especially the fine art students, and that bloke Claude Beardsley. He's from London you see. They're not as sociable as the local ones, I find. David's lovely though, always having a laugh and acting silly."

"Yes, I've noticed that. You say Claude comes in. What does he buy?"

"Oh, sandwiches, which we make up for him specially, the same as Mr Hamphlett. He has posh ingredients like smoked salmon and mayonnaise and so on, because he's from London."

"I bet *he* doesn't eat crisps and peanuts. Do you have to do him sticks of celery and raw carrots?"

"No, he usually has a bag of plain crisps. He isn't a creature of habit like Mr Hamphlett, but whatever he has, he usually has a bag of plain crisps to go with it. That's why he's getting a bit big round the middle. I told him not long ago that he's putting on weight, and I said it was almost certainly the crisps. Every day since he came here years ago he's had a bag a day, and it can't be good for you. I remember one day he said he fancied a change, and asked for nuts, but the next day he was back on the crisps again. Addicted you see. That's the trouble with Londoners I think, they get addicted more easily, what with….."

Snibboh interrupted her flow. "I'm sorry Mrs Timmins. When did he buy the nuts?"

"Oh when he was deputy head. I remember because Mr Hamphlett had been in as well, just before, for his usual, and I said to Claude, 'What's this, having a change?' and he said he'd decided to ease off the crisps as he'd taken my criticism to heart, you know, about getting a bit overweight, and I said, 'Well you're hardly going to lose weight eating nuts' and he said, 'I thought they were good for energy and better for you than crisps', and I said, 'No they're not because they're covered in salt and you'd be better off eating the unsalted monkey nuts', and he said, 'To hell with it, I like salty crisps and I'm sticking with them, and I'll have to jog round West Park instead.'"

Snibboh paid for her goods and thanked Mrs Timmins very much. She headed for the door, but paused to speak to the shopkeeper.

"Oh, one last thing. Do you still keep in touch with the lad who prepared Mr Hamphlett's sandwiches?"

"Not really, but I've got his number. He had a bit of a breakdown when he realized that he might have been responsible for a death. He took it badly."

"Can you do me a favour and ring him? Tell him we've proved beyond a shadow of a doubt that he was not to blame. I think that will help to heal his mental problems. I'd be grateful."

And with that she continued her march towards Chapel Ash, with a spring in her step.

* * *

At The Regency Gallery, guests were beginning to arrive in ones and twos. The proprietor, Martin, and his assistant Kirsty were handing out glasses of Bucks Fizz, and a girl from the catering company was wandering around with a silver tray loaded with sausages and cheese and pineapple on cocktail sticks. David and Dylan arrived just as Snibboh walked around the corner, and the three entered together, the two students greatly buoyed by the sight of her neatly pressed uniform. Having some time left before she was officially off duty, she resisted the alcohol, in spite of David insisting that no one would ever find out. She did, however, help herself to half a tray-full of tuna and sweetcorn vol-au-vents, just to keep her going, causing David to muse that, should she ever become pregnant, her husband would surely have to do triple shifts in order to keep her in foodstuffs.

Several familiar faces had now arrived, and a few older people David didn't recognize. These must be the ones he'd posted invitations to, with a little help from Jim Weston, who'd kindly searched college records for addresses. David mingled with the forming clusters of people, but gave no indication that he had been the brains behind the event. He had given strict instructions to Martin that he was to inform any interested parties that The Woverhampton Society of Artists had paid for the gallery, the framing and the refreshments, and anyone interested in purchasing work must approach the artists directly.

By eight o'clock the gallery was heaving with invited guests, many of whom were curious as to who The Woverhampton Society were. It seemed strange that no one in the room had actually confessed to being a member, or submitted a picture for

203

the exhibition. Usually, private views were entirely manned by interested parties, namely the artists themselves and their partners. So far, nobody seemed to have unearthed a single contributor.

Kieron Hastings arrived with his colleagues, the Limp Lisper, Mike Sambrokes and Claude Beardsley, followed shortly afterwards by Jim Weston, who'd called in at The Castle first for a quick one. David signalled to Martin that proceedings could now begin, so the gallery owner clapped his hands to silence the cacophony that is inevitable when thirty or more artists are thrown together in a small echoing room with dozens of bottles of cheap Spanish wine and a buffet.

"Ladies and Gentlemen!" he began. "It's good to see you all here tonight. Help yourself to the food and drink. There's no limit. If that runs out, we'll get some more. The first, and probably the last exhibition of The Wolverhampton Society of Artists is awaiting you upstairs in the main gallery."

The guests filed upstairs and spilled into the long narrow gallery, making their way around the walls. The girl from the catering company had ditched the cocktail sausages on sticks, and was on hand with vegetable samosas, sausage rolls and various hors d'oeuvres. The noise had subsided a little now, replaced with the hushed reverence of thirty-odd artists studying the pictures on offer. Suddenly there was an indignant cry from a gentleman with a beard at the far end of the room.

"This is *my* painting. It's been missing for three years! What's going on?"

Claude, who was still downstairs finishing his Bucks Fizz, sauntered upstairs to see what the commotion was all about. He arrived to more cries of recognition. Laurence Fuchs had just let out a string of mixed expletives as he discovered his own gory masterpiece, now lavishly framed, hanging in the centre of the long wall. Dylan Weldon nearly choked on his red wine as he arrived at his beautifully framed pencil drawing.

What had been initially a trickle was swelling into a tidal wave of righteous indignation, with artist after artist threatening to call the police, and demanding explanations. Snibboh, sensing that a riot was imminent, appealed for calm, and assured people that all would be revealed in a few moments. Claude walked into a room full of seething artists who were baying for blood. He took one look at the first painting to greet him and realized - for he was not a slow-witted man - that he was in the mire. His face, previously a healthy rose madder pink, thanks in no small part to the alcohol he had just guzzled down, was now an ashen Payne's grey. He scanned the room, looking for David. Their eyes met. Claude's were seething with fury, like a wolf that had been cornered, while David's just looked sheepish and embarrassed. He turned away and whispered to Dylan, who turned to face Claude, flashing him a look calculated to kill.

The girl from the catering firm chose precisely the wrong moment to offer Claude a samosa. He grabbed one from her tray and stormed out of the gallery, flinging it across the room as he left and catching David on the bridge of the nose, making his eyes water. David though, was made of sterner stuff, and a mere samosa to the nose was well worth it for the pleasure of seeing Claude riled - a clear indication of his guilt. Besides, compared to the earlier black eye he'd received from the man in the toilets, samosas were small beer indeed. His only concern was the look that Claude had given him. It was the look of a man that knew precisely who'd stitched him up, which indicated that the samosa attack had been well-aimed rather than random. Now there was a very real danger that Claude could re-appear, armed with a sausage on a stick.

The other guests may have interpreted this stormy walk out as the pent–up emotion of yet another artist who had discovered a stolen piece up for sale, for they paid it no heed. Meanwhile, downstairs, Claude was just about to hurtle through the front door when Martin blocked his way, and presented him with an envelope.

"I'm in a hurry!" barked Claude, shoving him out of the way, but Martin, who was built along the lines of an all-in wrestler, held the door shut and insisted that he read the contents, adding that that there was no time like the present.

Claude tore open the envelope and was confronted by an invoice. It read:

* <u>Acorn Catering Services</u>.

*Thirty bottles of wine.*

*Two crates of Banks's Mild.*

Buffet for fifty people.

* <u>Regency Gallery</u>.

*Mounting and framing of fifty-seven works of art.*

*Hire of gallery for private view.  Total; £1,500. 50p*

Martin smiled sweetly. "Payable within a week, Mr Beardsley, and there'll be no more said about it. Oh yes, and one other thing. It might be a good idea to retire in order to spend more time with your family, don't you think? Good evening to you!"

Claude, rudely, didn't reciprocate, probably because it was far from being a good evening from where he was standing. He stormed out and was lost in the night. Upstairs, a riot was about to ensue, when WPC Hobbins, called for order.

"Folks! I have some good news for all of you, if you'll be quiet for a second. We have apprehended a burglar who has, for some time now, been stealing works of art from the college. We have been able to trace all the pictures, and Martin, the owner of this excellent gallery, has kindly framed all the works for you, at the guilty party's expense of course, to make up for the inconvenience. If you would prefer to retrieve your artwork now, please do so. Those who wish to leave their pictures on display and are interested in selling them through the gallery, please let Martin know before you leave. In the meantime, help yourselves to the food and drink, and let's celebrate a happy conclusion. If you will raise your glasses, I give you The Wolverhampton Society of Artists. This could be the start of something big! Finally, if anyone sees Mr Beardsley, who left before this good news was announced, maybe you'd like to fill him in after Whitsun."

# CHAPTER 15

## Five Go Mad in Devon

Claude Beardsley, it was fair to say, was not a happy little bunny rabbit. He picked up the ceramic plate depicting two kittens in a basket, an 'ironic' gift that Kieron Hastings had bought him for his last birthday. Previously it had served only to beautify and enhance his home, with its hand crafted twenty-four carat gold edge and its 'pay no money now until you are completely satisfied' attitude to life which Kieron had found so endearingly enchanting. He had read the 'Playful Kittens' poem on its reverse side and ached to possess it, in order that he could send it as a birthday gift to a person who would surely cherish it forever.

'Forever' was probably a tad optimistic for ceramic items entrusted to Claude. Most of them only had a life expectancy of around two weeks. He held the plate upside down by its far edge, with the bulk of the thing pressed up against the underside of his arm, discus style, and launched it with a fair bit of passion at an antique Greek bust sitting on his sideboard at the other end of the sitting room, decapitating same with deadly accuracy.

"I'll give you ironic, you supercilious little twat!" spat the curmudgeonly head of department, as he searched for another item to vent his spleen on. "How about this for ironic? Of all the things I could have lost my job for, I have to resign for borrowing a few pictures, the least of my bloody problems."

208

Claude was smarting badly from the private view fiasco the previous night. He knew there was no option now but to fall on his sword, which meant that he would have no means of paying the mortgages on his many properties, and virtually no chance of securing another teaching post. He knew damned well who had been behind the event at the Regency Gallery, but there was nothing he could do but pay the huge invoice and hand in his resignation after the Whitsun break. David Day had virtually ruined his life, and he would pay dearly. Something was puzzling him, however. Why hadn't this nasty little grinning guttersnipe just informed the police and let *them* sort it out? He seemed to be well in with the young police constable after all. The bitch was actually at the event with him, but instead he had organized this charade of an art exhibition to humiliate him and extort vast sums of money. This made no sense, but in a strange way he was grateful. Any police interference would have been far more costly, so in a way he'd been allowed to get off light.

If only they had been aware of what had really been happening. His one consolation was that no one was doing any really serious digging. The policewoman had been doing a few routine enquiries, but he had expected that to happen. She'd been to see Gertie and asked to examine Jack's vehicle, but that was all. Had he been thinking a little more clearly, he'd have bashed the front of Jack's car around a little, but it was not the end of the world. It was feasible that Laurence's father could have died without denting the thing. Unlikely, but feasible – he was just skin and bone after all, and probably only weighed a few stone, if one discounted his boffin-sized brain. Perhaps the police suspected that Jack had used another vehicle and were looking into it. Little did they know that they had actually been standing next to the car that caused the accident when they examined Jack's. Another delicious little irony.

More troubling was the fact that this interfering little bitch had called on Leonora and her brother. Leonora was empty-headed and knew nothing anyway, but Laurence was another matter. This strange and stupid bastard had used his father's van, instead of some anonymous old car. Why hadn't he driven up to the multistorey in a bright pink double-decker bus and done the job properly? He could have decked it out in fairy lights too, to make sure everyone noticed it. Laurence was proving to be a liability, and might have to meet with a road accident at some point, just like his unfortunate father. At least now the van was somewhere where it would never be found. The forensics boys would have a field day, whatever one of those was, if they ever located it.

Claude sat down by the window and stared into the street, deep in thought. It was truly incredible how his situation seemed to be getting more and more complex by the hour. What was it Shakespeare had said? "Oh what a tangled web we weave, when first we practice to deceive."

He had never intended to kill Kingsley Hamphlett, but when the man burst into his office that day and confronted him about sleeping with Gertie, Claude could see his career going down the toilet in front of his very eyes. This usually placid, easygoing character had suddenly become a thorn in the flesh; a barrier between the two things he really had his heart set on, the Head's job and Gertie, in that order. Now Kingsley would make such a fuss that his promotion chances would be negligible; Claude had come to rely upon the rumours that he was being thought of as Kingsley's natural successor when he retired the following year.

The proverb about killing two birds with one stone had always impressed Claude, and here was a perfect example of how that proverb could be demonstrated. A light sprinkle of ground peanut was neither here nor there to the average man, but to Kingsley it was the end of the road, especially as he wouldn't be able to find his syringe when he needed it. The plan was foolproof, and when the police discovered that the sandwich shop employee had been eating peanuts earlier in the day, it was as if God had tapped Claude on the shoulder and whispered his tacit approval.

What Claude hadn't expected was Gertie's reaction. Women were complex creatures, heaven knows, but for a woman who was thoroughly bored by her husband, she certainly seemed distressed when he died. These females didn't know what they wanted till it was gone. Ever since Kingsley had keeled over and choked in his little rowing boat, all she had done was weep and wallow in guilt the whole time. The woman was no longer worth the effort, and it was high time, thought Claude, that he moved on to pastures new, especially now that his job was on the line. The sensible solution was surely to sell all the properties and live in France. He could open a small hotel and organize painting holidays for tourists, especially rich female ones.

Had everything ended there, Claude felt sure life would have slowly become less complex, but life, as John Lennon once said, is what happens when you're busy making other plans.

Gertie's irritating son, Jack, was the next Hamphlett to come storming into his office, accusing him of having an affair with his mother and bad-mouthing him all over the college. He was warned about his wild accusations, but the boy was a loose cannon who needed a lesson in manners. Not that Claude intended to do anything about it. One killing was more than enough for him. No, far better if the obnoxious Laurence would do that particular favour for him. As a first year, Laurence had been at The Crypt one evening, trying his best to seduce a young girl student who curtly informed him that she would far rather sleep with a capybara. Claude had been sat at a table near the bar watching this drama unfold as he sipped his gin and tonic, when he noticed that the thick-skinned fine art student, far from skulking away with his tail between his legs, was over at the bar buying a pint of lager and a glass of red wine, presumably in a last ditch attempt to soften the girl up a little. Either that or he'd developed a serious alcohol problem and was buying his drinks two at a time.

It was then that Claude noticed a little sleight of hand which he knew would stand him in good stead at some future date.

Laurence produced a small piece of folded paper from his inside pocket and began to unfold it in a very furtive fashion. He emptied what looked like white powder into the red wine and quickly stirred it with a cocktail stick, before returning to the girl and offering her the drink.

Claude watched as the girl eventually and begrudgingly accepted the drink, but seemed to be telling Laurence to go away, which he did. Around half an hour later, he saw Laurence return to the table and try once more to seduce the girl, who this time appeared to have had a serious change of heart, and now found him irresistible. Shortly afterwards, they were seen leaving the club together, the girl somewhat unsteady on her feet.

Over the year, Claude had observed this creepy student using the same technique on numerous occasions. He was also aware that there was a rumour circulating the campus that several attractive girls had woken up after a wild night at The Crypt with throbbing heads, memory loss, missing valuables and worse. It didn't take a genius to put two and two together. All this was excellent news for Claude, for it meant that Laurence could be relied upon to help out when he was needed, but even Claude couldn't expect a student to come running and volunteer to murder a fellow student, just because of a bit of blackmail. It would take something altogether more potent to do that. Fortunately the solution was handed to him on a plate by the same benevolent God who had sanctioned the peanut incident.

It was Gertie's fault. He was clear about that. Ever since her husband had died, she had been less forthcoming, sexually speaking, and this had upset Claude greatly. He was feeling bitter, twisted and resentful. So much so, in fact, that he decided one evening to take a night off from seeing Gertie in order to visit the seedier side of the town so that he could link up with a young lady who never said no, as long as the fee was agreed beforehand. He pulled up at the kerb, and after a brief bit of bartering, she jumped inside and Claude drove off in the direction of West Park, which offered a certain amount of privacy. As he drove in that general direction, he became cognizant of a loosening around the midriff, and before he knew it, his belt was off, the trousers down and the privates were on parade. Clearly, here was a young girl who enjoyed her work, and was eager to get down to the task in hand. Claude, being only made of flesh and blood, was soon elsewhere, mentally speaking, and not concentrating as he should on the task of driving. Luckily, it was a very quiet evening and the roads were all but empty, with one important exception.

Wilfred Fuchs was returning home from a meeting, and was, as usual, in a world of his own making, and mumbling incoherently to himself. It would have been rather comforting to imagine him at that precise moment, calculating that 'the power of the impromptu orgasm's effect on a vehicle's accelerator was directly proportionate to the level of jaywalker disintegration'. He would have been so gratified to know that his theory was correct.

Claude, who had never experienced such explosive sex, ordered the lady of the night to remain within the vehicle, hastily pulled up his trousers and staggered outside to survey the damage, which was serious. The bald headed coot under his front spoiler didn't look too bright either. Always a firm believer in the adage about discretion being the better part of valour, Claude shot back into the car and disappeared as quickly as his wheels could carry him, explaining to his companion that he'd run over a badger. Luckily, the lady's head had been well below the dashboard when disaster struck, so she hadn't seen a thing. After a brief choking fit, she felt able and willing to continue her duties, and Claude was once more on Cloud Nine. The lecturer had paid for an evening's entertainment, after all, and he was damned if some doddery old loony was going to spoil it.

It was only the following day when he realized that his accident could be another Godsend, and it was an ill wind that blew no one any good. All he had to do was convince Laurence that, with his own two eyes, he'd witnessed Jack kill his father and Jack's demise was as good as guaranteed. The problem was, he knew Laurence might well prefer to go through the official channels

213

and inform the police. Then Claude hit upon his brainwave. Laurence was impulsive with an evil streak. The police, Claude goaded, would simply lock Jack up for a few years. It was, after all, a hit and run, and not a premeditated murder. He'd probably get out after three years for good behaviour. Was this any way to punish a sneering alcoholic who had killed his and Leonora's beloved father? Besides which, if the police were involved, Claude would have to give evidence, and then everyone would know he'd been with a prostitute, which would spell disaster for his new relationship with Gertie.

No, Laurence would be better off dealing with this himself, and Claude could advise him how best to do so. He'd set Jack a project which involved him being on the roof top car park, a place he wasn't too enamoured of due to his fear of heights. All Laurence had to do was drive up there and pretend to be interested in what Jack was doing. Then, when he was preoccupied with looking through the lens, bash him across the back of the head with an iron bar and sling him off the roof. It was simple. The top floor was hardly ever used. All he had to do was drag him into his vehicle and wait till there weren't any shoppers around, either down below or up on the roof. Then haul him over the edge to finish him off, if he wasn't dead already.

Unfortunately, the best laid plans of mice and men 'gang aft agley' as Rabbie Burns often pointed out, and the rooftop was uncharacteristically swarming with shoppers, due to a sale at the department store below. It was six o'clock before the coast was clear, which meant that Laurence had to amuse himself by taking pictures, or hanging sheepishly around his father's old van, whistling, whilst a stiffening corpse lay within.

* * *

Claude's attention now returned to David Day. Rosie and Gilda, two more of Claude's ever-growing list of blackmail victims, had also made a pig's ear of a simple task. He was beginning to think that he was surrounded by rank amateurs. This cretinous Day was

214

trouble, and needed to be taken out of the equation quickly, before he caused any more migraine attacks. The dykes would have to travel down to Devon and do the job right this time, or risk the consequences.

As if to underline this last thought, Claude reached for an imitation Delft jug and threw it out of the window at the foul cat that was always hanging around his shed.

\* \* \*

WPC Hobbins had a call waiting for her in interview room two. She picked up the receiver.

"Snibboh, it's me, David," said David.

"Sergeant Snibboh to you, son," she relied proudly.

"What?"

"I've got my promotion. The bosses think I'm doing well and I've been rewarded. I'm so chuffed!"

"Congratulations! You deserve it. Due in no small part to your excellent work on the Jack Hamphlett case."

"Yes. They've given me more time to try and sort this out. I've explained everything to them and they think it's high time we talked in depth to our Mr Beardsley. The net is closing in."

"Snibs, I think that's a big mistake, if you don't mind me saying so. He's a cunning old fox. The second he gets a sniff that we're after him for something more serious than stolen artworks, he'll be off. You need something more concrete."

"I have something. I discovered that he bought peanuts from the corner shop."

"So what? I did."

"Yeah, but he doesn't like peanuts."

"Ah!"

"Add to that his repaired car, and an obvious motive. Let's not forget motive. With Kingsley out of the way, he becomes head of department and bags the widow into the bargain. Not a bad result for thirty pence."

"Thirty pence? There you take me into deep and unfathomable waters."

"The price of a bag of ready salted nuts."

"Oh. I was confused because I only pay twenty-three. You must be talking about the big bag. Look, I still think we should wait and let him hang himself. At the moment, he isn't aware that you or I are on to him. He can't be, but I must confess, when that samosa made my eyes water, it didn't look like a random shot. It had my name written all over it, and he gave me such a bloody look. Do you think somehow I gave the game away?"

"I don't see how."

"Nor me, but even if I did, that's all he thinks I know about. I've got a brilliant idea which I'm sure will hand him to you on a plate with watercress around him, but it means you can't go in making him suspicious just yet. Can't you plead with your bosses to hold back?"

"Yes, but only if your plan is a corker, and guarantees an arrest. God! They'll make me an inspector if I nail a murderer!"

"Exactly!" agreed David. "Now listen carefully, because I have to fly. I'm just about to set off for Devon, so I don't have much time……"

\* \* \*

The trip to Dittisham took five hours. It should have taken half that time, but thanks to Suzanne's map reading, they made a slight detour via Cumbria. As they arrived in the village they were met by a view straight from a picture postcard.

The sun was high in the sky and the river twinkled with a million fairy lights. Swifts darted about maniacally, dipping into the water to take a sip with consummate skill and grace. Suzanne's theory was that they were all deceased members of the Red Arrows display team, reincarnated as birds, but David felt that this was highly unlikely. The white sails of hundreds of yachts charged this way and that, occasionally capsizing and soaking their owners. Herons floated majestically through the cloudless sky, and little children stood along the little jetty with their crab lines and buckets, squealing with delight as more and more of the creatures succumbed to the temptation of raw bacon. The smaller children sat in pushchairs rubbing ice cream cones into their heads while their parents, burnt bright red by the vicious midday sun, downed pints of shandy at the harbour-side pub. In short, God was in his Heaven and all was right with the world.

Honeysuckle Cottage, and its Siamese twin, Rose Cottage, were a short walk up from the jetty on the right hand side, set back from the tiny steep road that led up the hill and out of the village. In typical Devon style, one was a pastel blue colour, and the other a pastel pink, topped off with a dainty thatched roof. The front garden of Honeysuckle Cottage, not surprisingly, was full of honeysuckle, whereas its twin preferred roses. David unloaded the suitcases from the back of his old Mini, so graciously returned by Len for the Whitsun break.

"Well, this is just wonderful!" enthused the dreamy young artist, who was prone to get a bit emotional about England now and again. "What a place! The simple pleasures, eh? A Devon cream tea, and then an evening of catching crabs."

Suzanne wasn't so sure about this last detail, but she let it pass.

"Look David! In the eaves of our cottage. That's where the swifts are nesting. Have you ever wondered how they make those nests? How do they keep the first twig in place, till they get back with the next one?"

"I wish you'd listen occasionally," sighed David wearily. "I explained this to you in Stratford. Sorry, no I didn't, my mistake. Er, shall we carry the bags in, get freshened up, and then pop down to the pub for some dinner?"

Suzanne eyed him thoughtfully, while David, flushing red, nervously fiddled with the key and pushed open the door. There was an immediate smell of damp.

"Probably not aired up. I bet no one's been down here for a while. We'll soon get it warm. Jim says there's a log fire."

"It looks a bit dank inside. The outside looks better."

"Oh, it'll be fine, I'm sure. Jim wouldn't rent me a pigsty would he? I'll turn the lights on."

A bare forty-watt bulb flickered on. The sitting room was small, with a threadbare and burnt Persian-style rug in front of a dusty open fire. The furniture, such as it was, was of the Second World War period, commonly referred to as 'Utility'. A crooked bookshelf held such delights as 'Steam Trains of the nineteen-fifties' and a black plastic folder full of 'useful' leaflets for the Devon holidaymaker. Suzanne's cursory search revealed must-see venues including, 'The Button Museum. (A collection of interesting buttons through the ages)', Bee World, (Observe the fascinating world of bees), Barometer World (Barometers through the ages) and Garden Gnome World, (Every type of gnome set in beautiful gardens).

"We'll be going down the pub a lot then," she remarked somewhat waspishly.

David threw the cases down and meandered upstairs to check out the sleeping accommodation. He came back down a few seconds later to find Suzanne in the tiny kitchen putting the kettle on. He sidled in and coughed his little nervous cough.

"Erm. Do you want the good news or the bad news?"

"I hate when you say that. Good news."

"Right. The bedroom isn't too bad, but it smells a bit damp and the sheets look like nylon."

"Shit! If that's good news, the bad news is going to be pretty bad."

"There's a miniature frog on the window ledge."

"I can live with that. I hate ornaments, as you know, but if it's…"

"It's a real frog. But miniature. I think it's a baby."

Suzanne gave him a wild look. "You KNOW that I hate frogs. If this is your idea of a joke…"

"It's a tiny baby frog. It's actually very cute indeed. It's probably half an inch long, if that."

"Are you sure it's not a newt? It sounds too small for a frog. If a frog was only that big, it would still be a tadpole. Did it have a tail? If it did it was a newt or a tadpole."

"It was a frog. I know what frogs look like. Shit! There's another one."

Suzanne screamed even louder than David had done at the cinema, when The Weird Woman handed him his wallet. A minute green frog was casually hopping across the work surface, seemingly without a care. Three more were waiting to greet him at the bread bin. Suzanne, true to her sexual stereotype, was now on top of a stool with her hands clasped to her mouth.

"Get them out of here or I'm leaving! David! Now!"

"I like frogs. They're harmless."

"Now!"

"Okay. I'll put them in this saucepan."

"No you bloody well won't. Not if you want me to do Spaghetti Bolognese. Flick 'em out of the window with a piece of card."

David dutifully rid the kitchen, sitting room and bedroom of frogs, which at the last count, numbered over thirty.

He went in search of the bathroom and came back moments later, ashen faced.

"There's a bath with a cheapo shower tap thingy. The shower curtain is officially white, but the bottom third is green. There is a colony of mini-frogs living in the bathroom. I suppose it's because they like damp conditions. I've just evicted another sixteen and there's a squashed one under the door. I intend to kill Jim Weston with a potato peeler, very slowly."

An hour later, every last frog had been removed, the shower curtain soaked in bleach and a fire lit in the hearth. Suzanne, meanwhile, was busy hoovering away at the chairs to remove dog hair, and had so far managed to find enough to create a small Labrador from scratch. They eventually slumped down exhausted and sat quietly listening to the crackle of the logs burning in the fireplace.

"Why do all these places promise so much and offer so little?" asked Suzanne. "They look marvellous in the brochures, but they're all the same. It's like Christmas. Never as good as you think it's going to be. Did you spot the coat hangers? Two wire ones and a padded pink thing that once belonged to Barbara Cartland. I'd read a book and put my feet up but I don't think I fancy 'An Otter in my Hand Luggage' by Bernard Braithwaite."

"Tell you what," said David, who was feeling guilty for inviting her to this fleapit. "Let's get cleaned up and go down to the Harbour Pub for some dinner. Then we'll turn in early and I'll make passionate love to you in a little bedroom overlooking the river, to the sound of seagulls. Then tomorrow I'll catch crabs."

"Not from me you won't. And seagulls don't make that noise at night. They're all in bed. Come on then, big spender. There's a gammon and pineapple down there with my name on it."

A simple but well cooked dinner and two bottles of Liebfraumilch later, David and Suzanne staggered out of the pub and walked to the end of the jetty to gaze silently out across the Dart. In spite of Jim's cottage, this was a lovely place. There were no amusements and only one pub, but it spoke to David's depths. The sky was clear, with more stars than either of them had ever seen before, and there was no traffic noise. The only sounds were the creaks of moored rowing boats and the occasional strain of live folk music coming from the pub bar. Bats dive bombed them as they hunted for insects on the wing, or the odd mini-frog, for those with more substantial appetites.

"I haven't seen anywhere near enough of you lately," whispered Suzanne, as she clung onto his arm.

David suddenly became engulfed with a most potent and overwhelming feeling of joy. It was as if he had experienced a moment of extreme clarity, when everything around him suddenly made perfect sense. Here lay the answer to the world's problems, here in lovely old Dittisham on a creaking old jetty on a perfect summer evening. Life wasn't about money, or ambition, or world domination. It was about little things. Someone who loved you holding your hand, rubbing your back without being asked to. It was about watching this beautiful world go by, and taking the time to see nature happening in all its glory. It was about sunsets and twinkling lakes, eating good dinners and occasionally having too much wine, making love, looking at stars, Italian pizzas, full moons and crazy bats. He wondered if Stalin ever took the time to dangle his feet in the river Dart, or catch a crab in a plastic bucket. Did Adolf Hitler ever sit in an Austrian meadow with Eva Braun and watch the butterflies flitting around? Surely anyone who could appreciate the small things wouldn't want to destroy half of the planet. Maybe if they'd accepted the young Adolf into art school, he'd never have had any desire to rule the world. Blessed be the meek, for they shall inherit the earth. Whoever said that knew a thing or two about life. It was probably Shakespeare. Either him or Oscar Wilde. The only problem was that the earth would almost certainly be ruined by the time the meek got to run the place.

"Let's go back to the cottage and get naked," he leered, the Liebfraumilch kicking in, now that the cold night air had got to him. "We could do it in front of an open fire, like James Bond always does."

"Not with those cinders shooting off all over the place. It'll have to be between the nylon sheets. We'll be full of static. It might be nice."

They ricocheted back up the hill, bouncing off a hedge here and a fence there, until they reached the front gate of Honeysuckle Cottage. David fumbled excitedly with the key and they tumbled in, pleased to see that the fire was still going nicely and the old place was feeling a little more hospitable. They staggered upstairs, cleaned their respective teeth, and began to kiss each other in the bathroom doorway.

"It's been too long," smiled Suzanne, as she removed her T shirt and jeans and slid under the sheets. David stared at her moonlit body and became quite overcome with love. He took off his clothes and slid in next to her, rubbing her lovely shoulders gently and kissing her once more. Suzanne raised her arms above her head and clasped the rails of the old brass bed. She knew this simple act drove David to distraction.

"Touch me," she whispered.

His hand slid under the sheets and down over her flat stomach. She sighed in his ear as he did so, which made him very excited.

"Touch my spot."

His hand slid lower. "Is that nice?"

"Touch the spot."

"I am. You're very wet. Oh God! You're lovely."

"You're not on it."

222

"Yes I am. Jesus! It jumped. IT'S A FROG!"

Suzanne's blood curdling scream could be heard in Dartmouth. She leapt out of bed and switched on the light. There was one left, and it was hopping about under the top sheet.

"That's it David!" shrieked Suzanne, grabbing her T shirt. "We're going next door."

"We can't just go round there at this time of night," reasoned David. "We'll go first thing in the morning. I've got the keys for the other party when they arrive, so we *could* swap cottages, but who says next door will be any better? At least I've got rid of all the frogs here, apart from this one. Look! I'll go over the place with a fine-toothed comb, right now, okay?"

Suzanne was on top of a chair again. She flashed him an expression that was part grimace, part nod. David's warning about the potential state of Rose Cottage had hit home, as he hoped it would. He rounded up the amorous amphibian and re-united it with its colleagues, before proceeding to execute a fingertip search, police-style, of every nook and cranny in the house.

While he was diligently going about his duties, Suzanne opened the bottle of brandy she had packed for the trip, and shouted up to David that she intended, by way of calming her frayed nerves, to get a stiff one inside her, prompting David to shout back that he had also been thinking pretty much along those lines before the frog showed up. A good hour later, he pronounced the hell-hole completely devoid of frogs, and, for that matter, toads, newts, spiders, scorpions, lizards, bats and snakes. Only then did she cautiously slide back into the bed, but David could tell by her body language that his night of passion was going to be shelved. Her jeans, cardigan and raincoat were also a giveaway.

The next morning, they were awakened by the sound of seagulls shrieking, plodding and no doubt shitting all over the roof, after their hearty breakfast of homeless mini-frogs. It was a sound that

223

David was rather fond of, but only in small doses. He gazed down at his sleeping girlfriend, who appeared to be wearing most of her clothes all at once and looking decidedly flushed. He wondered to himself whether this overdressing was protection against frog attack, or due to the fact that the entire cottage only had three coat hangers.

The early morning sun streamed in through the flimsy curtains, leaving white-hot bars of light on the duvet. He peeled the top sheets back and began to unbutton Suzanne's clothing, partly to prevent her from over-heating, but more so because he wanted to see her naked body bathed in the streaks of brilliant light. She opened her eyes and asked what he was doing.

"Good morning," he smiled. "It's okay, I'm a doctor. You've had a nasty shock, but you'll be okay once you've got a little something inside you."

"Little being the operative word, doctor."

"Now now. How about a nice sausage, for starters?"

"Cocktail variety?"

"At the moment, I admit, but not for long. I wish you wouldn't tease me about that. I'm getting a complex. Whenever I used to walk into a room full of women at some party or other, I'd be too terrified to try and chat any of them up, because I thought they all somehow knew my todger wasn't very big and they'd all start laughing. Crazy isn't it?"

"Not really! I used to go around telling them."

"Thanks."

"Pleasure! And talking of pleasure, can you shut up and get on with it? I want my breakfast."

Ten minutes of passion later, they were in the cramped kitchen, trying to work the toaster. The first two slices had catapulted out from the machine and landed in the sink, two feet away, thankfully putting the fire out. Suzanne had managed to catch the second two in mid air, but they were marginally tougher than Welsh slate. David decided to adjust the slider on the side of the toaster by one notch, the result of which was a strange buzzing sound which preceded a dramatic flash from the plug.

After weighing the pros and cons carefully, they decided that the promise of fresh toast was far outweighed by the threat of a Duncan-style near-fatal electrocution, and they deemed it best to stick to corn flakes until they had learnt the ropes.

"If we had some eggs," suggested Suzanne, "I could do omelettes. Maybe I could pop up to that little corner shop at the top of the hill and buy a few, while you make a pot of fresh tea, if the kettle works."

David gingerly tested the kettle by flicking the switch down with a long wooden walking stick that he'd found in the hallway. This particular electrical appliance, at least, was in good working order, for the time being. He gave Suzanne a few pounds and waved her off up the hill, while he searched the house for tea bags. Half an hour later she returned, looking somewhat smug, with a dozen eggs and a few bits and pieces from the store. She handed him the change.

"They've undercharged you," said David.

"No they haven't," she assured him. "I got the eggs for nothing. There's this great house up the hill, and it's empty. It could be lovely if it was done up, but at the moment there are chickens clucking about all over it. It's got a huge old derelict barn building next to it, and they're all in there, running wild. There's eggs everywhere, so I took a dozen."

"What? You'll get us arrested, woman. They have to belong to someone. Chickens don't just form a limited company and go it on their own. Did anyone see you?"

"Two women were walking down to the jetty, hand in hand as it happens, but I'm not prejudiced, as long as they don't try it on with me. They might have noticed me just leaving, but I don't think they spotted me nicking off with any eggs. For all they knew, I was looking the place over with a view to buying it, because it's got a sale board up. Stop panicking anyway, you're like a girl!"

After a reasonable breakfast, all things considered, Suzanne insisted that they have a nose next door, as David had still got the keys. Jim had told him that he could have first choice on the cottages, so he'd tossed a coin and gone for Honeysuckle. The other party weren't due until later that afternoon, so if Rose Cottage was a bit better, they could quickly swap over.

On first impressions, it was indeed cheerier inside. The kitchen was lighter and slightly better equipped, and the reading matter far superior. Some previous occupant had bequeathed twenty ex-libris copies of P.G. Wodehouse novels, so as far as David was concerned, it was a done deal. Rose Cottage also had one very important strategic advantage. It was ten yards nearer to the pub, and with a hill as steep as Dittisham's, this was no idle whim. Conquerors of Everest, Kilimanjaro, Mont Blanc and the like, who had long since hung up their crampons and retired to Dittisham, still had a healthy respect for that gradient. What clinched the deal though, was a singular lack of amphibians. Quite what had enticed those little green chappies into Cottage One was anyone's guess, as was the vexed question of why they had turned their noses up at Cottage Two.

David lugged around the clothing and provisions and lit a fire to air the place.

"I'm going to enjoy this week," he said happily. "I intend to chug up to Dartmouth in a hired boat, and then chug back. In between molesting you, and believe me, that will be often, I will while away the hours with a glass of dry white and a Jeeves book. Of an afternoon we'll indulge in the simple pleasures, with a crab catching contest and an ice cream. Then, when the sun has gone over the yard-arm, whatever that is, we'll saunter down to the pub and eat dinner, followed by a stroll in the moonlight, a sensual snog, and more sex. I am doing nothing of an artistic nature, because when we get back, we're straight into the degree shows which will mean stress and chaos. Then there's the small matter of seeing Claude Beardsley face the music."

"What's that humming sound?" asked Suzanne, subtly changing the subject from David's mooted sexual Olympics. "It seems to be coming from the kitchen ceiling."

David sauntered into the kitchen and cocked an ear.

"It's electrical."

"What does that mean? It's electrical."

"It sounds like wiring making a noise in this false ceiling. Wiring often does that."

"Does it bollocks! What are you now? An electrician? I've never heard electricity do that, apart from those bloody great pylon things in fields."

"Fair point," agreed David. "But you must admit, it's definitely an electrical type of hum."

He climbed onto a tall kitchen stool and put his ear to the pulpboard ceiling tile. The hum's epicentre seemed to be directly above him, and it appeared, unless this was just a strange coincidence, to coincide with a small brown stain in the centre of the tile, a fact that he pointed out to the girl steadying his stool down below.

"Poke at it then," advised the girl, who was by nature, scientific in her approach to such phenomena. So he did.

David's finger pushed right through the stained tile, which had the same consistency as Marmite. The humming sound suddenly became at least twice as loud. He hurriedly withdrew the digit, for fear of being severely 'Duncan-ed'. He jumped from the tall stool and observed the hole that he had made, as if expecting something to happen.

Something did. A wasp crawled out from it and ran a critical eye over the two people below. Then it went back.

There is a very popular film, starring Michael Caine, about the Zulu uprising, called, logically enough, Zulu. It tells a story about a small garrison of men who have been warned that a mighty Zulu army is marching in their direction, and escape is nigh on impossible. The garrison, frightened senseless, commit to reinforcing the old place as best they can, and sing snatches of 'Men of Harlech', just to keep their spirits up, until the inevitable happens. The look-out spots a thin line of Zulu warriors on the horizon and the men galvanize themselves into action, forming two lines of redcoats and squirting a drop of WD40 on the old Gattling gun. The Zulus charge down the slope and get stuck in without delay, throwing assegais, hacking the soldiers to bits and so on, while the brave little garrison fight for all they're worth and send the devils packing. So far so good. They are exhausted but pleased with a job well done. Band-aids are dispensed, aspirin consumed, and a few rounds of 'Men of Harlech' sung. The casual observer, however, would have warned them not to count their chickens too soon. These Zulu chappies were determined individuals, and not prone to giving up, just because a few had been shot dead with muskets or speared up the jacksie with a bayonet.

The look-out, who had the world-weary look of a fellow that had already got his eight hours graft in and was looking forward to a beer, a bully beef sandwich and a good kip, had decided to take one last peek through his brass telescope before turning in for the night. To his horror, he saw that there were some twenty thousand more of the buggers lined up on the ridge, this time banging their spears against their shields and chanting a blood-curdling ditty in a very aggressive fashion that he didn't much care for. No one recorded his exact words, but one can bet good money that he uttered several choice expletives that he wouldn't have wished his grey-haired old mother to hear.

This was, as near as 'damn it', the scenario that was being re-enacted on the ceiling tiles of David and Suzanne's kitchen, with the aforementioned pair cast in the roles of Michael Caine and Stanley Baker, and the twenty thousand angry wasps taking on the Zulu warrior parts. They may have only been one inch Zulus without an assegai between them, but they did have incredibly sharp spears attached to their rear ends and they weren't afraid to use them. The air above David's head was fast turning black, and the noise was petrifying. He had inadvertently poked his finger straight through the middle of a huge nest, and the wasps were feeling threatened. To bolt for the open spaces was, with David and Suzanne, the work of an instant. Once outdoors, with the cottage door firmly shut, they stared, saucer-eyed into the kitchen window, which was now black with the little devils.

"Can you clear this one up for me?" asked Suzanne, close to hysterics. "What are wasps for?"

"Beats me!" replied David. "I understand bees, but these bastards...."

"What on earth are you doing here?" asked an all too familiar voice. Dylan Weldon was standing at the front gate, unnoticed in the chaos, accompanied by Kathleen and two suitcases.

"What on earth are YOU doing here?" responded David, his question equally valid, if somewhat lacking in originality.

"I rented Rose Cottage from Jim Weston," Dylan replied, "So that I could have some peace and quiet to finish my sculpture project and do a bit of walking before the degree shows. At least the walking option is still a possibility. What are you doing in my cottage, or should I say, not in my cottage?"

"I'm glad you agree that this is your cottage," said David, with some passion, his voice broken with raw emotion. "You can keep it. It's got around seventeen million wasps living in it. That's my cottage, next door, which has no wasps at all, but there was a colony of mini-frogs, before I asked them to seek other accommodation."

"Well I'm not living in a cottage full of wasps," replied Dylan adamantly. We'll doss in with you and the frogs. I can cope with frogs."

"You have to be joking. There isn't room to swing a cat in there. There's not even room to swing a frog, or even a wasp. It's bijou, to use a Mrs M word. Talk about 'A plague on both your houses'. I can't remember which of Shakespeare's characters came up with that line, but I bet he lived in Dittisham."

"What seems to be the problem?" asked a new voice. It belonged to a middle-aged gentleman in a straw hat and a cravat.

"Wasps!" said David. "Forty-nine million of them."

"That's lucky," said the Straw Hat.

"I fail to see how that can be," said David, exasperated.

"It's lucky because I'm not a blacksmith," smiled the man.

"They're not all locked up," whispered Kathleen, cryptically.

"Is anyone looking after you?" asked David sympathetically. "A carer?"

"It's lucky I'm not a blacksmith, or a fireman," added the Straw Hat.

David shook his head. "No. Still don't get it."

"It's lucky, because I'm neither of those professions, but what I am, by trade, is a pest control officer."

David sank theatrically to his knees and prayed. "Thank you, Jesus!"

"And I saw you young folks screaming and flailing around, like you was auditioning for our Morris-dancing troupe, and I thought

230

to myself, "That'll be bees then. Only I was wrong. It was wasps."

"Yes."

"And I knows how to get rid of wasps."

"Then don't let us stand in your way."

"But there's a snag."

"I knew there would be."

"It's going to cost fifteen pounds."

"Bloody hell!"

"Look on the bright side my friend. That's less than a farthing per wasp."

"Okay, if you put it that way, it's worth it. When can you start?"

"Now. It'll take an hour."

"Good, we're off down to the pub."

The Harbour Inn was alive and kicking, which in Dittisham meant there were three anglers in the bar playing darts and two holiday families eating scampi and chips. David, Suzanne and Kathleen commandeered a barrel and perused menus while Dylan went to the bar, returning moments later with four pints of Guinness.

"So," he began. "Which place shall we take, Frog Cottage or Wasp Cottage?"

"You may as well have Frog Cottage now," said David, "being as all our luggage has been taken to Wasp Cottage. Besides, every last mini-frog has been found other accommodation, the place is well-aired at last, and the shower curtain is no longer a threat to the nation's health. Let's drink a toast to Jim Weston. Bless him!"

"The one consolation," said Dylan, trying his hardest to be reasonable, "Is that it only cost us fifty quid for the week."

"Gnah!" snarled David, enigmatically.

"He charged you loads more didn't he?" asked Dylan, grinning quite unnecessarily, in David's opinion.

"I don't want to talk about it, right?" said David, potentially breaching Nick's copyright. "Anyway, what are we all going to do, now that fate has thrown the four musketeers together?"

"Well," said Dylan, "I don't want to be a party pooper, but I've loaded tons of modelling clay into the back of Kath's car, because I'm going to work on my self portrait project for my degree show. I've painted my face in several styles, such as Renaissance, Cubist, Impressionist and so on. For the centrepiece of my space, I want to model my head in clay, so that there's a bit of '3D', just to show how versatile I am."

"Nice idea," said David, "But personally I wouldn't ever carry modelling clay on the back seat of a car." He winced at what was obviously still a painful memory. Kathleen began to look fidgety, and asked Dylan to drink up and help unpack.

"The rest of the time," continued Dylan, ignoring her completely, "I want to do some walking. I was in two minds whether to come here or have a dirty weekend in Wales."

"I like Macynlleth, you see," added Kathleen.

"You like your WHAT licked?" asked David, taken aback. He had no idea that this forthright young lady had such a serious speech impediment. Kathleen's face flushed as red as her hair. She buried her head into her Guinness till it subsided, and emerged a full minute later with a frothy moustache.

"Well, let me know when you fancy a bit of company," said David. "We can hire a motor boat and go to Dartmouth, or do a bit of crabbing."

"Fantastic!" agreed Dylan. "We'd better get off and unpack then. Good luck with the wasps. At least they're Wolves fans!"

"Explain."

"Well, they'd all got Wolves strips on. See you later."

And with that, they were gone.

David and Suzanne drained their drinks and left, just as the two ladies Suzanne had spotted earlier walked in.

"The one's quite pretty," admitted Suzanne, "but the other is only borderline female. She's the type who fails the Olympic shot-put random blood test."

David laughed. "That reminds me of a great joke that Jim Weston told me last week. A woman goes to the doctor because she's worried about excess hair. The doctor examines her extremely hirsute stomach, and enquires how far the hair spreads. The woman replies, "Right down to my bollocks!""

Laughing like a pair of navvies, they strolled up to the two cottages, waving to their friends, who were busy unpacking. Straw Hat emerged from Wasp Cottage carrying the large ceiling panel with the marmite-like stain on it. Attached to its upper side was a huge grey ball, which he brought over to show them.

"See this here? This great big structure is their nest. See, it's honeycombed, just like a beehive. You stuck your finger right into the epicentre. It's a miracle you ain't been stung senseless. Give me another quarter of an hour to clean up the mess and remove the deceased, and it's all yours."

David thanked him profusely and begrudgingly parted with the cash. They decided to while away the time by walking up the hill to the post office cum general store and buying a few postcards to send home. David liked to keep in touch with his little brother, and was feeling guilty because, what with one thing and another, he hadn't seen much of him of late.

"We'll need oxygen soon," complained Suzanne, gasping. "That place set back from the road is where I found the eggs. Do you fancy a peek? There's no one living here and the place is up for sale. We can have a nose around. If anyone asks, just say we're interested in buying the place."

* * *

Gilda had just returned from the bar with a pint of Guinness for herself and a brandy and Babycham for Rosie, who was sitting at a cast iron pub table with a two piece snooker cue case under her arm. A rustic type from the poolroom, upon spying the cue, called over to her, asking if the two ladies would care to challenge him and his even more rustic-looking friend to a game of doubles.

"We don't play," called Rosie. "This isn't our cue; we're just delivering it to a friend of ours in ze village."

The rustics came over, intent on a spot of flirting.

"Let's have a look at it, girl," demanded the more vocal of the two. "It looks like a nice 'un. Expensive, judgin' by the leather case."

"Piss off!" snarled Gilda, and there was something about the way she said it that left them in no uncertain terms that she meant it. They promptly pissed off, as instructed.

"Zis whole situation is getting me down," she whispered, downing her pint in one mighty gulp. "I vill be glad ven ve haf completed our side of ze bargain. Zen, maybe, he vill leave us alone."

"At least our blackmailing friend, whoever he is, has found us accommodation, Gilda. He said that he has rented ze old house for a week, so that ve can have ze use of it, even after our work is done."

"Maybe zat is a good idea, Rosie. No one would suspect the couple on holiday a few houses further up ze street. It's best to stay put, ja?"

"Ja, I think so too, but I'm a little worried about zat couple who just left ze pub as ve arrived. Did you see zem? Zey are friends of zis David Day and haf ze cottage next door. The woman was nosing around our house ven ve arrived in ze village."

"It's nothing to vorry about, Gilda. She vas probably just looking because ze house looks empty and has ze sign in ze front garden. Zat's all! Ze English are nosy people."

"I hope you are right. Shall ve haf another drink, and then christen ze bed?"

"Natürlich, Liebchen."

*　*　*

"Ah, it's sold," said David, examining the 'For Sale' board. "It's empty at the moment though. You can tell."

"Here's the old barn I got the eggs from," said Suzanne. "The place is really run down, but it could be a cracking house if someone spent a few quid on it."

They sneaked into the barn, which had ancient exposed beams and wonky roof slates that let in brilliant bands of white light full of swirling dust. The room was crammed with old garden mowers, oil cans, rusting bicycles and general junk, plus a platoon of very vocal hens. The floor was constructed of large quarry tiles covered in dirty straw, and several hens were fluttering around making a raucous din. A derelict old red van stood in the centre of the barn, which, judging by the state of it, was where the hens slept at night. One door was missing, and there was straw inside the cockpit and all over the ripped vinyl seats. Hens had nested on the passenger seat and inside the rear compartment, and there were eggs everywhere.

"Told you," said Suzanne. "These eggs would just be wasted if we didn't have them. I'm going to get some for Dyl and Kath."

She tried the rear doors of the van, which were unlocked, and reached inside.

"Look at this," she smiled. "One of these hens has used an old hat as a nest. It's got three eggs in it."

She carefully removed a black bobble hat and placed the eggs into a plastic carrier bag hanging on a nail nearby. As she was doing so, she spotted a small white label inside the hat, with the initials 'L.F.' written on it in biro.

"Let me see that," said David. "Shall we take it home with us? We could give it to our friend Laurence as a present from Devon. It's even got his initials inside!"

David's face suddenly became thoughtful. Suzanne always knew what this particular expression meant. He would come over all dreamy and vague, and not respond to questioning. He walked around the van, rubbing the paint with his fingers.

"Whoever did this did an awful job. It's been painted by hand with a brush."

"Typical old farm vehicle if you ask me," said Suzanne. "These folks don't concern themselves with aesthetics like us poncey artists. As long as it does the job."

David grabbed a rusty trowel from the floor and scraped at the paint along the side panel of the van.

"Humour me," he said. "I've just had a completely mad idea."

The deep scrape revealed the van's original colour, which was a rich Winsor Green.

"If these farmer types aren't concerned about aesthetics, why bother to paint a van another colour, and crudely at that? I don't get it."

He continued to scrape away, the paint peeling off in long strips now, like the skin on a dirty old potato. Evidence of bright yellow sign-writing was now clearly visible. Perhaps, he reasoned to himself, the owner had purchased the vehicle from a trader and wished to cover over the previous owner's details. As more and more letters were revealed, it was apparent that this was no ordinary van. Had David been appearing on the popular 60's television quiz show, 'Name that Van', he would surely have won the fortnight's holiday in Skegness, the speed boat *and* the canteen of cutlery, because he had worked out the answer with only three letters on the board. They read:

VIN

Which, of course, would have been most witty and amusing to a French contestant. He realized that this word may well be the beginning of VINEYARD, VINEGAR or VINTAGE, to name but three, but he was willing to bet his life that he knew what was under the red paint. What wasn't so clear was how or why. There was absolutely no logic to it. If it *was* Vincent Gough's van, what on earth was it doing in a barn in the very village he had chosen to visit for a holiday? Claude had no known association with the place, and neither had Laurence, as far as he knew, but it was a hell of a coincidence that Jim Weston did. Was this property one of his new acquisitions? That would certainly make sense, as he already owned two more in the same lane. Was, then, Jim part of the cover up, and in league with Claude and Laurence?

David feverishly scraped away, watched with great amusement by Suzanne, who was beginning to think that he had gone completely mad.

"Ten minutes ago someone told me off for trespassing on private property," she recalled. "Is this the same person who is now trashing someone's old van, for no obvious reason?"

But David was mesmerized. The sign-writing now read:

VINCENT GO

This was enough to convince him. He stopped scraping and turned to Suzanne.

"We've found it! I don't know how we've found it, but we've found it! It's like I was sent here by a higher force, to solve this foul murder, because that is what this is. I know it now. That smiling, slimy villain. That damned supercilious git who runs our course is a killer, and so is Laurence Fuchs, or I'm a Dutchman."

"And all this because you found an old van? Fancy a bit of Edam? Nice clogs you're wearing!"

"Look," confessed David. "There's a lot I haven't told you about what's going on at our college, because I didn't want to worry you, but this old van is important evidence and the police will need to be informed. I know this policewoman who's on the case, and I'm going to have to call her."

"Oh yeah?"

"It's not like that, stupid," he lied. "We need to skedaddle now, just in case anyone turns up and finds us trespassing. Grab your eggs and let's go."

David and Suzanne returned to Wasp Cottage just as Straw Hat was emerging with two black bin bags.

"All yours!" he smiled. He doffed his hat and set off towards the pub in order that he could convert his wages into cider.

"I bet he planted those wasps before we arrived," sneered David. "They're probably specially trained circus wasps and they're really his pets, and that's how he…."

"Shut up, David."

"Okay. Shall we drop in on Dyl and Kath, to see how they're getting on?"

Dylan was upstairs in the bedroom by the window, working on his sculpture. Still in the formative stages, it was nevertheless beginning to take shape. Having never ventured into 3D before, he was justifiably proud of the start he had made and thoroughly enjoying the experience. Kath, he explained, was down at the Harbour Inn buying some cans of Guinness and using the facilities. Frog Cottage's lavatory had suddenly erupted, Vesuvius-like, and then ceased to function.

"If I need a crap in the middle of the night," explained Dylan, "be warned that I may be doing a bit of breaking and entering, so lay off the baseball bats."

"If you so much as fart in our cottage," warned his friend, "you will be a mass of contusions. I'll have a look later. My dad taught me all about lavvies. It's probably just the ballcock."

David explained that he needed to use the public call box at the top of the lane by the stores, so Suzanne made a cup of tea and settled down to a good book in the tiny front garden. His first call was to a trusted friend.

"Hello Laz. How ya doin'? Look, I need you to do me the biggest favour I've ever asked. Dig out a train timetable and get yourself to Dartmouth around midweek, if you can. We'll put you up at our cottage, feed you and ply you with drink. Yes, I *know* you've got a car, but I want you to come by train, and there's some stuff I need you to bring. The weather's lovely down here, so think of it as a free holiday. No, I haven't got sunstroke. Just do it!"

His next call was to Snibboh, who was doing reams of paperwork at the station.

"Snibbs. It's me, David. I'm on holiday in Devon, and I've got incredible news. Stall your lads until I get back. I have evidence now that will sink him, so lay off and don't scare him into hiding, whatever you do. You could inform Gertie that you've thoroughly investigated Jack's death and you're convinced that it was just a tragic accident. That should lull him into a false sense of security. This might sound paranoid, but we don't know who we can trust, so we'll give this little operation a code name. How about D-Day? Very apt, if you don't mind my saying so. I'll ring again with more details, later in the week. Bye, Sarge!"

David, being a student, only had one twenty pence coin left. He asked Directory Enquiries for the number and dialled. He had to be brief.

"Hello, Mike? Thank God you're in. It's David Day. I've got something very important to tell you. Something you won't believe, and I need your help. When you hear the beeps, can you phone me back on this call box number? What do you mean, I'm a cheeky bugger? This is life and death!"

* * *

It was yet another idyllic summer's day, and in spite of the excitement of his discovery and the worries of the degree shows and D-Day, there was something so wonderful and innocent about Dittisham that David felt completely relaxed. Dylan was engrossed in his sculpting and Kath was trying to top up her tan in a battered old deckchair; not a wise move when one is white skinned and heavily freckled. Often, her attempts to look bronzed and fit had left her looking as if she had been sunbathing inside a colander.

David and Suzanne agreed to meet up with them later in the afternoon to hire a boat and cruise into Dartmouth to look around the shops, but until then, they grabbed a couple of lines kindly donated by a previous inmate, and armed with two rashers of bacon, went in search of crabs.

Those familiar with this enchanting pastime will know that this is not some awful blood sport. It relies entirely on the greed of these crustaceans, which will apparently do just about anything for a bit of Danish bacon. The trade-off, such as it is, is entirely acceptable to them. The holiday-maker dangles a line into the water by the jetty with a rasher attached, and waits for a minute or so. He or she then hauls up the line, to find at least two or three small crabs clinging on for dear life. The line is then shaken vigorously until they fall into the plastic bucket carried by the holiday-maker for this purpose. It is not entirely clear whether the crab is so brainless that it keeps falling for this simple lure, or so clever that it realizes the worst that can happen is to spend an hour in a plastic bucket in return for copious quantities of bacon, before it is eventually released into the wild to repeat the process ten minutes later. Whatever the reasoning behind it, the sport is great fun for both parties, and no one comes to any harm. In most crabbing Meccas, an hour will yield a decent haul of crabs, often reaching double figures. Dittisham, however, is something special in crabbing circles. It is the crab capital for the cognoscenti. Here, if one has not netted fifty in an hour, one is either a rank amateur, or one has omitted to attach the bacon.

By four o'clock, David and Suzanne had amassed a private collection of some sixty-seven crabs, ranging in size from an inch to giants of eight inches. Such was the mass of crabs that Suzanne was sent back to the cottage for another bucket. Celebrating a job well done, they treated themselves to an ice cream each and dangled their feet in the cooling waters, hoping that the few remaining crabs weren't partial to strong cheese. It was then that Suzanne had her brainwave.

"Why don't we challenge those two to a crab catching contest tomorrow?" she suggested. "You know how Dyl loves a gamble with snooker and so on. You could have a wager that the team with the most crabs in one hour buys the dinner."

This was good stuff. The subject was broached during the afternoon's boating expedition to Dartmouth, and was universally well received. The competition was pencilled in for Monday afternoon at two p.m., subject to weather, and on their return, Dylan was so fired up that he and Kath went out with a bucket each to get some practice in before dinner.

That evening in the pub, Dylan's mood had changed, prompting David to ask if he was feeling okay. Dylan sipped a contemplative Guinness and tried to articulate his innermost thoughts.

"I'm a bit worried that I may be going insane."

This was not what David was expecting. He tried his hardest to look concerned and sympathetic.

"You see," explained Dylan, expanding on his theme, "they say it begins with paranoia. Thinking everyone is out to get you and so on. Seeing things is another popular symptom, I'm told."

"And you've seen things?"

"I'm not sure. Do you remember when I got shoved in the canal? You all joked that I was just pissed and I fell in, but I definitely saw two women running off across a field. One was nice looking and the other looked like a Russian wrestler."

"I remember you saying."

"Well, when I roadied for the band at The Crypt, I saw them there as well. Hanging around, all furtive looking."

"Hardly surprising. They're probably students at the college."

"Granted, so what are they doing in Dittisham then?"

"They're here now?"

"Yes. I'm sure I just saw them walking up the hill. I was in my bedroom looking out of the window, and I could have sworn it was them. The ugly one even glanced up at my window menacingly."

"Dyl," said David, "you may be drinking too much of that stuff. Why would two women be terrorizing you? They're not old girlfriends settling a score I take it?"

"Hardly. Especially not the ugly one, and I don't recognize the pretty one."

"Maybe it's just a coincidence, and they're here on holiday."

"Maybe, but it was the look she gave me as she passed. If I could be sure it was the canal pair, I'd go and confront them, but I don't want to make a fool of myself. For such a small place, there are a few coincidences going on, if it is them."

242

"Tell me about it," agreed David, offering no explanation for his comment. "I'm absolutely convinced this is nothing to worry about. They are not out to get you. You're just paranoid, that's all."

"Oh, well that's good news anyway!" Dylan drained his drink and perused the menu. "I don't know whether to go for the scampi, the scampi or the scampi. What are you having?"

"I'll have the scampi."

"So will I then. Get the next round in."

They left the pub at eleven and returned to the cottages, tired but happy, having arranged to meet after breakfast the next day to go to the beach. Dylan turned on his bedside lamp and decided to read a little before going to sleep, but Kath was exhausted and was gone as soon as her head hit the pillow. After ten minutes he too was flagging, and he was soon reduced to reading with one eye and going over the same sentence twice, neither of which were making sense. Abandoning his thirst for knowledge, he began to doze.

\* \* \*

An hour later, in the ink black Dittisham night, Gilda and Rosie were hiding behind a large privet hedge outside Frog Cottage, observing with interest the silhouette of Dylan Weldon at the bedroom window. Gilda carefully opened her snooker cue case, took out the two sections of sniper rifle and began assembling them, while her partner in crime handed her the night sights.

"Schnell bitte!" hissed Gilda. "He von't be zere forever."

"Es ist zu dunkel hier. Ein Moment!" replied her prettier counterpart, handing her the sight with trembling hand. "Okay. Alles in Ordnung."

Gilda fastened the sight to the top of the rifle and peered through it at the window, adjusting the focus until it was pin-sharp. There was a thin white muslin curtain obscuring her view, but there was no mistaking the man's profile. She trained the cross hairs on where she estimated his temple to be, took a deep gulp, and squeezed the trigger. There was a sharp cracking sound, followed by a tinkle of glass, and the figure at the window keeled over slowly, with a resounding thud. Looking around nervously for a reaction to this late night commotion, and thankfully seeing none, Rosie and Gilda quickly packed away the deadly rifle and disappeared into the black night, back to their holiday cottage a hundred yards up the hill.

\* \* \*

David and Suzanne were in the kitchen, eating cereal, when Dylan burst through the door.

"Paranoid eh?" he bellowed, causing David to choke on his cornflakes. He rose unsteadily from his seat and began to turn blue, prompting Suzanne to rush to his aid and slap him heavily on the back twice. This didn't appear to improve David's condition in the slightest, so she put her arms around his waist in order that she could perform the Heimlich manoeuvre, something she had always wanted to have a go at.

Dylan, who couldn't understand what was happening, rushed forward to help, just as Suzanne squeezed hard under David's ribcage. The results were instantaneous and spectacular, much to her delight and Dylan's dismay. Two huge gobbets of half-digested cornflakes came out of David's mouth like shot from a double-barrelled shotgun, catching Dylan squarely in the face. Remarkably, each gobbet landed perfectly in the middle of each of Dylan's round, John Lennon-style spectacles, rendering him temporarily blind. He removed them and squinted, mole-like, at his stricken friend, who was gasping for air.

"What the bloody hell do you want to come in here scaring the shit out of me for?" he yelped with some passion. "I might have died then, you stupid sod!"

Dylan wiped the offending sludge from his specs on David's tablecloth and spoke.

"You said I was paranoid, and I'm not!"

"I never did. It was you who said you were paranoid, and judging by this performance, you were right."

"Those lesbians are out to get me, the bastards! What have I done to them? That's what I want to know. Come and look at this!"

David and Suzanne filed out of the kitchen behind Dylan, who strode purposefully back to his own cottage, mumbling as he went.

"It's the Guinness," whispered David sadly. "It's finally done for him."

Dylan shot up the narrow stairs four at a time and stormed into his bedroom.

"Look at this. It's ruined. The lesbians have blown my bust to kingdom come. You were the one who warned me not to carry modelling clay in a car, and you were right. It explodes! Either that or it's lesbians out to destroy me."

"Slap him Kath," shouted David. "He's hysterical."

"You'd be bloody hysterical if someone had exploded your sculpture after it took you ages to do. Look at it. I woke up this morning to find the window smashed to smithereens and my bust on the floor all exploded looking, with shards of bloody glass poking out of it. Explain that, if you think it's just me being bloody para-bloody-noid."

"Okay, okay, calm down," begged David, rubbing his friend's shoulders. Let's get it back onto the table and see what caused it."

They righted the upturned table and hauled the clay back into position again, carefully avoiding the many slivers of glass.

"Someone's chucked a brick through the window and caught it straight in the brow," said David, puzzled. "This isn't an area for vandalism. It's genteel Dittisham for God's sake. What's going on?"

"It's lesbians!" whined an inconsolable Dylan.

"Whatever they threw is still lodged in the clay, judging by this," David estimated. "Look, there's no exit wound."

He dug into the clay with his hands, and finally emerged with the offending article. "I apologize," he continued, clutching his furrowed brow. "You may well be paranoid, but in fairness, you have a lot to be paranoid about. This is a bullet."

The other three clustered around to get a better view.

"Who would hate Dyl enough to throw a bullet at his bust?" asked Kath, somehow missing the gist.

"They didn't throw it, you stupid sod," shouted Dylan. "It was shot out of a bloody gun, and I have a feeling that it could well have been me they were aiming at."

"Well why did they shoot at a thing that patently looked nothing like you then?" asked David, somewhat bitchily under the circumstances.

Kath was trying to make amends for her earlier foolishness. "Did you say lesbians?"

"Yes. One pretty one and one that looks like a brick shithouse in dungarees. I'm convinced they're following me, trying to cause me serious damage, but I haven't got a clue what I did to deserve it. They probably hate men, and because I'm a perfect example of one, they resent me."

"That makes sense. Perfectly logical," nodded David.

"I'm going to get the bastards," snarled Dylan. "The hunted turns hunter."

"I saw two women who fit that description down at the pub, when I went to use the loo," said Kath. "They were in the loo as well, while I was in the cubicle, and I overheard something interesting. If it *was* the same two, I think I know how you could get them back."

"How many teams of pretty and ugly lesbians are operating in Dittisham this week?" asked Dylan, exasperated, his voice an octave higher than usual. "Of course it's them!"

"Okay, let's stay calm," pleaded David, who'd got quite enough on his mind without lesbian assassins. "Why don't we finish our breakfasts and then stick together today. We'll go to the beach, and then go crabbing as planned, and stay vigilant. It's probably just a student prank, but you never know. Perhaps this perfect specimen of manhood spurned the pretty one at a disco ten years ago, and she turned her back on all men after that and became a lezzer, obsessed with killing the man that broke her heart."

"Thanks!" said Dylan, desperately trawling his memory in case his friend's loony scenario had a grain of truth in it.

* * *

After an uneventful but calming morning at the beach, they returned to Dittisham for lunch and the crabbing contest. Armed with four buckets and crablines, they sauntered down to the jetty, Dylan constantly glancing over his shoulder as they walked.

The competition got off to a brisk start, with honours fairly even. By three, David and Suzanne had amassed just over thirty crabs, with Dylan and Kath close behind with twenty-seven. After a brief interlude for drinks, the second half began. Inspired by the Guinness, Dylan rallied dramatically by netting a further forty-seven, leaving David needing fourteen in the last ten minutes to stand a chance. He rose to the challenge, however, and now it was almost neck and neck to the finish line, with only two or three crabs the difference. Kath, who was designated timekeeper, as she was the only one who had remembered to bring a watch, called a halt, with David declaring victory. Dylan, a keen sportsman, was unconvinced, and demanded a re-count. It was then that Suzanne spotted a couple of women at the far side of the jetty hiring a motorboat.

"Er, lads, do you see what I see?"

Dylan glanced round. "Quiet! Act natural. That's them; I'm positive. This is perfect. I'm hiring a boat."

Ignoring calls to be careful, Dylan ran over to another boat operator at the opposite side of the jetty and slipped the man a five-pound note. He hissed at the others to hurry up, and bring their belongings with them.

\* \* \*

Rosie and Gilda had decided on a boat trip along the Dart so that they could see Agatha Christie's house, which was a big tourist attraction on the river. Rosie had originally shown an interest in the local custom of crabbing, but noticed that her normally hard-as-iron soulmate had blanched when she had suggested it to her whilst washing their hands in the lavatories at the Harbour Pub.

"I'm afraid," confided Gilda, "that I can't join you if you wish to do that. I haf a confession to make. I haf a very bad phobia, which has haunted me since I was a child. I am so embarrassed to admit zis, but I haf a morbid fear of crustaceans - I am terrified of them. I sink it began when my grandfather, as a joke, prepared my lunch one day under one of those silver domed things that they use in expensive restaurants. He pretended to be ze waiter and lifted it with a flourish, saying 'Voila!', and underneath was a crayfish, but it was still alive. I had many nightmares after zat, and ze feeling never went away."

\* \* \*

Dylan grabbed the steering wheel and powered the boat in the direction of Gilda's craft, causing the normally smooth waters of the Dart to churn up, rocking the moored vessels nearby. Within a minute or two he had drawn alongside. Gilda had been concentrating on steering, but turned around to see what kind of madman was causing her boat to buffet about erratically. The Germanic swearwords froze on her lips when she saw who was staring angrily at her.

Dylan let go of the steering wheel just as the boats collided, and held onto Gilda's boat with one hand. She was about to bring her powerful arm crashing down onto his, when she saw him reach for the first red plastic bucket. With one smooth movement, he emptied the first consignment of crabs into the boat, and was gratified to see this huge and seemingly indestructible woman reduced to a quivering wreck in seconds. The second bucket was emptied over Gilda's head, causing immediate and quite spectacular results. One small crab had found its way down the front of her bra-less T shirt and had latched onto a large and hirsute nipple, trying its damnedest to snip it off, as if it were the tip of a Havana cigar. Another had tangled itself hopelessly in her hair and was exploring the possibility of escaping into her ear. The third bucket consolidated Dylan's efforts, and by now he was of the opinion that a fourth would be wasted on her, as she was currently as hysterical as it was possible to be. Feeling it was a shame to waste it, he emptied the fourth and final bucket over Rosie, just for good measure, and sped away towards the jetty before they could think about retaliation.

Handing the boat back to a startled boatman, the four stood watching - along with most of the population of the village – the drama that was unfolding in the middle of the river. Gilda was standing up in the boat, which was rocking violently from side to side, screaming at the top of her voice and performing some sort of frantic tribal dance routine as she did so. Rosie was trying to get her balance in order to stand up and help Gilda, but the vessel was rocking so badly now that this was proving impossible. Then, quite suddenly, she catapulted to her feet, only to be punched senseless by the flailing Gilda for her efforts, causing her to fall into the Dart. Gilda, sensing that here could be her escape route, jumped in after her, still waving her arms about like a demented windmill, oblivious to the irony that she had chosen to dive into a river that was crammed full of crabs in order to avoid them.

"And there's more where they came from if I ever see your ugly bloody face round here again!" called Dylan triumphantly, knocking the dust from his hands.

* * *

An hour later, Rosie and Gilda were seen heading out of the village, en-route for Düsseldorf in their battered old Volkswagen, Gilda still hyperventilating and weeping inconsolably in the back seat. Dylan had beaten them, but he still had absolutely no idea why they'd been so horrible to him in the first place, and now, probably never would.

After Dylan's would-be assassins had left with their tails firmly between their legs, his paranoia subsided to an acceptable level, and he earnestly set about the task of re-building his sculpture, pausing only to take on essential supplies. He was a keen gastronome who liked to cook with alcohol, (sometimes even adding food to it) and had volunteered to organize a barbecue in Frog Cottage's front garden to welcome Laz to the fold, as a welcome change from the Harbour Inn's scampi.

David and Laz arrived tired and thirsty from the railway station to be greeted by what could only be described as a carnival atmosphere. Kath was serving chilled drinks from a crab bucket filled with ice, while Dylan busied himself with hotdogs and steaks. Suzanne, in the meantime, had not been idle. With a few rolls of multi-coloured crêpe paper purchased in Dartmouth, she had fashioned five garlands in the Hawaiian tradition and was dancing around, doing what she fondly imagined was an authentic south sea island dance, handing out the garlands as she did so.

"Aloha, Laz!" she called as he approached the front gate. "This barbecue is in your honour!"

"Thank you!" called Laz, grabbing his first beer of the night from Kath. Ignoring the pungent aroma of seafood wafting from the can, he demolished the beer in seconds and started work on another.

"I still haven't got the foggiest why I'm here, but thank you anyway. I hope you've organized a nubile young Tahitian bare-breasted beauty for me, because otherwise I'll feel like a bloody gooseberry."

"Sorry old pal," laughed Dylan. "We did have a couple lined up but they caught a bad dose of crabs and went home."

"So why am I here, apart from the fact that I'm great company?" asked Laz.

"I have a project for you," replied David. "There's a derelict van up the hill that won't start. You used to be a car mechanic. Do you reckon you could start it up and enable us to get it home?"

"Ah!" smiled Laz. "So that's why I had to bring my tool box. Sorry to disappoint you lads, but someone in my position isn't allowed to get his hands dirty, or risk breaking fingernails anymore."

"And what, prithee, *is* your position? A bogus art student who can't draw?"

"Give my catty young friend a saucer of milk," replied Laz, feigning deep hurt. "How about bona-fide music student?"

"Explain."

"Well, Kieron Hastings saw right through my deceit, but after our gig at The Crypt he introduced me to a friend of his at Birmingham Conservatoire, who can recognize talent when it creeps up and bites his arse. Ladies and Gentlemen, I am now a first year guitar student, and no longer a rag and bone man who robs old ladies."

"Straight up?" asked David, giving him the eye.

"Straight up, my 'Doubting Thomas' friend, so can I propose a toast? To students. God bless us!"

David wasn't exactly keen on students, in spite of being one himself, but gave his oldest friend a hug nevertheless.

"Fantastic! Sometimes we're too close to see the wood for the trees, or whatever the bloody expression is. It's as plain as the nose on your face that you were born to be a musician, and with a nose like yours it couldn't have been much plainer."

"There's just one problem," sighed Laz. "Dave, I don't know an easy way to say this, so I'll just blurt it out. I have to leave the band. The Conservatoire is going to be tough, and I'll have to spend every waking moment doing my grades and practising. I don't think I'll have any time spare to rehearse from now on."

"That's ironic," smiled David. "I was the one who was panicking about leaving, and the very person who was most into it is the one to break the band up. Laz, you have to do what you have to do. Maybe Nick, Ken and George will carry on, if Duncan decides to retire gracefully. And talking of whom, how is the little charred fella?"

"Crispy!"

"It's a shame."

"He'll survive, but he's gone off the idea of stardom for now. I think he had a cathartic experience and decided to become a born-again accountant instead."

"I suppose it hit him like a bolt out of the blue," sniggered David.

Laz was astute, and could read between the lines. He was getting an almost subliminal message from David that he wasn't too keen on the singed singer.

"I hope you like your hotdogs well done," shouted Dylan, who appeared to be loading sticks of solid graphite into buns.

Laz opened his bun and studied Dylan's effort with less than total enthusiasm.

"Talking of Duncan," he mused, "I think I've just found his todger."

Suzanne gave the hotdogs a miss and decided to wait till the chicken was ready.

* * *

The following morning, all was quiet. It had been a late night, with copious quantities of alcohol consumed, and all through the house, not a creature was stirring, not even a frog.

First to emerge was Dylan, who was trying to understand why he had a slab of stilton measuring three inches square by one inch deep in the back pocket of his jeans. He removed the crumbling, stinking mess and sat contemplating it in silence over a strong coffee, hoping to God that he hadn't somehow consumed his wallet by mistake the previous night.

Next to surface was David, who looked ashen. He joined Dylan in the kitchen of Wasp Cottage, and helped him to study the cheese.

"But we didn't buy any stilton, Dyl. That's the strange thing," he observed, his hand clasping his chin. Had they been actors in a made-for-television suspense thriller, the sound track would have struck up with a dramatic 'DA-DA- DAR!' However, as this was real-life, the comment was met with a far less interesting knock on the front door. Suzanne entered, clad in a crumpled dressing gown, her eye make-up smeared down both cheeks.

"Ah Sooz," groaned David, "Dyl's found some cheese in his pocket."

She gave the distinct impression that she could add nothing of any worth to the on-going discussion, but the look of earnest concentration on her face suggested that she was on the brink of airing a brand new topic for debate.

"Charcoal is apparently carcinogenic," she eventually volunteered, grasping for the nearby work surface, as if the complex sentence structure had taken it out of her.

"Is that so?"

"Yes. Maybe Dyl's hotdogs were so burnt, they caused you to hallucinate, and there isn't any cheese."

David weighed this. "If that is so, why can we all see this block of cheese on the table, and also smell it?"

"What blonk of cheeds?" asked Suzanne, who seemed to be experiencing some difficulty in both removing the kettle lid and enunciating her words.

Laz arrived, and everyone agreed that they had seen healthier corpses.

"Oh, you've got my stilton," he mumbled. "I was looking for that. I'm going to take a shower and grab some strong coffee, and then I'm going to mend this van, unless I die in the next five minutes, which is on the cards."

An hour later, looking only marginally better, David and Laz struggled up the hill and into the old barn. Laz opened the van's bonnet and peered sagely at its innards, testing various parts with various gadgets, whilst David looked on with interest, like an old man studying a tense game of chess in a café with a wise look on his face and absolutely no idea what was going on.

Irritated by having David constantly under his feet, Laz asked him to sit in the driving seat and turn the ignition key when asked. The first ten or so times produced the harsh and unpromising 'her-her-her-her-her' sound of the knackered vehicle mocking its repairer, but Laz was made of sterner stuff. After fiddling with something that might or might not have been called the differential cam-sprocket bearings, followed by several other fundamental tests, the rusty old engine finally spluttered to life.

"You're a genius!" cried David, punching the air with delight. "What was up with it?"

"No petrol, you twat," came the bad-tempered, hung-over reply.

The wildlife of Dittisham, previously left undisturbed for centuries, was having to get used to its temporary new neighbours, who seemed intent on ethnic cleansing on a grand scale. First the frogs had felt the backlash, followed by the wasps and crabs. Now it was the hens' turn. Suzanne and Kath arrived with bowls of water and scouring pads, while David and Dyl tried to relocate the foul collection of fowl. This was proving harder than they had first imagined, as two or three birds would be evicted from the cab, only to find their way into the back seconds later. These would be chased, clucking maniacally, from the back, while six others were busy sneaking back via the cavity where the door should have been. Eventually though, after a concerted effort, both hens and their oval offspring were shunted out into the field behind the house, and after a bit of bad language, settled begrudgingly in and around an outside lavatory with a corrugated roof. It wasn't the most savoury place to bring up a family, but beggars can't be choosers.

The remaining days were filled with sunshine and much laughter. Guinness and scampi were consumed on an epic scale, Alka-Seltzers were swallowed, Jeeves books were read in dusty old deckchairs, sculptures were worked on, crabs were caught and duly returned, and caught once more, ice creams were licked, beds were tested, boats were sailed and occasionally sunk, and photographs were taken, until finally it was Saturday morning, and time to go home. Kath loaded up her car while Dylan carefully carried out his pride and joy, glancing this way and that for hidden snipers. Suzanne cleaned the kitchen, which was something Jim Weston had never done, and David and Laz filled

Vincent Gough's van with fuel, ready for its epic voyage. After a tearful farewell to two cottages that had been so awful at first, and were about to become fond memories, the cavalcade moved out, leaving Dittisham to fall once more into a deep sleep. Straw Hat waved goodbye, and immediately began to install a wasp's nest for the next occupants. The Old Rectory lay empty, (except for a gang of determined hens who had already sneaked back into the barn) waiting patiently for a new owner who would never show. Somewhere deep in the grass verge, ninety-seven mini-frogs cheered, some flashing 'V' signs, while others shed tears for their fallen comrades, devoured by seagulls.

The trip home passed uneventfully, at least by David's standards, though Laz did have a little explaining to do when the remaining van door disassociated itself from the van on the M5 just past Weston Super Mare, shredding a passing panda car's tyres at seventy miles per hour. Luckily, Laz was born with dark skin and black curly hair, which helped greatly with his "Me mechanic. Me no spik English. You aska my boss," routine. Luckily, the officer was so traumatized by his near-death experience that he omitted to check for current tax and MOT, tyre tread limits, working indicators and headlamps.

"I did *have* headlamps," explained Laz, on arrival at David's house. "It's just that they were in the back of the van."

Once David had greeted his parents, hugged his brother and handed over the packs of fudge with 'A present from Dartmouth' printed on the front, he rang Mike Sambrokes to see if things had progressed while he was away.

"I've been hard at it, Dave," said Mike wearily. "It took some sorting out, I can tell you, but the majority of it is completed now. Claude called us all in for a meeting during the holiday, but I was in anyway, working on project D-Day. He asked what I was up to, but I just said I was catching up with degree show photos for the students, and he seemed satisfied. It happened as you said it would. He's announced that he's standing down at the end of next week, and John Law will take over. Apparently, he's going to spend more time with his family. His health is poor, he keeps getting migraines and Gertie wants to leave the town for good. Wolverhampton's got too many bad memories. They want to settle in France."

"I bet they do."

"He just wanted to slip away, but I suggested a farewell party at The Castle on Friday, and all the others agreed. It was really funny, because he kept saying he didn't want a fuss, and we all said, 'Nonsense, you have to have a good send off!' You should have seen his face, but he had to agree to it, just to shut them up!"

"Excellent! Well done, Mike. You're a genius!"

"We'll see about that. It's going to be tight trying to finish it off before Friday. I'll have to work nights."

"Thanks Mike. I won't forget this, but more importantly, you know you're doing the right thing."

This was good news indeed. Now it was time to phone Snibboh.

# CHAPTER 16

## The A.V.'s the thing

"I'm shitting myself!" proclaimed David, rather too loudly. The old lady in the next booth was 'tut-tutting' audibly over her egg custard.

"Thanks for sharing that with me," frowned Snibboh, tucking into her beans on toast. "How do you think I feel? If we've got this all wrong they'll rip my stripes off my arm and horse-whip me on the steps of my club."

"What, Wolverhampton Working Men's Club - that fine old institution? Look, we're in this together now and we need to hold our nerve till tonight. Then, hopefully, it'll all be over and we can concentrate on what we do best. This is playing havoc with my degree show work, you know."

"Just think," smiled Snibboh, stroking his hand. "If you hadn't accosted me with your banana, none of this would have happened. You'd have been beavering away at college and I'd have been chasing petty thieves through precincts. Now I'm on the verge of catching my first murderer."

"Don't count your chickens I always say. Actually, I don't always say that. Last week in Dittisham, I kept telling everyone *to* count their chickens, but that was only so as we didn't accidentally bring one home in the van."

Snibboh looked towards the heavens, exasperated by David's convoluted sentence structure, but only got as far as a slightly stained polystyrene ceiling tile.

"Has Mike finished?"

"Yes, God bless him. He's been running around like a headless....well, you know, and he phoned me last night to say he'd finally tracked down the last few bits and pieces and everything was ready. Did you order beans on toast?"

"Yes."

"Then why are you eating beans on toast? I'd send it back and demand the wrong meal."

"I think the strain is beginning to tell. Who's coming tonight?"

"Most of the graphic design and illustration bunch, loads of lecturers. It'll be a really big do. Mr and Mrs Wood, the new landlords, have opened up the big function room with the French windows at the far wall. Dyl's down there now, covering the entire wall with white backdrop paper which Ken got for him from the photography studios. We'll use that as a giant screen. Mo's down there now too. He's set up the band's P.A. so that we can have some music, announcements and speeches and so on. Mrs Wood's done loads of food. SHIT!"

The old lady in the next cubicle began 'tutting' furiously.

"What have you forgotten?" asked Snibboh nervously.

"No, no. I haven't forgotten anything. I've just been hit by a thunderbolt. Do you remember my strange afternoon with Mrs M, when she touched the camera and went into a trance? At the time I thought she was just spouting random extracts from Shakespeare and mixing up her Hamlets with her Macbeths. She said that none of woman born would harm the king, until Birnam Woods moved to the castle at Dunsinane. At least, that's how the story goes, if I remember rightly."

259

"Well?"

"Well cop this, copper! The new landlord of the pub is Bernie Wood. The Woods have just moved to The Castle, and guess what? It's in Dunsinane Street, at the back of the college."

"Bloody hell!"

"So she wasn't talking rubbish, was she? The bit about 'None of woman born shall harm him.' That's a reference to the hero of the story who turned out to have been born by caesarean section, and so technically wasn't born of woman. I can't imagine she meant anything by that. I was born naturally. I know that."

"Yes," said Snibboh, "but I wasn't."

They stared at each other in silence. Neither was a strong believer in the supernatural, but Mrs M's prediction was spot on, and seemed to galvanize their resolve. There are, after all, more things in heaven and earth than are dreamt of in your philosophy, as someone once said.

\* \* \*

It was six-thirty, and the room was ready. A huge sheet of white paper filled the far wall, with a lectern and microphone just in front and to the left. Mr Wood had pinned up tinsel and balloons to give the room a party atmosphere, and his wife was busy covering over the pool table so that she could use it for the buffet. Down the other end of the room, Mike Sambrokes was assembling the carousel for his audio-visual presentation.

David arrived with Snibboh, who had changed into her best party dress and let her hair down. Nodding nervously to Dylan and Mo, he darted down the room to have a word with Mike, and check that everything was in good working order. The guests were filing in now, with Jim Weston one of the first to arrive. He smiled and came over to ask how the holiday had been. David had long since forgiven him for the frogs and wasps, and told him that a wonderful time had been had by all. Sensing that David looked a little pre-occupied, Jim sauntered up to the bar to greet Edwin Binks, who was sitting on a bar stool sipping a half pint of bitter shandy.

"Evening Edwin. How's your love life?"

"Fantastic!" replied the spotty-faced and usually reticent art student. "I took your advice about going round to my girlfriend's parents' house with the wine and the flowers and so on."

"Never mind that. Did you get to shag her?"

Edwin reddened considerably at his forthright lecturer's turn of phrase. "I wouldn't put it quite so crudely Jim, but yes. We finally made love, thanks to you, and it was the most wonderful experience of my life, and Stephanie Marie's, of course."

Jim eyed the young man suspiciously. "That's a coincidence. My daughter's called Stephanie Marie."

Laurence Fuchs was next to arrive, his face, as usual, like thunder.

"Good evening!" smiled David sweetly.

"Piss off, wanker!" replied Laurence, heading for the bar.

"Revenge," whispered David to Snibboh, "is a dish best eaten cold. He's here. That's good enough for me."

Conspicuous by his absence was Claude Beardsley, who was still at Gertie's house, storming around her sitting room like a particularly aggressive bull in a very small china shop.

"Hurry up woman, for God's sake," he snarled. "I want to get this bloody awful evening over with so I can sod off and never see the bloody college again."

"I won't be long," she said patiently. "I need to change this dress. It's got a damned spot of red wine on it and it won't wash out."

261

"For God's sake!" shouted Claude. "It's a few cheese sandwiches at The Castle, not a night at the opera. Forget the damned spot. No one will notice. There'll probably be more where that came from before the night's out."

She acceded to his request and grabbed her bag, giving him her best 'I love you but I don't like you' look.

\* \* \*

The room was comfortably full now, and everyone was ready to welcome the guest of honour. Kathy and Suzanne, who had arrived together, were at the bar, buying drinks for themselves and their boyfriends, but David was too nervous to drink, for the time being at least. Then the door opened and in walked Claude and Gertie, triggering a noisy cheer from the room, and a few tense glances from the cognoscenti. Mrs Wood hurried out of the kitchen with a large, iced cake in the shape of a palette, with blobs of coloured icing to represent oil paint, each speared through the middle with a candle. Kieron Hastings led the assembled multitude into a rousing version of 'For he's a jolly good fellow,' and called for a speech.

"No speeches!" shouted Claude, desperately trying to look happy. "Just have a drink on me at the bar, and I'll catch up with you all as the night progresses. Enjoy yourselves!"

David, who had spotted Suzanne struggling to carry too many drinks, made his way over to the bar to help, and relieved her of two pints of Guinness. As he turned, Laurence, who was just arriving at the bar, collided with him, sending most of the Guinness down Laurence's clean white shirt.

"You cretinous bastard!" yelled Laurence, flicking the surplus liquid from his clothing. Why don't you look where you're going, you and your vacuous whore?"

"What...did you say?" David asked with a chillingly quiet voice that belied his inner-rage.

"I said, you and your vacuous whore. Are you deaf as well as thick?"

"What's going on here?" asked Claude, who had appeared behind them en-route to the bar.

"This little shit just threw drink all over me," explained Laurence, shoving David in the chest and sending him reeling backwards, upsetting several other drinks in the process."

Claude stared intensely at David. It was a look that said, 'why are you still alive?'

"Come on you two. Don't spoil my big night with a silly argument over a spilt drink. Kiss and make up."

"Easy for you to say," growled Laurence. "This bastard's ruined my best shirt."

"I'll ruin your face in a minute," retorted David, quite out of character and trembling like a leaf. Suzanne had never previously known him to be overly chivalrous, and she wasn't sure this was such a good idea, given that Laurence was well over six feet tall, loved to paint entrails and had psychopathic tendencies.

"Now now!" appealed Claude, flashing Laurence a steely glance. "Why don't you settle this amicably? I'm sure it was an accident after all. Tell you what. Play a game of darts. If Laurence wins, David can buy the drinks all night, and vice-versa."

"I don't play darts," snarled Laurence, unconvinced.

"Okay, play pool. You're good at that," suggested Claude hopefully.

"Not as good as I am," smiled David.

By now, a small crowd had gathered to watch the altercation. Mo sidled up to David and whispered in his ear.

"Drop this Dave. You're in danger of ruining the whole evening. Let it drop."

"No worries, Mo. It's just a game of pool. It won't take long. Then we can get on with the presentation."

"Excellent!" said Claude. "I'll get you both a drink. We don't want any unpleasantness on my last night, gentlemen."

"That would be awful," agreed David, through gritted teeth. "Tell you what, Fuchs-Face, let's make this more interesting. Fifty quid says I beat you."

"Don't make me laugh. I play snooker for the Institute first team."

"So it's a bet?"

"Fair enough. Fifty quid it is. I'll fetch two cues."

Word was now spreading around the room that a grudge match was about to get under way, and soon there was a large crowd around the pool table, which meant that poor long-suffering Mrs Wood and her young barmaid had to remove the buffet and take the sheet of plywood off again. Claude returned with two glasses of white wine which he placed on a shelf next to the pool table. Laurence went over to his drink and took a sip, moving it away from David's.

"Yours is on the left," he sneered. "I'd hate for us to get them mixed up. Here's your cue. I got you the bent one."

Dylan, having got wind of this impromptu grudge match, had been busying himself setting the balls up and taking upon himself the responsibilities of referee. He tossed a coin and asked Laurence to call.

"Thank you gentlemen," he announced. "Mr Fuchs to break."

Laurence broke off, leaving the white fairly safe in the baulk area. David studied the table and went for a loose red near the top cushion. He chalked his cue and took aim, but instead of a nice smooth 'thud', he was greeted with an inelegant 'clank'. The white ball skewed sideways and failed to hit a single object ball.

"Two shots," called Dylan, who was relishing his role as referee, and positively aching to be asked to clean the white.

David, red-faced with embarrassment, examined his cue.

"Hang on a minute!" he shouted. "Someone's tampered with this. The tip's been partially severed. It's hanging off."

Dylan took a look. "That's odd. It wasn't like that an hour ago, because I was playing with it."

The scarlet in Laurence's cheeks almost matched the crimson of David's.

"I'll fetch my two-piece from behind the bar," shouted Mr Wood, eager to see fair play in his new pub. David quickly assembled the cue while Laurence played his free ball. David stepped up to the table and took on a difficult red, potting it and lining himself up nicely for the next. Laurence filled in the time by trying to soak up the Guinness from his ruined shirt with a serviette. He had quite a bit of time on his hands, unfortunately, as David also potted the next two reds and was on the third. He stepped back from the table and chalked his cue, to give himself time to think. His mouth was dry, and he was acutely aware of the many pairs of eyes trained on his every move. Sidling over to the shelf, he picked up his white wine.

Mo was in the front row of the crowd, watching intently. He called out with some urgency, just as David raised the glass to his lips.

"Dave, don't drink that wine!"

Laurence glared at the huge Asian.

"Why not?" asked David, reasonably enough.

"Because it's Blue Nun, and it's warm! It's bloody horrible, I had some earlier. Have a swig of my Banks's Mild for now, and I'll get you something better."

He handed his friend the drink. Mr Wood eyed him with suspicion, wounded by the slight.

David potted the red and missed his next ball, allowing Laurence back to the table. He seemed distracted, however, and his yellow ball missed the pocket by several inches. David responded by potting another easy red and missing the next. Laurence, by now sweating profusely, aimed at a loose yellow, blasting it into the pocket. He turned to Claude, with a slimy smile that said, 'Now watch me go'. Unfortunately, while he stood gloating over this last shot, he had omitted to observe the path of the white ball, which had cannoned into the black and sent it careering across the table towards the centre pocket. As he turned his attention back to the table, the smile disappeared from his bony, bearded face, just as the black disappeared down the hole.

A resounding cheer echoed around the room, leaving Laurence in no doubt as to what the majority of the clientele thought of him. He pushed his way angrily past onlookers, but David wasn't finished. He called over to the defeated entrail specialist.

"Excuse me. There's the small matter of my fifty quid."

"You'll have to whistle for it," spat Laurence. "I don't have any money on me."

To assorted boos and jeers, he sought solace in a dark corner and brooded over his warm German wine.

Mike Sambrokes caught David's eye and nervously tapped his wristwatch. David scanned the room for Snibboh, who was scanning the room for him. They nodded knowingly to each other, and David stepped up to the microphone, calling the crowd to order.

"Ladies and Gentlemen," he began. "Tonight is a very special night, because we are here to say goodbye to our head man, Mr Claude Beardsley. It's been a difficult time for Claude, having to take over from his friend Kingsley Hamphlett in such tragic circumstances, and it's been made doubly difficult by the heart-rending suicide of Jack Hamphlett. This little presentation is our way of saying goodbye. After this, we'll cut the cake and you can help yourselves to the buffet. Dylan - the lights please."

The room was now in semi-darkness. Mo located the introductory tape, which, thankfully, this time wasn't still in David's back pocket. He inserted it into the player, and seconds later, a gentle orchestral piece by Debussy wafted across the room. The huge paper screen flickered into life, with a scratched old sepia photograph of a chubby baby, scowling at the camera and lounging in a sand pit.

David read from his crib notes.

"Claude Beardsley was born in Camberwell, London, in nineteen-thirty. Even then, he could be grumpy."

A polite titter rippled through the audience. This whole audio-visual presentation was a complete surprise to them, and they were enjoying the prospect. The carousel clicked, and a new image was on screen. This time a colour photograph of a teddy boy.

"Is it Oliver Reed, or maybe Marlon Brando? Neither, it's Claude, aged seventeen, and heading for art college. Nice D.A., Mr Beardsley!"

Claude sat in semi-darkness holding Gertie's hand, his previously gloomy countenance now replaced with something much more benign. This was a nice and unexpected tribute, and he was touched that someone had gone to so much trouble. A smile formed on his lips. Slide after slide followed, with pictures of Claude at college, standing in front of his abstract paintings, skiing down Swiss mountains and raising glasses of red wine in trendy London wine bars, sporting hairstyles and clothing that perhaps he would rather have forgotten. There was even a shot of him chatting to David Hockney at a private view. The crowd were loving every minute and cheering each new image - especially if their head of department looked a bit silly. Claude was in a good mood now, waving regally at his hecklers and slurping his wine.

Next up was a photograph of Kingsley Hamphlett with his arm around Claude.

"Here's the old boss and his right hand man," announced David. "This was taken a few years ago, judging by Claude's waist line."

More cheers from the crowd. Another slide showed Kingsley seated in a rowing boat on West Park.

"And here's the boss relaxing in a boat, eating his sandwiches as usual. God bless him!"

The slide had now changed to a picture of a packet of nuts.

"And here's what ended his life."

Gertie turned to Claude, looking upset. This was in poor taste. Another slide showed a recent shot of Claude, smiling at the camera.

"The Kingsley is dead. Long live the King."

This was greeted with quiet mumbling. Gertie was becoming a little distressed, and Claude began to feel his collar nervously. The next slide showed a picture of Wilfred Fuchs next to a whiteboard, studying some unspeakably complex formula. Laurence, who had been gazing at the screen with total lack of interest, suddenly leapt to his feet.

"Ten points if any of you know who this is," asked David. "It's a pub quiz!"

The next slide showed a photograph of a car.

"And here is Claude's car. You'd think he could afford better on his salary. Mind you, it does look better now that the front wing's been repaired."

A photo of a young lady in a very small skirt followed. It looked as if it had been snapped without permission by a paparazzo.

"Oops! How did that one get in there?" grinned David. "She's a well known lady of the night. Moving swiftly on…"

Now they were looking at a picture of Jack Hamphlett with his arm around Leonora. Claude had gone white now, and was sweating profusely. Laurence just stood and stared at the screen, occasionally glancing towards Claude. Dylan stood impassively half way down the room near the side wall, following events closely and marking reactions to the presentation, like a head teacher in assembly.

"And now a sombre moment, as we all remember Jack, who never let the fact that he was dead stop him taking photos in his bobble hat. I've got it here as a keepsake, with his initials inside. L.F."

He showed the hat to the audience, who by now were, to say the very least, perplexed. Laurence and Claude exchanged worried looks, whilst Gertie just sat sobbing and looking down at the floor.

David signalled for Dylan to turn the houselights on.

"And now we come to the highlight of our presentation," he announced, moving the microphone and lectern to one side. A chill wind blew through the room, as Mo quietly opened the French windows outwards into the courtyard, behind the paper screen. Suddenly, there was a roar of engine noise, and crashing through the screen came Vincent Gough's old van, with Laz at the wheel.

The first rows of audience screamed and leapt back for fear of being mown down. Mr Wood stood saucer-eyed in disbelief, as the pungent fumes from the stricken engine's rusting exhaust system began to fill the room. Laz turned off the ignition so that his friend could conclude his presentation.

"Voila!" shouted David. "The van that was used by the killer of Jack Hamphlett, for this was no suicide. It was murder most foul, as in the best it is, but this, most foul and unnatural, eh Laurence?"

Laurence dashed towards David, stopping as he reached the cake to grab the knife that Mrs Wood had left by its side. He made a lunge at his antagonist, but was confronted by Mo, who stood between them.

"Is this a knife I see before me, Laurence?" asked Mo. "I think it's best if you give that to me, before anyone gets hurt."

WPC Hobbins, accompanied by Reg and Donald, slowly edged around the room to assist, but they couldn't get there quickly enough. Laurence, sensing that trouble was closing in, lashed out at Mo, who ducked with expert timing, rose again and felled Laurence with a single blow to the jaw, causing him to drop like a sack of potatoes, unconscious before he reached the floor.

"Thanks Mo!" called David, shaking visibly. "You're like an HB pencil."

"What?"

"An HB pencil. Hard and black."

With this impromptu sideshow entertaining the crowd, Claude seized his opportunity and quietly left his seat, only to be confronted by Gertie, who grabbed his leather jacket, demanding to know what the strange presentation had been about. He roughly shoved her out of his way and dashed for the door, reaching it before Donald, Reg or WPC Hobbins could head him off. Slamming it behind him, he ran towards the exit, but found his way blocked by two police officers who had just arrived.

Like a wounded bull he charged up the staircase, desperate to get away from his tormentors. On the first floor landing now, he could hear the thunder of size eleven police boots on the staircase behind him. There were two doors to choose from, just like Alice in Wonderland. Or was it Through the Looking Glass? Come on! Think! That one's no good, it's the lavatory. There's no way out from there. Try this one. Good! It's unlocked. Bad! I'm falling, just like Alice, down and down the rabbit hole until.......CRUNCH!

Claude fell, just as Jack had fallen, out of the old loading door and onto the plastic corrugated roof, but their trajectories had differed somewhat. Whereas Jack had fallen heavily straight through the sheeting and hit the deck, Claude had fallen standing up, his feet crunching through the roof either side of a four by two inch support beam.

Those who follow the noble game of cricket often wax lyrical about the minutiae of the sport, such as the eccentric nature of the terminology, with fielding positions such as 'Silly Mid On' and 'Slips'. They get especially dewy-eyed about the comforting sound of leather on willow.

There is, in sharp contra-distinction, nothing comforting about the sound of testicles on pinewood. It creates a rather stomach-churning squelching noise which often causes the onlooker to turn away, or bite the knuckle, and so it was with constables Donald and Reg, who had just arrived at the loading bay door. Their colleague, WPC Hobbins, however, had not chosen to follow them, feeling that three was a crowd, and had used her wily feminine intuition, coupled with a working knowledge of the pub's layout, to direct her to the back yard, where a large, leather-jacketed Oliver Reed look-alike was suspended, his two legs poking through the corrugated roof and thrashing around in agony. She quickly dashed back into the function room and screamed for Mo to bring the black two inch Gaffer tape that he used to stick down amplifier leads to the stage floor. She then returned breathlessly to find that Claude, though not in peak form, was desperately trying to get his legs out of the roof and make his escape. Thinking on her feet, she grabbed both flailing legs, catching a fruity one to the nose for her troubles. Despite the eye-watering pain, she hung on for dear life, suspended above the floor by some six inches. This was having a devastating effect on Claude up above, who began to issue a high-pitched wail that chilled the blood. Mo arrived with the Gaffer tape, but couldn't find where it started on the roll, much to WPC Hobbin's chagrin, as she was getting kicked senseless and kneed in the face. Eventually, after what seemed an age, Mo triumphantly released the tape and began to wrap it around Claude's legs, until he was trussed up like a mummy. Sensing that Claude was at last secured, the plucky WPC released her grip and fell back to earth, she knew not where.

She was quickly joined by David, Dylan and Laz, who helped her off the floor and began wiping blood from her bruised nose with serviettes borrowed from the buffet.

She stood up, straightened her dress, and spoke.

"Claude Beardsley. I am arresting you for the murders of Kingsley and Jack Hamphlett, the manslaughter of Wilfred Fuchs and the theft of seventy-three works of art. You do not have to say anything, due mainly to the fact that your bollocks are lodged somewhere in your stomach at the moment, but anything you do say may be used in evidence against you. Do you understand?"

"Gnah!"

"Very well! Take him down, Donald."

David returned to the brightly-lit function room, where a deathly silence fell as he entered. It was not a pretty sight. The makeshift screen was in tatters, and a great big decaying old van with both doors missing occupied the space where the dance floor should have been. The first two rows of chairs and tables were upended, with drinks and broken glass all over the floor. Groups of students and lecturers stared around the room in total disbelief at what they had just witnessed.

David spoke.

"Well, I think that went well. It's a shame to waste all the food that Mrs Wood has prepared. Let's have a party and I'll try my best to explain what's happened."

Mo took out the intro tape and replaced it with 'Motown Classics' while Mr and Mrs Wood hauled the plywood sheet back on top of the pool table and brought out the buffet again. Mr Wood, looking shell-shocked, staggered over to David.

"I'm new here," he explained, "as you know. Is it like this every week in these student pubs?"

Mrs M, accompanied by Mike Sambrokes, walked over to David and planted a big kiss on his cheek.

"I'm so proud of you David. You nailed him."

"We couldn't have done it without you and Mike. Thank you both."

Out in the courtyard, Claude had been extricated from the roof and was handcuffed and on his knees next to Donald and Reg. Gertie had left the room in tears after being comforted by Mrs M, and was heading for Claude at a rate of knots. Just as the words, 'I can explain' were forming on his lips, she planted a perfectly executed drop kick between his legs, causing him to fold up faster than a Swiss army knife. His bloodshot eyes, which had only recently ventured forth from the safety of the back of his skull, retreated there with some alacrity. It was at this juncture that the officers removed the arrested man from the scene for his own protection, slinging his comatose colleague Laurence into the van with him to keep him company.

WPC Hobbins promised to catch up with the other officers in a few minutes, as she needed to pop back into the room and thank a few people for their efforts. She entered bloodied but unbowed, and was given a spontaneous round of applause by all in the room. David walked over to greet her and gave her a big hug.

"We did it Snibboh!" he said, punching the air. "I almost feel sorry for him now."

"Don't," frowned Snibboh. "Remember what he's done."

David coughed nervously.

"Erm, this is Suzanne. Suzanne, this is Snibboh."

The two girls smiled at each other and said 'Hello'.

"Hey," quipped David, sensing an awkward silence was about to ensue, "How about this for ironic? Kingsley Hamphlett was killed by nuts, and now his successor's nuts are killing him too!"

"I'm going to miss your sensitivity and tact," smiled Snibboh. "I'll leave you two love birds to catch up!" and with that, she was gone.

## CHAPTER 17

### Life is but a Dream

David and Dylan sat in the corner of The Castle bar smiling bittersweet smiles and sipping at their Guinness. There was something about a darkly lit pub on a brilliant summer's day that David didn't care for, but this day was all about nostalgia, and the setting was perfect. The beer glasses were twinkling like the river Dart on a Sunday afternoon, and everything was in soft focus.

Earlier that morning they had been at West Park playing mini-golf, just to take their minds off the degree show results, which were due to be posted on the ground floor reception notice-board at two o'clock. They had walked, trembling with anticipation towards the board, dreading a mark that was less than they had expected, but also secretly hoping that they would both achieve the same result, no matter what it was.

A heaving throng of students had beaten them to the notice board, making it impossible to see. Some were punching the air and hollering with delight, whilst others turned quietly away and disappeared down the corridor. There were tears of joy and tears of sorrow, but this was all part of the art school dance, which would go on forever, year after year.

Finally the two friends were able to push their way to the front, frantically running their nervous fingers down the alphabetical list. Whoever had devised this very public form of mental torture was obviously a sadist, but, just like a penalty shoot-out in a

World Cup Final, it was hard to deny that it didn't add a touch of drama to the proceedings. David was first to see how he'd done. A 'Two-One'. A tearful smile slowly stretched across his face. This was what he'd hoped for. No one seemed to have achieved a First, so he'd done well. Dylan whacked his old friend between the shoulder blades and offered up a relieved and extremely grateful 'Yes!' through clenched teeth. Honours even. A 'Two-One' for him too.

Now the winners, the disappointed and the losers were congregating in their favourite pub, some to celebrate, some to drown their sorrows, and some just to get drunk. Four glorious, crazy, magical years had come to an end after what seemed more like ten minutes.

Jim Weston sat on a bar stool, watching the world go by. Each year he'd say goodbye to them all, and each year thirty more arrived to start all over again. Dom Bentley sat a few stools away, with a beautiful blonde-haired woman in a black leather skirt. She kissed his cheek and disappeared to the ladies room. Jim sidled over and slapped his back.

"I don't know how you do it, Dom, but good luck to you. What a cracker! If you get bored with her, send her my way. God, what a pair of tits!"

Dom drained his pint and put his coat on. He smiled at his colleague. "Thanks! That's my daughter. We're off to grab a pizza. Bye!"

Mo, though not a student, had invited himself along to see how his college friends had fared, and was currently arguing with his girlfriend, Desdemona, in a dark alcove.

"Look! I found one of them monogrammed hankies I got you off the market in Ian's jacket pocket. You've been seeing him again."

Desdemona turned on the waterworks again.

276

"I haven't, I swear. Lay off me, you're smothering me, man."

"Don't start wiv the cryin', woman. I hate it!"

"Well, you never trust me. It's you I love, not Ian. Look! I got you a watch for your birthday."

"It's a bloody Casio. You *know* I hate Casio. Where did you get this? The petrol station?"

More tears flowed, followed by the usual over-emotional reconciliation. David glanced over at his muscle-bound friend and smiled a wry smile, grateful that his relationship with Suzanne was at least relatively smooth and free of hysterics, if a little lacking in raw passion on occasions.

All over the pub, different stories were unfolding. A group of Northern girls were crying their eyes out in a corner, emotional because they were going their separate ways after four years of sharing a house. Young men from Sheffield were shaking hands with young men from London, and taking one last affectionate pot-shot at each other's accents. It was the end of a magical time of freedom, romance, self-expression and excess. The world of commercial art was a precarious one, where only the strong survived. Now work beckoned, with all the boring, responsible, adult things that went with it.

It meant the end of Tweedledum's Café, with its crazy proprietors and even crazier customers, and the end too of all the one-night stands and college romances. There would be no more free football on Saturdays, no Jimmy Triplicate, no Weird Woman and no Katie Black, with her marvellous bra-free black T shirts. Gone forever was the surreal seventh floor and its barking-mad inhabitants, snooker at Glass Eye's place and pool at The Castle pub. Mike Sambrokes would disappear back into his bat cave and Mrs M to her materials storeroom, never to be seen again. There would be no more summer parties on canal boats and no more drippy Leonoras picking wildflowers and singing folksongs. They would never go to The Crypt again on a Saturday night, or go boating on West Park, and there would definitely, absolutely, positively never be anyone like Snibboh to brighten their lives.

David was getting more and more maudlin by the minute at the overwhelming realization that this was the official end of childhood - the moment when playtime finished and work began. Summer would never again be as hot or as long, and feelings never again so intense. He raised his glass and smiled at Dylan.

"To absent friends. To Kingsley and Jack Hamphlett, and Wilfred Fuchs. To Vincent Gough's van and William Shakespeare. To Laz, who as we speak is probably practising his plagal cadences in B Minor. To my hamster, may he rest in peace, and especially to our Snibboh, the best looking officer in Wolverhampton. It's been great!"

David and Dylan downed their pints and sat back in their seats, contented. Jodie Stone, a beautiful and buxom third year graphics student sashayed by on her way to the bar, winking at them as she passed.

"Bloody hell, Dyl," drooled David. "There's another thing I'm going to miss. Do you realize, there's only me and you in the entire third year who haven't slept with her?"

Dylan stared sadly down at his empty glass and sighed.

"I'm afraid it's just you, Dave."


THE END.

**Books in the David Day series (all written but released once a year).**

## A NASTY BUMP ON THE HEAD

Eleven-year-old David Day finds the curmudgeonly toy shop owner, Miss Kettle, murdered in her shop. He duly informs Scotland Yard, only to bump into her in Tenbury Wells the following week.

## MONET TROUBLE

First year art student David Day is persuaded to forge a Monet painting by the mysterious Lord Hickman, but unknown to either of them, several other artists have the same idea.

## VINCENT GOUGH'S VAN

An art college murder mystery of Shakespearian proportions, littered with psychic sewing teachers, entrail-painting students and lesbian assassins.

## THE CURSE OF TUTTON COMMON

David sets about trying to improve Britain's worst museum, and ably assisted by a cat named Hitlerina, he discovers an ancient Egyptian tomb in South Staffordshire.

## PAINTING BY NUMBERS

Thirty-year-old David is having a mid-life crisis, made worse by the fact that his art studio has exploded, and the ninety-year-old 'paint by numbers' enthusiast he has befriended is not what he seems.

## STEALING THE ASHES

Forty–year-old David Day overhears two Australian cricketers plotting to steal the Ashes, and, ably hampered by his best friend Laz, he tries his best to thwart their plans.

**…and a new novel featuring a new hero!**

## THE MYSTERIOUS TALE OF THE MISSING HOOF

Writer, Adam Eve hires a pantomime horse costume, but forfeits his deposit when he loses one of the hooves. His obsessive efforts to locate it create mayhem!

For more information, email gt@geofftristram.co.uk

279

## The David Day Fan Club

Those of you who have read a David Day book will know how addictive they can become. At first, you think you can take them or leave them – you are an adult with a modicum of willpower, after all, and no mere book is going to rule your life. Quite soon though, you realize that you've started reading a quick chapter while you're in the bath or the lavatory. From there it is but a short step to the torch under the bed sheets at midnight and the paperback hidden inside your desk at the office. You'll find yourself reading the final chapter extra slowly to make it last longer, savouring every word and even reading good bits twice. Then, when you can stall no further and the book is finished, you will go through an awful mourning process, whereupon an intense craving will kick in. You'll need more and you'll need it NOW. Bad-tempered due to the crippling withdrawal symptoms, you'll probably complain that the author isn't nearly prolific enough for your voracious appetite, and begin to call him rude names. Extreme cases have even been known to try and climb the walls in anguish. Friends will turn against you because you will insist on regurgitating the plots *ad nauseam* while they're trying to watch television. It will get so bad that you might seriously consider a spell in a clinic, or maybe a course of hypnotism.

Well, help is at hand. Why not join the David Day Fan Club? It's a bit like Alcoholics Anonymous. You sit around in a circle and confess, "My name is Deirdre Sponge and I'm a David Day fanatic." (Obviously, you don't say this if your name i*sn't* Deirdre Sponge. That was just an example.) Then the others get up and hug you, with a bit of luck.

If you email me at gt@geofftristram.co.uk I'll keep your name on file and let you know when a new book is due to be released into the wild. Unlike other authors who are now too important – people such as J.K. Rowling and Shakespeare for example, I promise to always be approachable, grateful and humble, and write back. That's with the proviso that you tell me my books are great, of course. I don't want any sour-faced old scrooges writing in to tell me I'm rubbish and that I deserve to be horse-whipped on the steps of my club. Maybe I could cope if you've spotted a glaring error, or a bit you didn't think made perfect sense, but obviously, I'd prefer it if you to told me how a paragraph had made you wet yourself on the train, or prevented you from leaping off a high building to certain death. You can suggest things that David can get up to in future stories, if you wish. I might even write *you* into a book. After all, most of my characters are based on real people, believe it or not!

Anyway, I'll leave it with you. The offer's there. You can lead a horse to water but you can't make it drink, as my Granny Bertha often tried to say. I hope you've enjoyed Vincent Gough's Van. It's The Curse of Tutton Common next, and if *that* doesn't make you laugh, I'll refund your money.

That was a joke by the way. You have to be so careful in this litigious age. I need the money for a new conservatory - I can't afford to give it back. The bookshops keep forty percent anyway. And another thing. Will you stop lending my books to everyone when you've finished them? Let them buy their own. I'm never going to be another J.K. Rowling at this rate.

*Geoff Tristram.*

Vincent Gough's Van is set in the mid 1970s at the Art College in Wolverhampton, a few yards from where Tarmac's Head Office was once situated.

In conjunction with the college, we initiated the Tarmac Prize – a prestigious award that Geoff Tristram, as a talented young art student, never won.

In an attempt to finally make amends some thirty years later, and to prevent him from remaining bitter and twisted, we have reluctantly agreed to sponsor his latest novel. In return for this, he has begrudgingly agreed to give us a very brief mention in the story, on condition that it didn't compromise 'the integrity of the writing'.

We hope you enjoyed the book, and could you please inform us if he didn't keep his side of the bargain, so that our solicitors can investigate?

# Tarmac ®

*Helping local talent to get noticed, in-between building the odd road here and there.*